Pokémon™

Ω RUBY OMEGA · α SAPPHIRE ALPHA

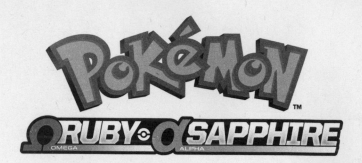

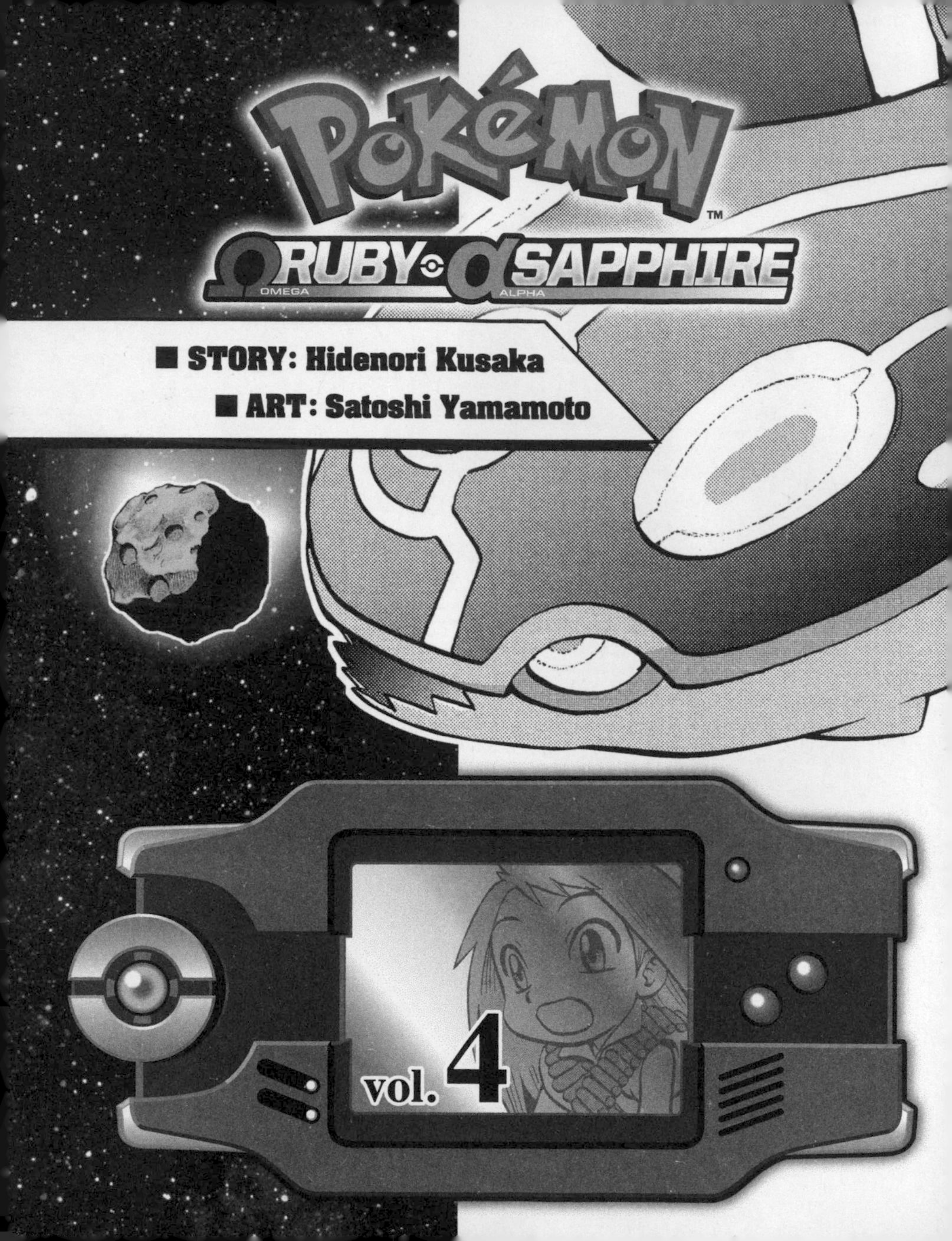
POKÉMON™
ΩRUBY OMEGA αSAPPHIRE ALPHA
■ STORY: Hidenori Kusaka
■ ART: Satoshi Yamamoto
vol. 4

Our Story Thus Far...

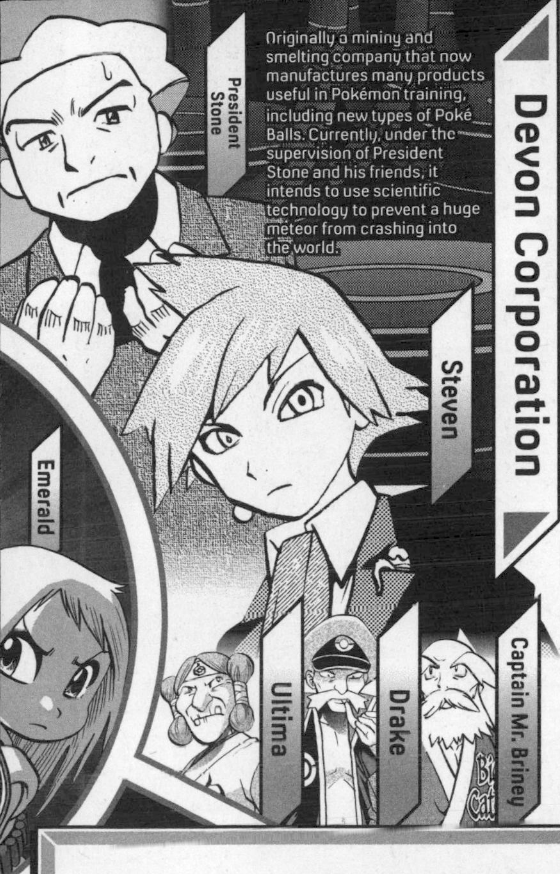

Devon Corporation
Originally a mining and smelting company that now manufactures many products useful in Pokémon training, including new types of Poké Balls. Currently, under the supervision of President Stone and his friends, it intends to use scientific technology to prevent a huge meteor from crashing into the world.
President Stone
Steven
Captain Mr. Briney
Drake
Ultima
Emerald

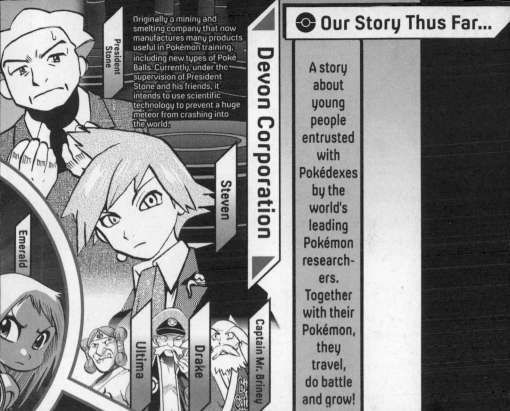

A story about young people entrusted with Pokédexes by the world's leading Pokémon researchers. Together with their Pokémon, they travel, do battle and grow!

In order to power a machine to prevent a huge approaching meteor from striking the planet, Steven Stone, president of the Devon Corporation, summons the three Pokédex holders of Hoenn to help him convert the life force of many Pokémon into Infinity Energy.

Meanwhile, the Draconid people claim they have a better method to stop the meteor, and their Lorekeeper, Zinnia, is determined to sabotage any other strategies.

When Ruby finds out that the Draconid People's key to controlling the meteor is Legendary Pokémon Rayquaza commanded by a Trainer it trusts, it dawns on him that this Trainer must be none other than... himself! Ruby heads down to Sea Mauville to meet Sapphire and the others, but Zinnia chooses that time and place to attack. And when Sapphire learns about the world's impending doom, she loses her voice from shock and is transported through a mysterious ring to...*where*?!

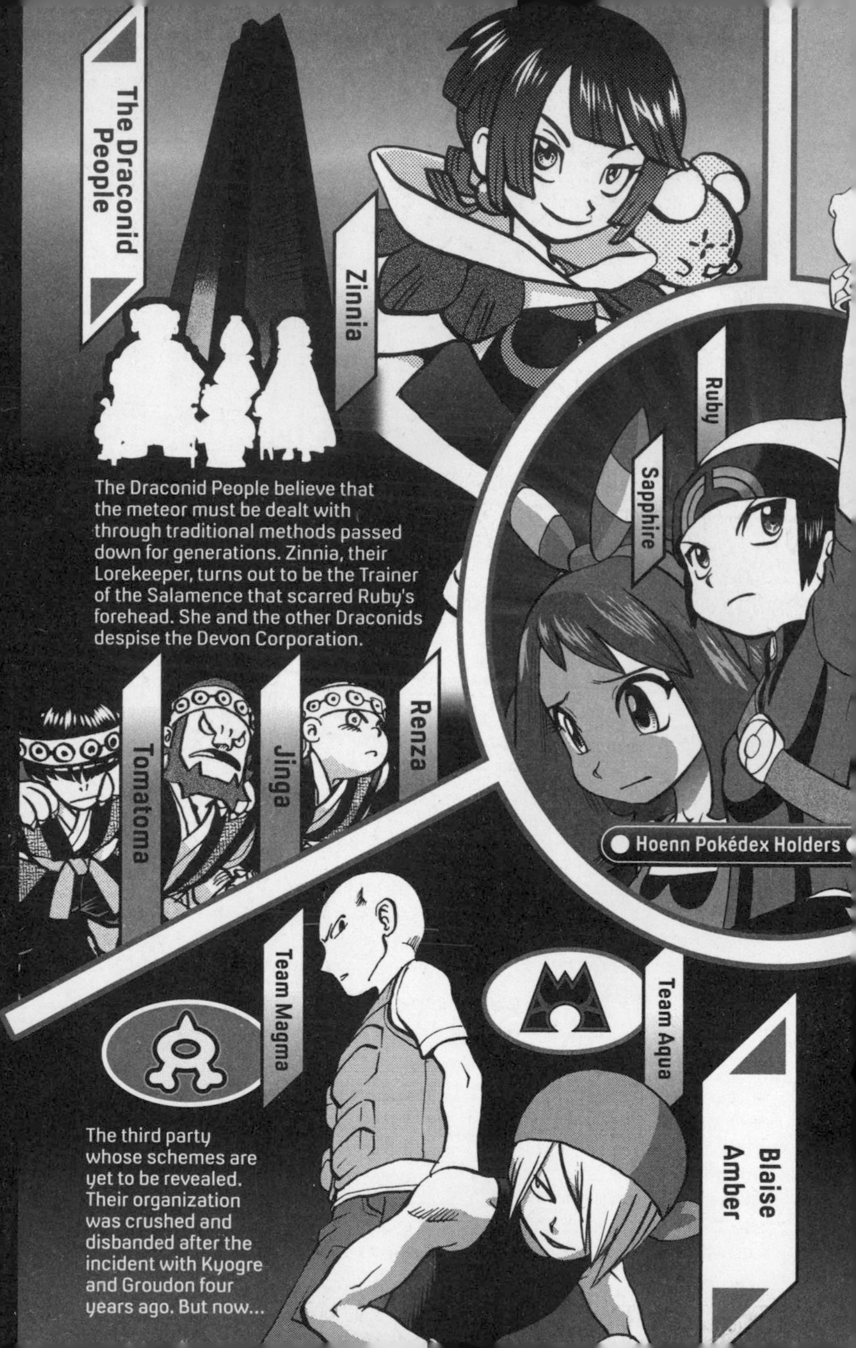
Hoenn Pokédex Holders
Ruby
Sapphire
The Draconid People
Zinnia
Renza
Jinga
Tomatoma
Team Aqua
Team Magma
Blaise
Amber

The Draconid People believe that the meteor must be dealt with through traditional methods passed down for generations. Zinnia, their Lorekeeper, turns out to be the Trainer of the Salamence that scarred Ruby's forehead. She and the other Draconids despise the Devon Corporation.

The third party whose schemes are yet to be revealed. Their organization was crushed and disbanded after the incident with Kyogre and Groudon four years ago. But now...

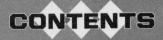

CONTENTS

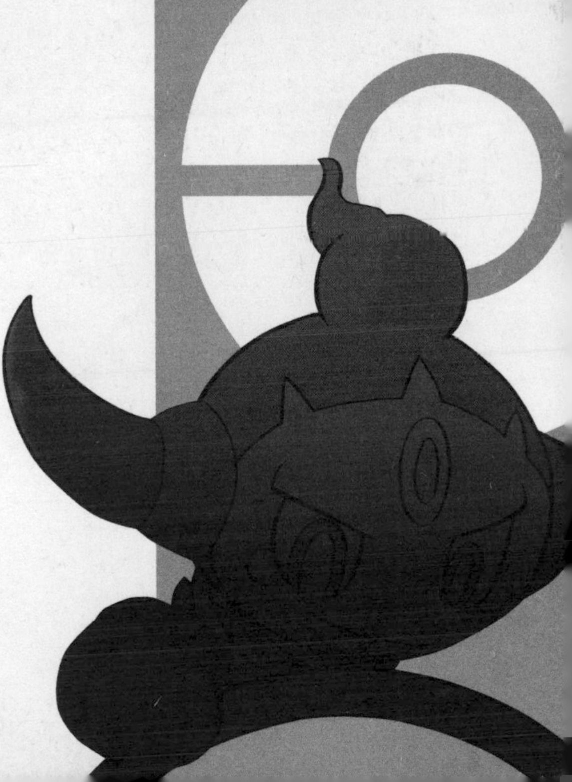

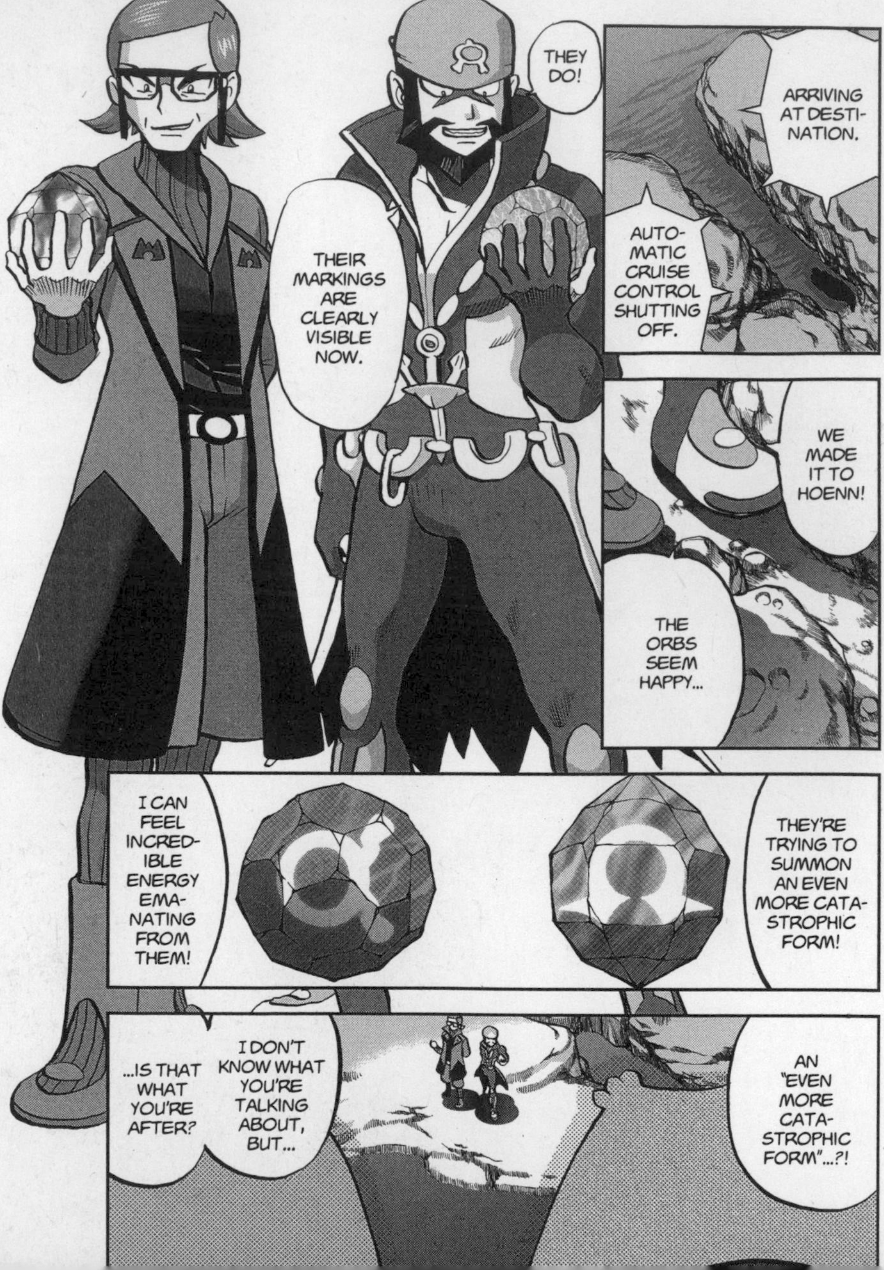
ARRIVING AT DESTINATION.
AUTOMATIC CRUISE CONTROL SHUTTING OFF.
WE MADE IT TO HOENN!
THE ORBS SEEM HAPPY...
THEY DO!
THEIR MARKINGS ARE CLEARLY VISIBLE NOW.
THEY'RE TRYING TO SUMMON AN EVEN MORE CATASTROPHIC FORM!
I CAN FEEL INCREDIBLE ENERGY EMANATING FROM THEM!
AN "EVEN MORE CATASTROPHIC FORM"...?!
I DON'T KNOW WHAT YOU'RE TALKING ABOUT, BUT...
...IS THAT WHAT YOU'RE AFTER?

Omega Alpha Adventure 11

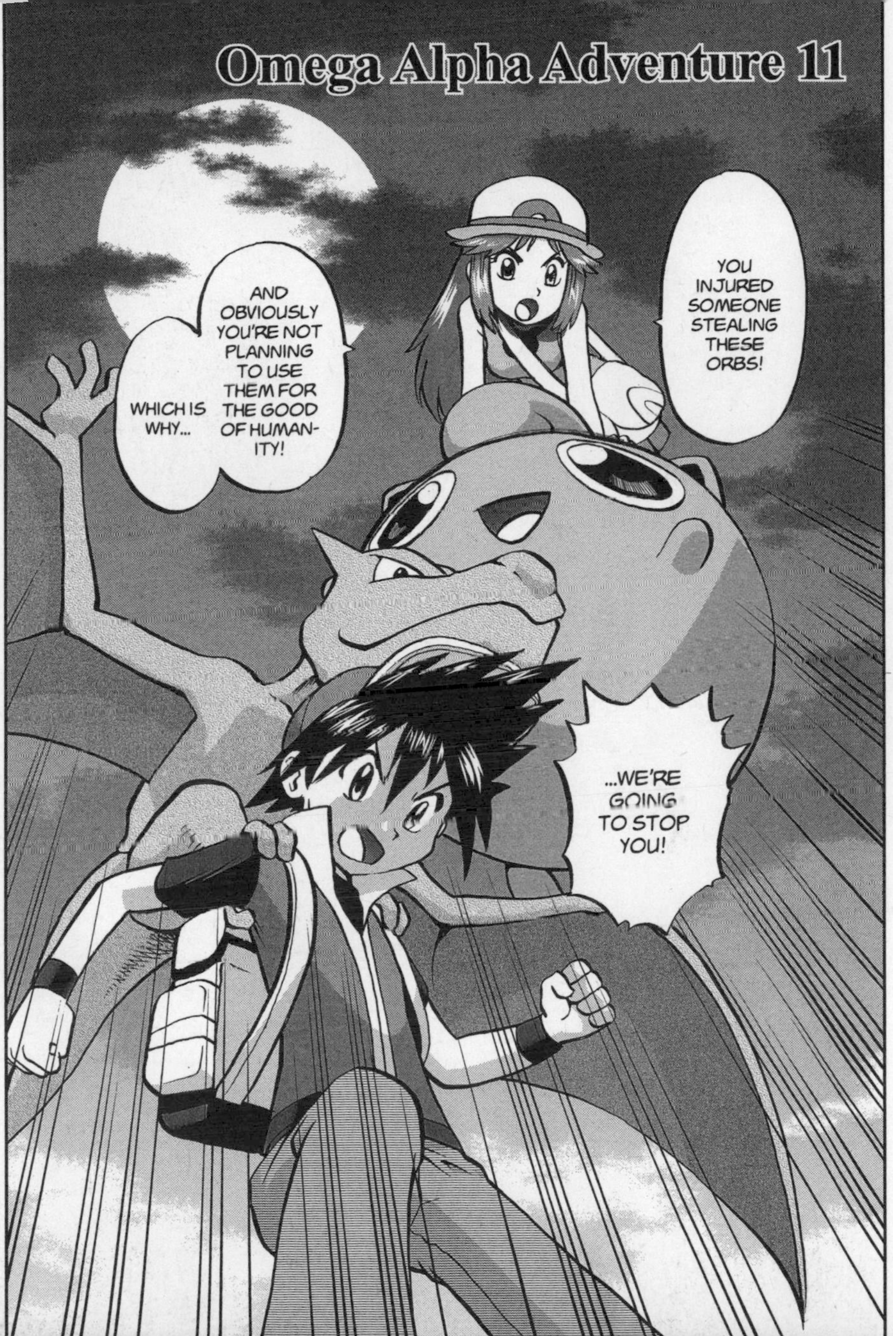
YOU INJURED SOMEONE STEALING THESE ORBS!
AND OBVIOUSLY YOU'RE NOT PLANNING TO USE THEM FOR THE GOOD OF HUMAN-ITY!
WHICH IS WHY...
...WE'RE GOING TO STOP YOU!

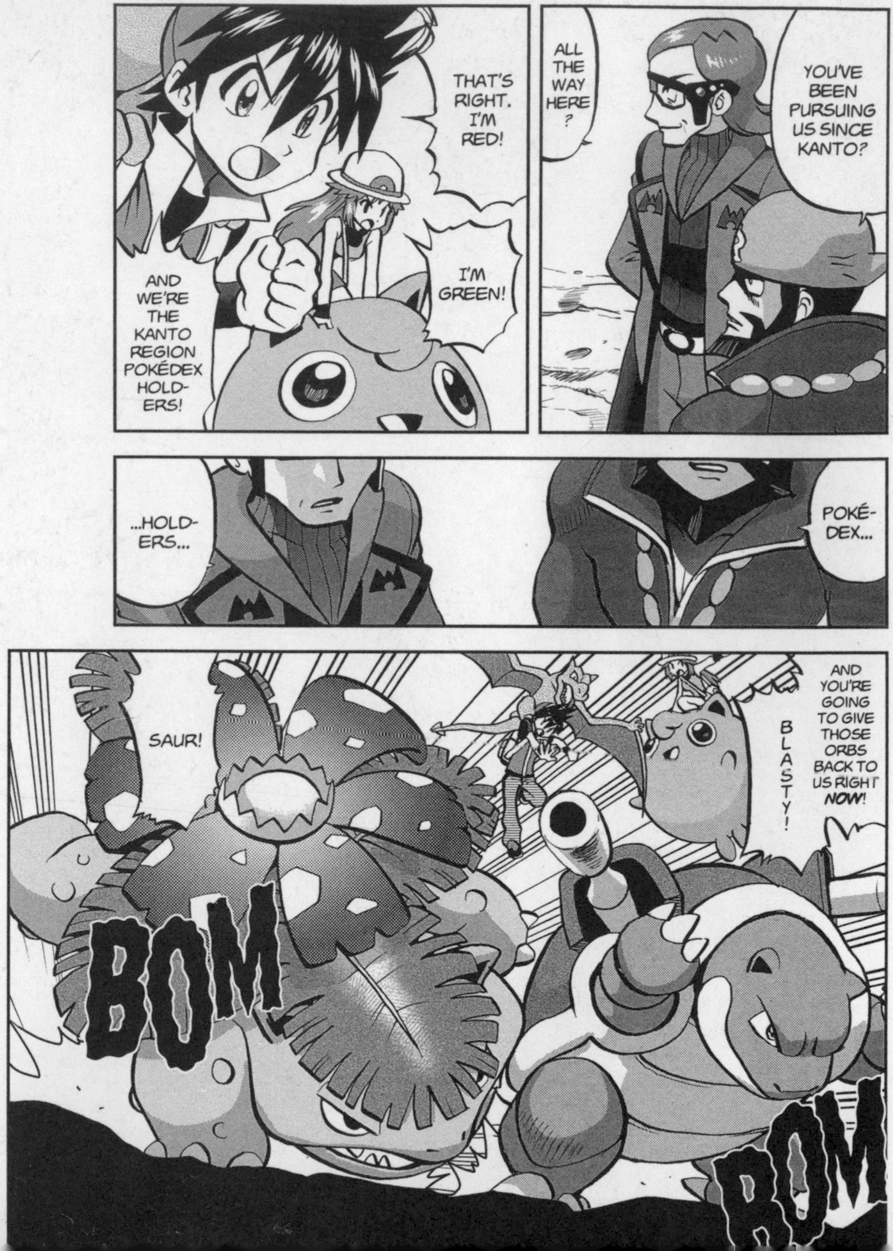
YOU'VE BEEN PURSUING US SINCE KANTO?
ALL THE WAY HERE?
THAT'S RIGHT. I'M RED!
I'M GREEN!
AND WE'RE THE KANTO REGION POKÉDEX HOLDERS!
POKÉ-DEX...
...HOLD-ERS...
AND YOU'RE GOING TO GIVE THOSE ORBS BACK TO US RIGHT *NOW*!
BLASTY!
SAUR!
BOM
BOM

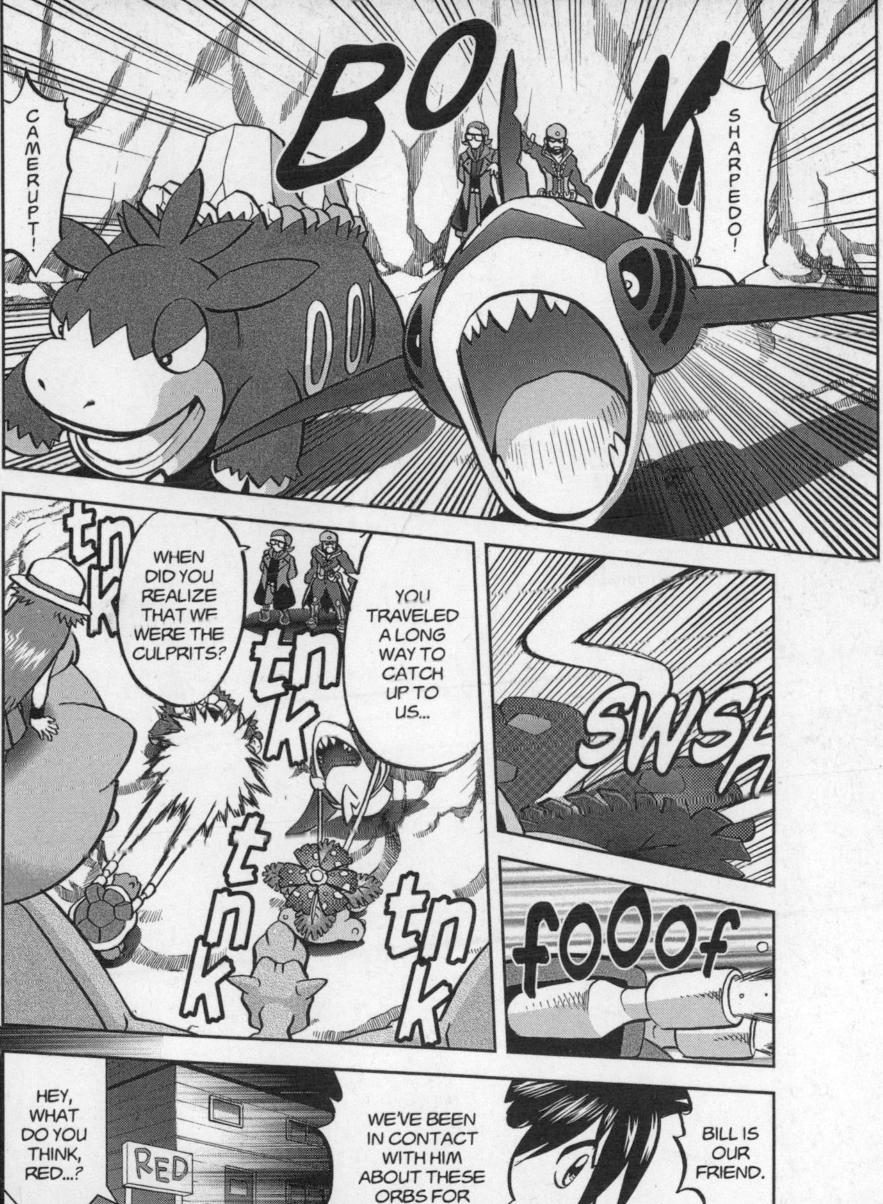
SHARPEDO!
BO M
CAMERUPT!
SWSH
fOOOf
YOU TRAVELED A LONG WAY TO CATCH UP TO US...
WHEN DID YOU REALIZE THAT WE WERE THE CULPRITS?
tnk
tnk
tnk
tnk
BILL IS OUR FRIEND.
WE'VE BEEN IN CONTACT WITH HIM ABOUT THESE ORBS FOR WEEKS NOW.
HEY, WHAT DO YOU THINK, RED...?
RED

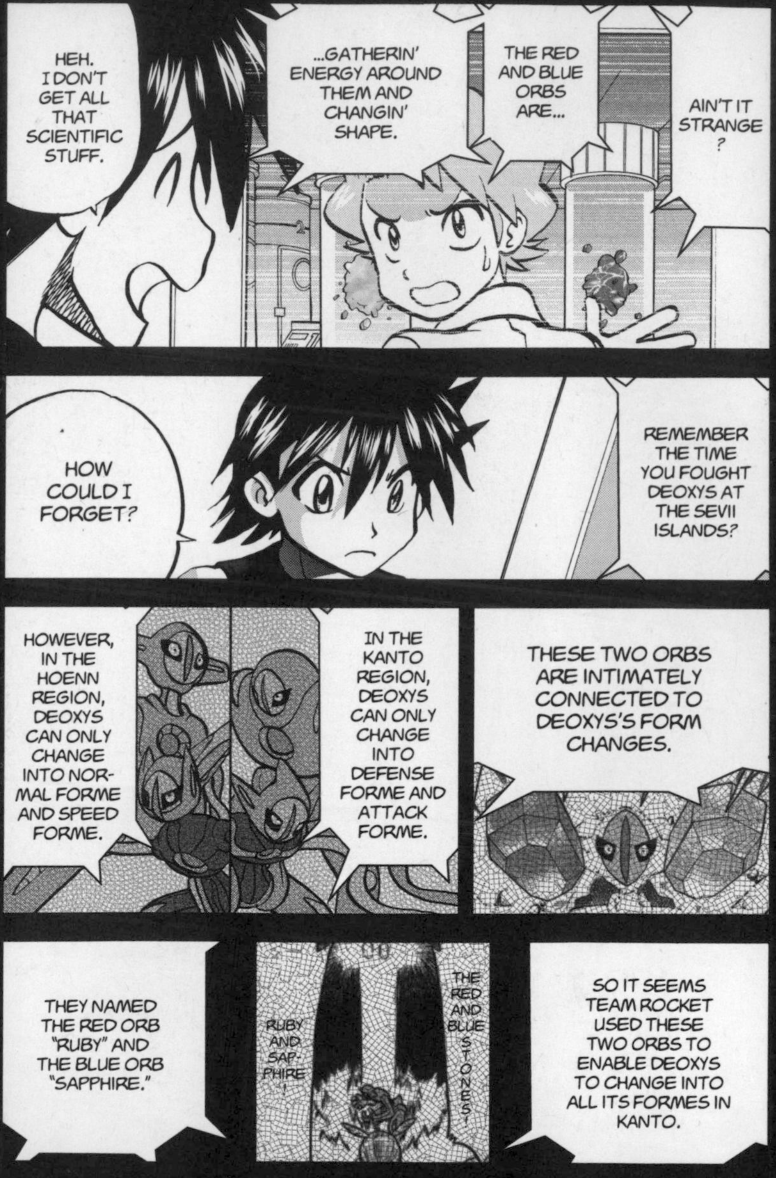
AIN'T IT STRANGE?
THE RED AND BLUE ORBS ARE...
...GATHERIN' ENERGY AROUND THEM AND CHANGIN' SHAPE.
HEH. I DON'T GET ALL THAT SCIENTIFIC STUFF.
REMEMBER THE TIME YOU FOUGHT DEOXYS AT THE SEVII ISLANDS?
HOW COULD I FORGET?
THESE TWO ORBS ARE INTIMATELY CONNECTED TO DEOXYS'S FORM CHANGES.
IN THE KANTO REGION, DEOXYS CAN ONLY CHANGE INTO DEFENSE FORME AND ATTACK FORME.
HOWEVER, IN THE HOENN REGION, DEOXYS CAN ONLY CHANGE INTO NOR-MAL FORME AND SPEED FORME.
SO IT SEEMS TEAM ROCKET USED THESE TWO ORBS TO ENABLE DEOXYS TO CHANGE INTO ALL ITS FORMES IN KANTO.
THE RED AND BLUE STONES!
RUBY AND SAP-PHIRE!
THEY NAMED THE RED ORB "RUBY" AND THE BLUE ORB "SAPPHIRE."

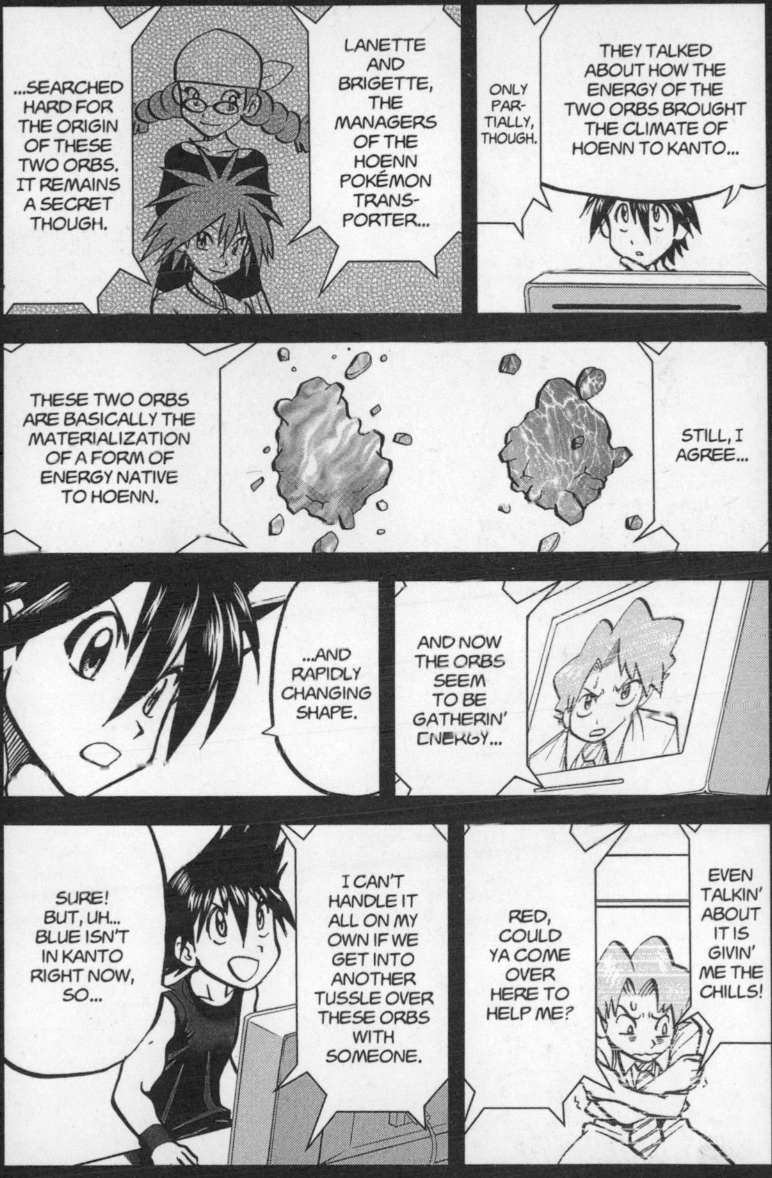
THEY TALKED ABOUT HOW THE ENERGY OF THE TWO ORBS BROUGHT THE CLIMATE OF HOENN TO KANTO...
ONLY PARTIALLY, THOUGH.
LANETTE AND BRIGETTE, THE MANAGERS OF THE HOENN POKÉMON TRANSPORTER...
...SEARCHED HARD FOR THE ORIGIN OF THESE TWO ORBS. IT REMAINS A SECRET THOUGH.
STILL, I AGREE...
THESE TWO ORBS ARE BASICALLY THE MATERIALIZATION OF A FORM OF ENERGY NATIVE TO HOENN.
AND NOW THE ORBS SEEM TO BE GATHERIN' ENERGY...
...AND RAPIDLY CHANGING SHAPE.
EVEN TALKIN' ABOUT IT IS GIVIN' ME THE CHILLS!
RED, COULD YA COME OVER HERE TO HELP ME?
I CAN'T HANDLE IT ALL ON MY OWN IF WE GET INTO ANOTHER TUSSLE OVER THESE ORBS WITH SOMEONE.
SURE! BUT, UH... BLUE ISN'T IN KANTO RIGHT NOW, SO...

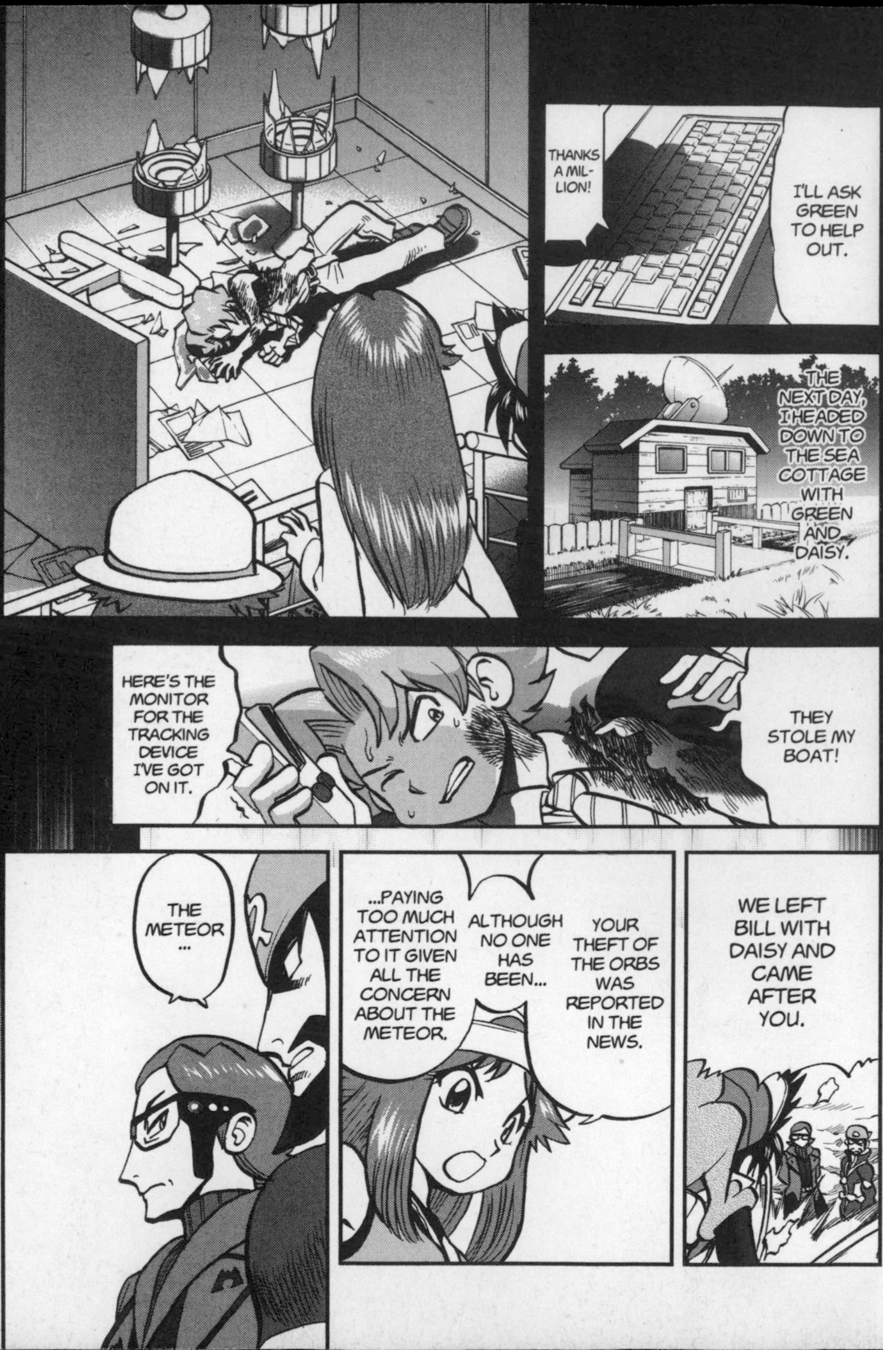
I'LL ASK GREEN TO HELP OUT.
THANKS A MIL-LION!
THE NEXT DAY, I HEADED DOWN TO THE SEA COTTAGE WITH GREEN AND DAISY.
THEY STOLE MY BOAT!
HERE'S THE MONITOR FOR THE TRACKING DEVICE I'VE GOT ON IT.
WE LEFT BILL WITH DAISY AND CAME AFTER YOU.
YOUR THEFT OF THE ORBS WAS REPORTED IN THE NEWS.
ALTHOUGH NO ONE HAS BEEN...
...PAYING TOO MUCH ATTENTION TO IT GIVEN ALL THE CONCERN ABOUT THE METEOR.
THE METEOR ...

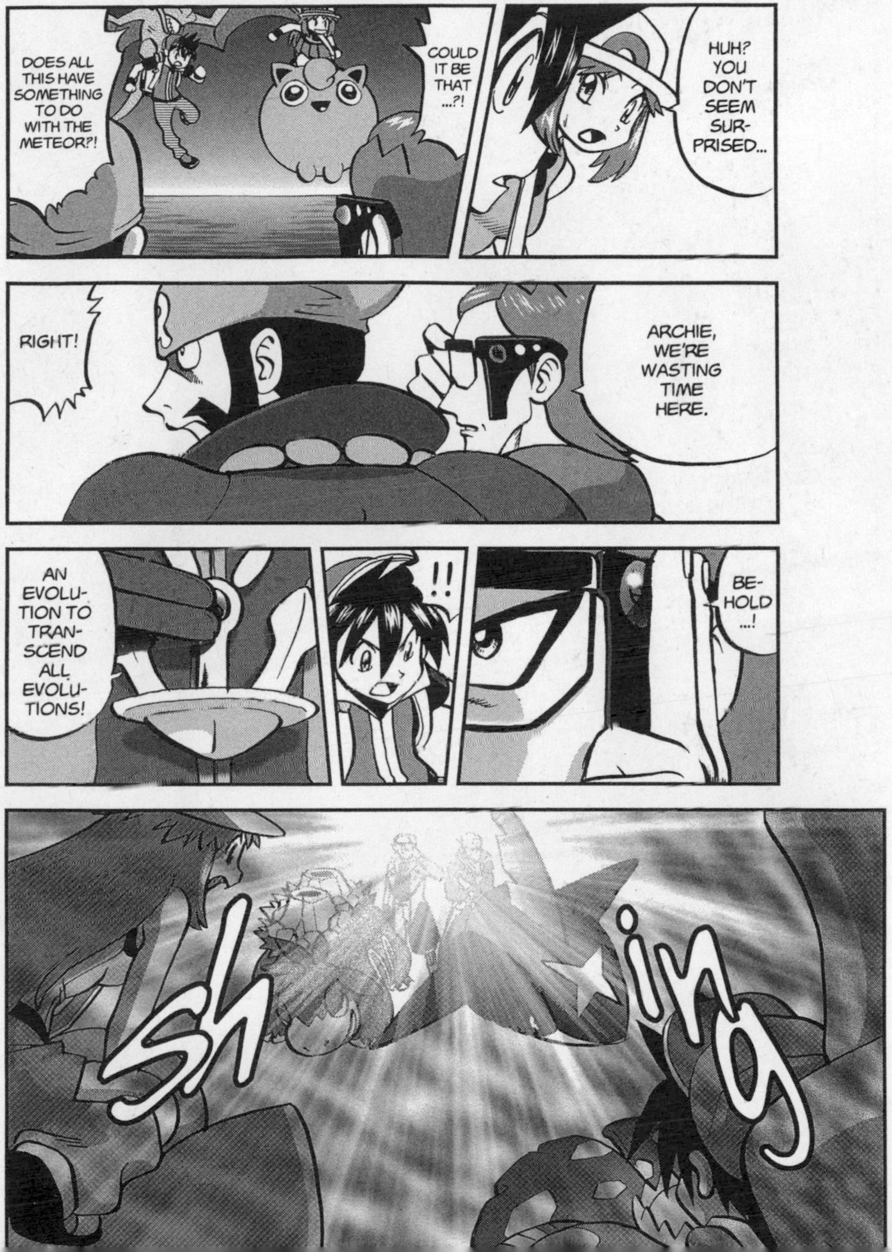
HUH? YOU DON'T SEEM SUR-PRISED...
COULD IT BE THAT ...?!
DOES ALL THIS HAVE SOMETHING TO DO WITH THE METEOR?!
ARCHIE, WE'RE WASTING TIME HERE.
RIGHT!
BE-HOLD ...!
!!
AN EVOLU-TION TO TRAN-SCEND ALL EVOLU-TIONS!
Shing

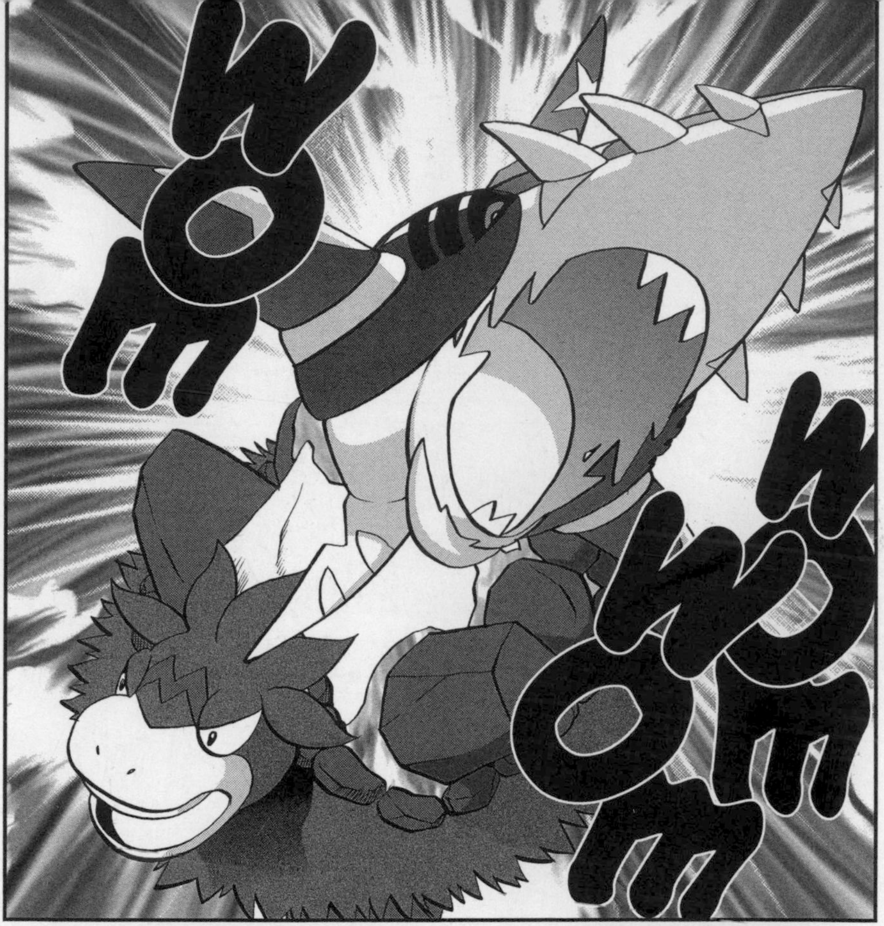
WOM
WOM
WOM

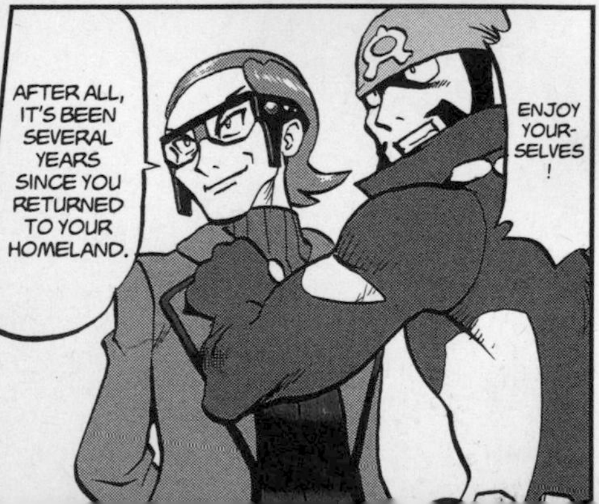
ENJOY YOURSELVES!
AFTER ALL, IT'S BEEN SEVERAL YEARS SINCE YOU RETURNED TO YOUR HOMELAND.

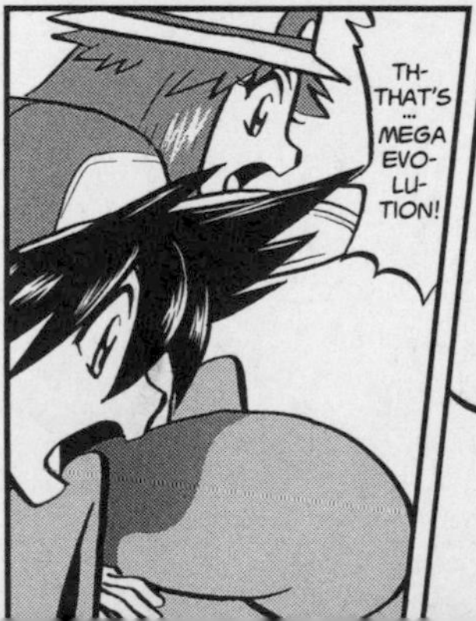
TH-THAT'S... MEGA EVOLUTION!

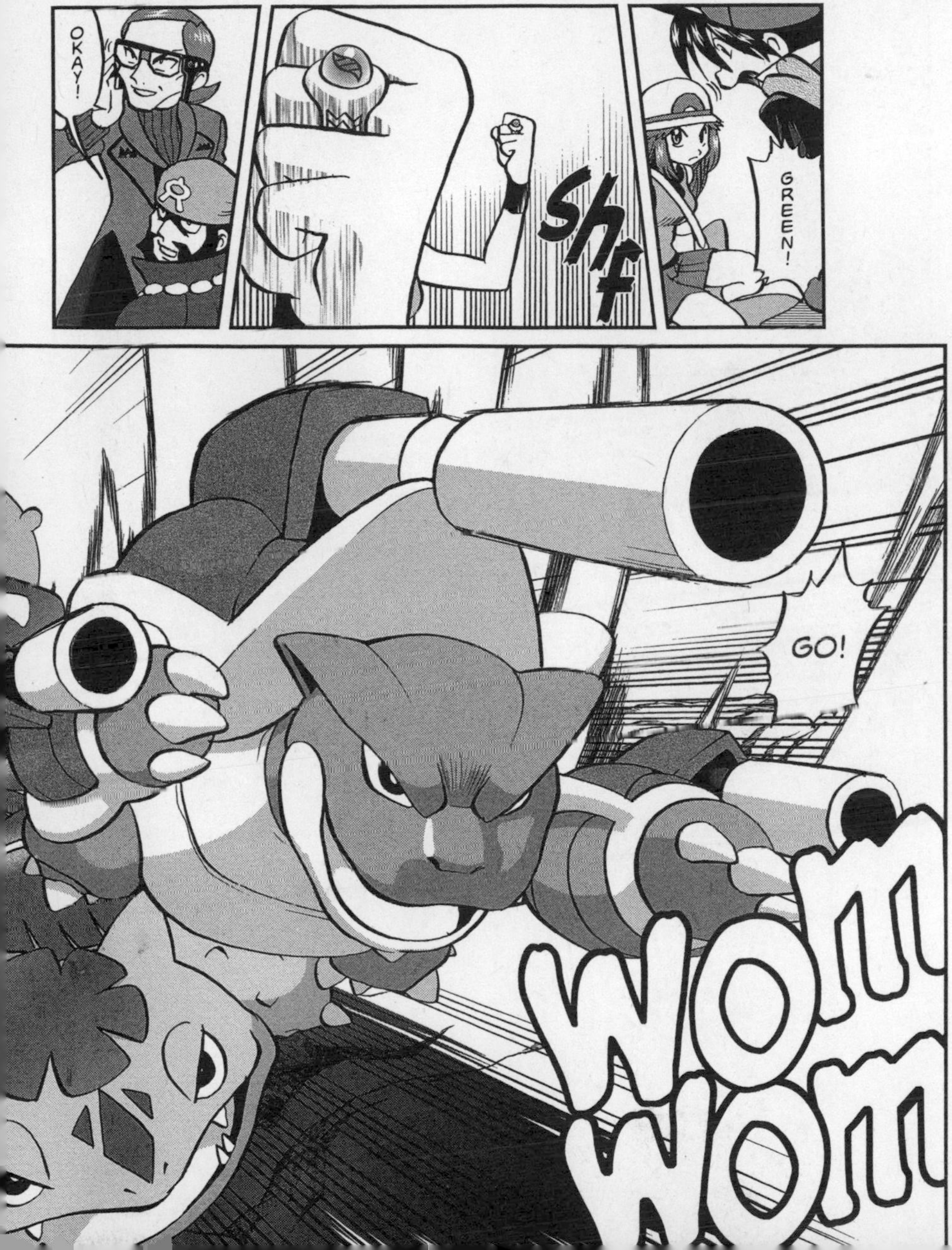
GREEN!
Shf
OKAY!
GO!
WOM
WOM

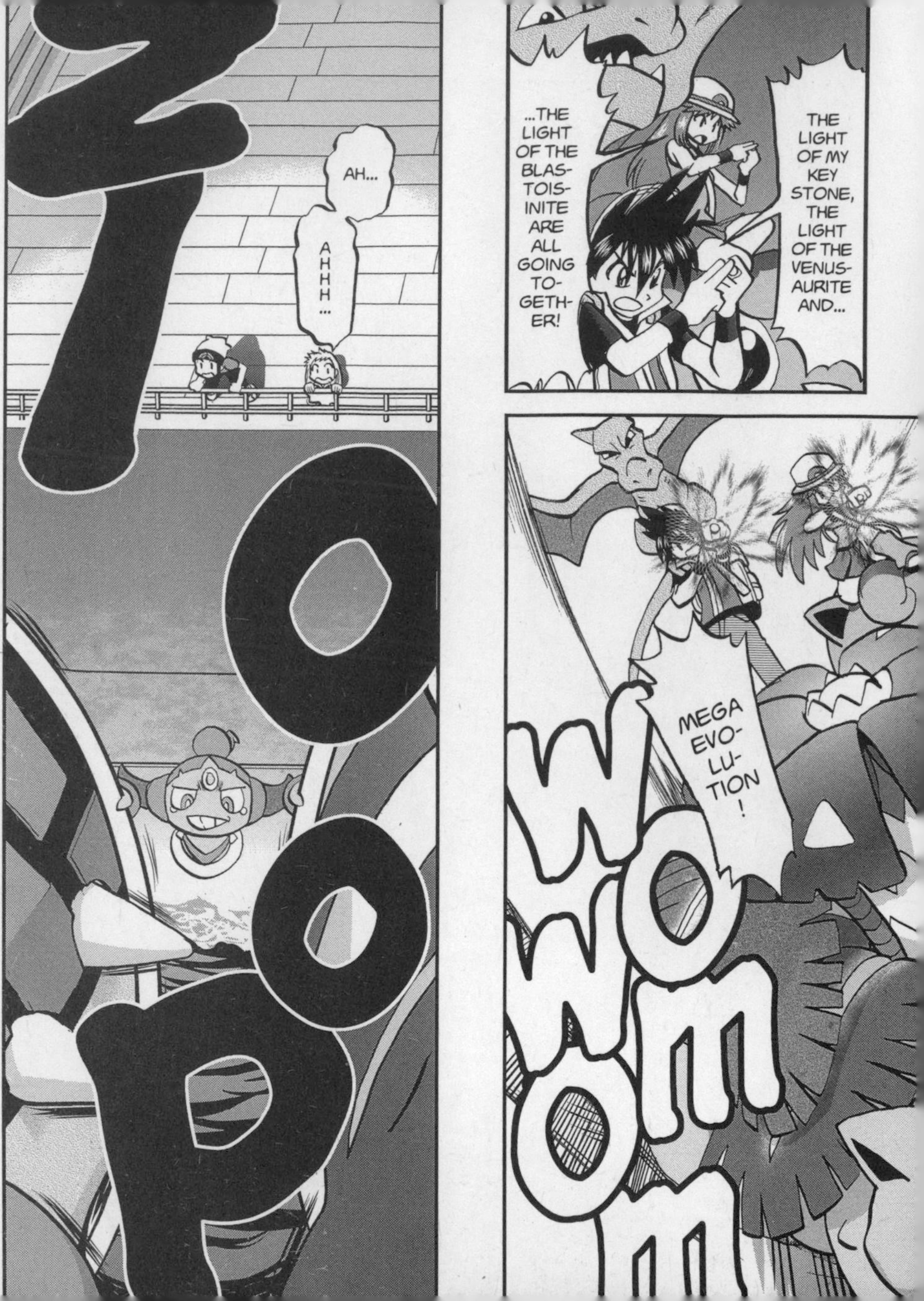
THE LIGHT OF MY KEY STONE, THE LIGHT OF THE VENUSAURITE AND...
...THE LIGHT OF THE BLASTOISINITE ARE ALL GOING TOGETHER!
MEGA EVOLUTION!
WOOM WOOM
AH...
AHHH...

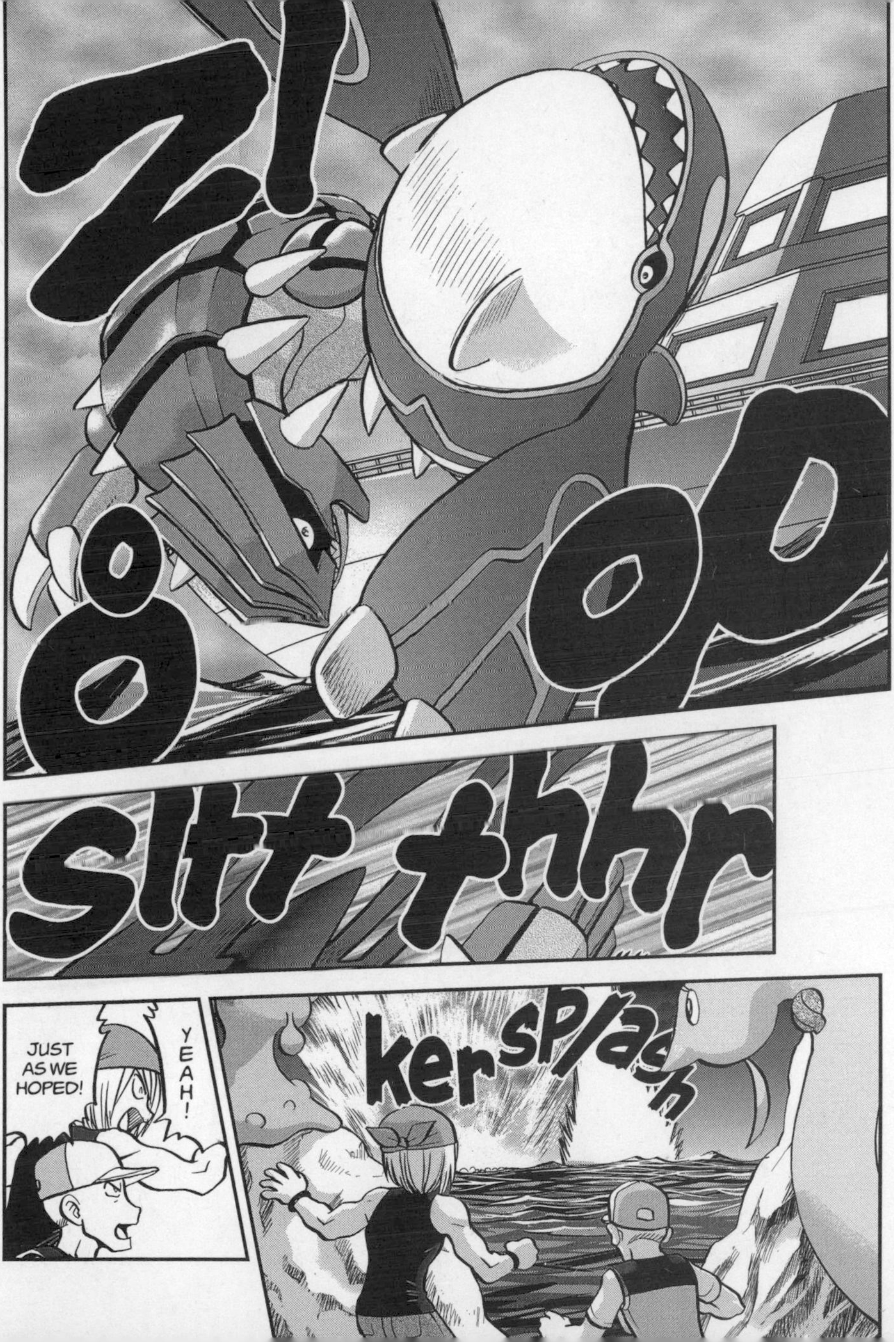
kersplash
YEAH!
JUST AS WE HOPED!

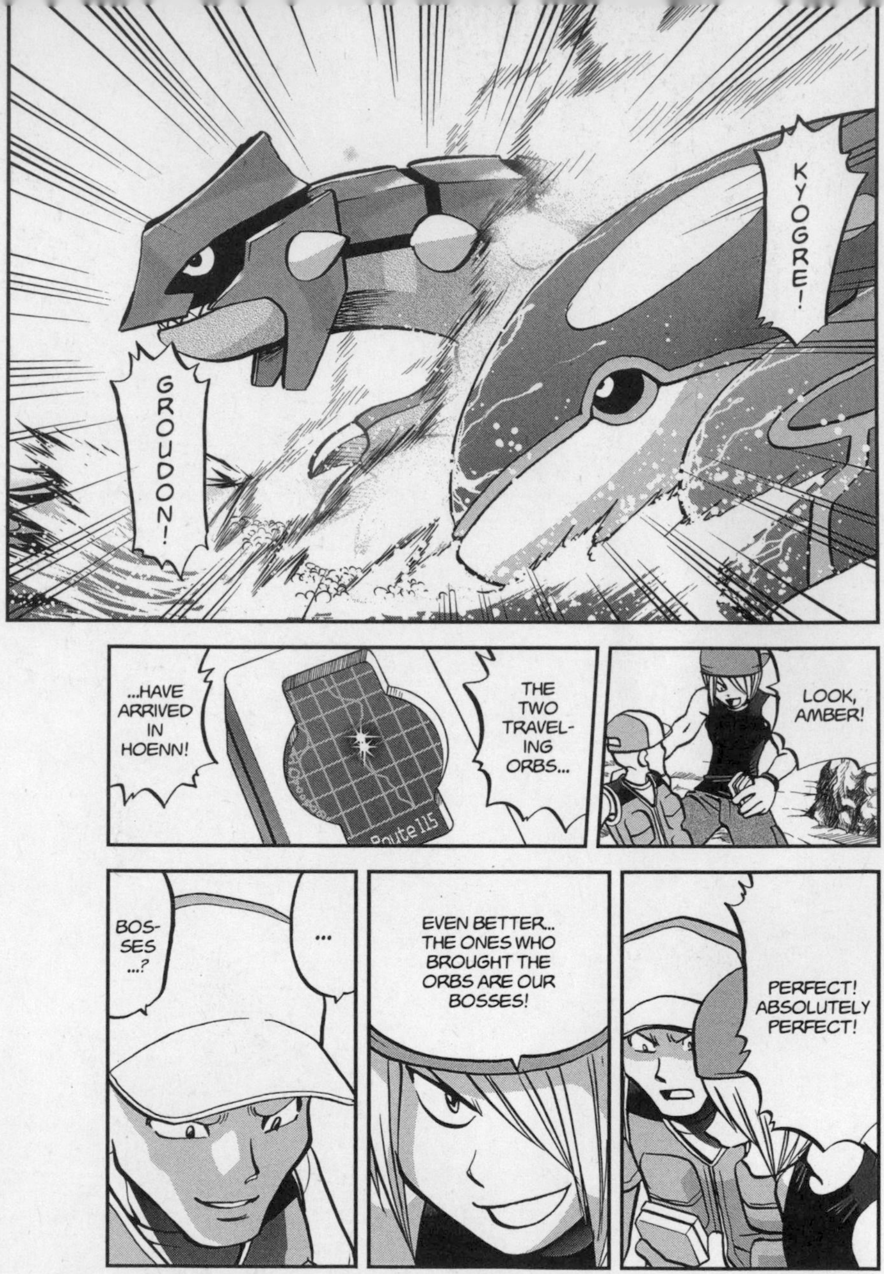
KYOGRE!
GROUDON!
LOOK, AMBER!
THE TWO TRAVELING ORBS...
...HAVE ARRIVED IN HOENN!
PERFECT! ABSOLUTELY PERFECT!
EVEN BETTER... THE ONES WHO BROUGHT THE ORBS ARE OUR BOSSES!
...
BOSSES...?

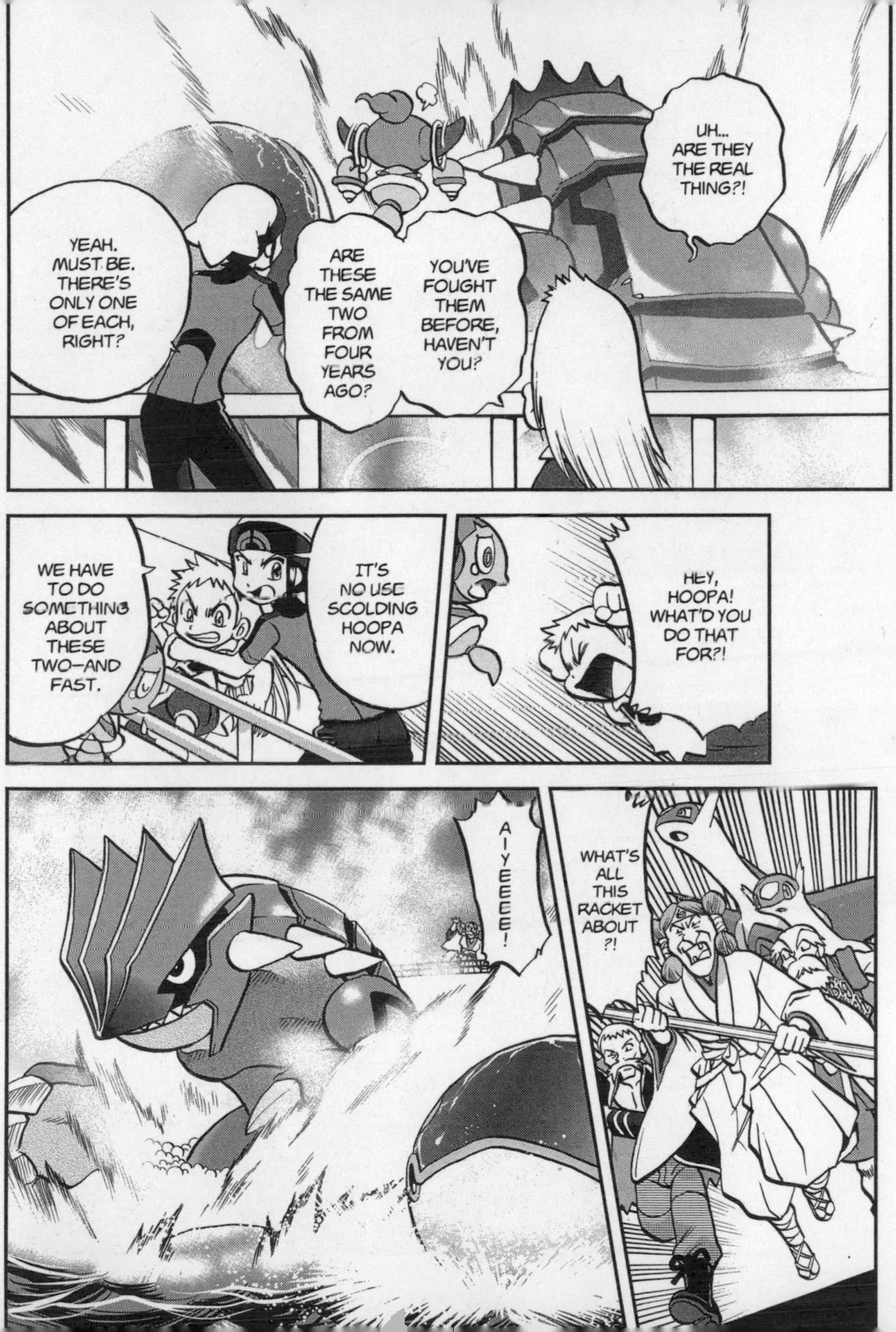
UH... ARE THEY THE REAL THING?!
YOU'VE FOUGHT THEM BEFORE, HAVEN'T YOU?
ARE THESE THE SAME TWO FROM FOUR YEARS AGO?
YEAH. MUST BE. THERE'S ONLY ONE OF EACH, RIGHT?
HEY, HOOPA! WHAT'D YOU DO THAT FOR?!
IT'S NO USE SCOLDING HOOPA NOW.
WE HAVE TO DO SOMETHING ABOUT THESE TWO—AND FAST.
WHAT'S ALL THIS RACKET ABOUT ?!
AIYEEEEE!

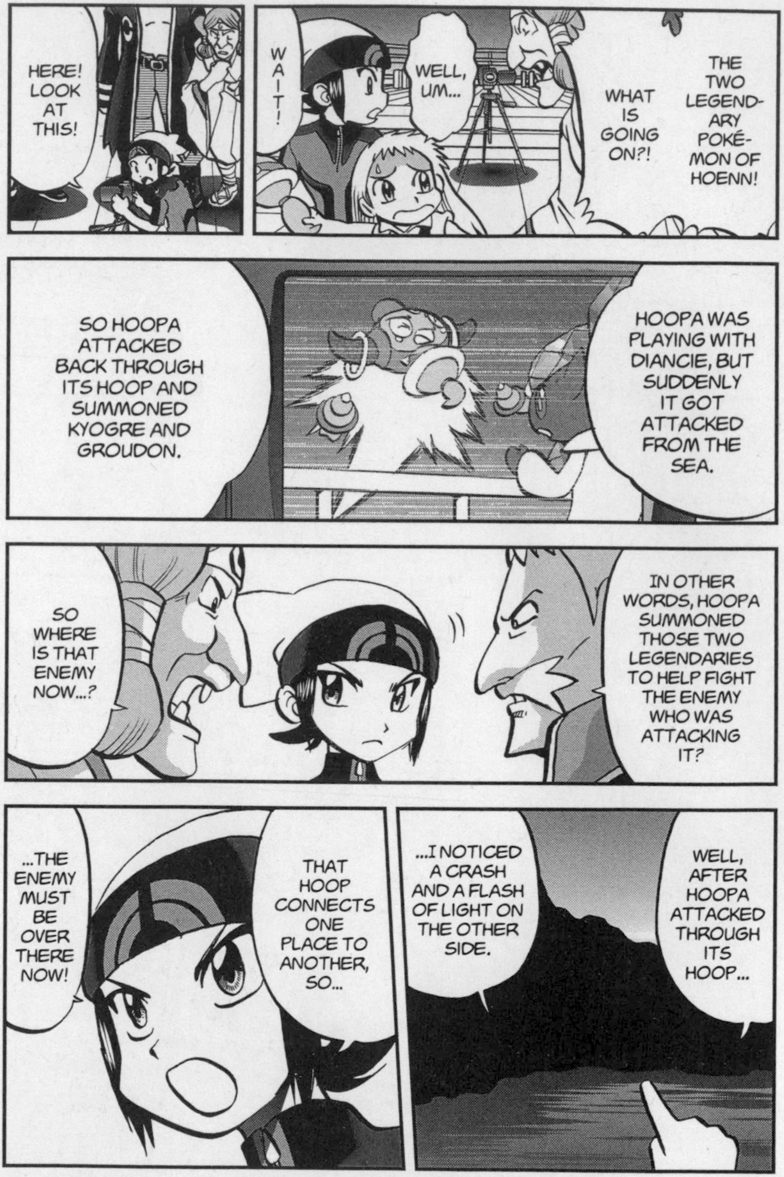
THE TWO LEGENDARY POKÉMON OF HOENN!
WHAT IS GOING ON?!
WELL, UM...
WAIT!
HERE! LOOK AT THIS!
HOOPA WAS PLAYING WITH DIANCIE, BUT SUDDENLY IT GOT ATTACKED FROM THE SEA.
SO HOOPA ATTACKED BACK THROUGH ITS HOOP AND SUMMONED KYOGRE AND GROUDON.
IN OTHER WORDS, HOOPA SUMMONED THOSE TWO LEGENDARIES TO HELP FIGHT THE ENEMY WHO WAS ATTACKING IT?
SO WHERE IS THAT ENEMY NOW...?
WELL, AFTER HOOPA ATTACKED THROUGH ITS HOOP...
...I NOTICED A CRASH AND A FLASH OF LIGHT ON THE OTHER SIDE.
THAT HOOP CONNECTS ONE PLACE TO ANOTHER, SO...
...THE ENEMY MUST BE OVER THERE NOW!

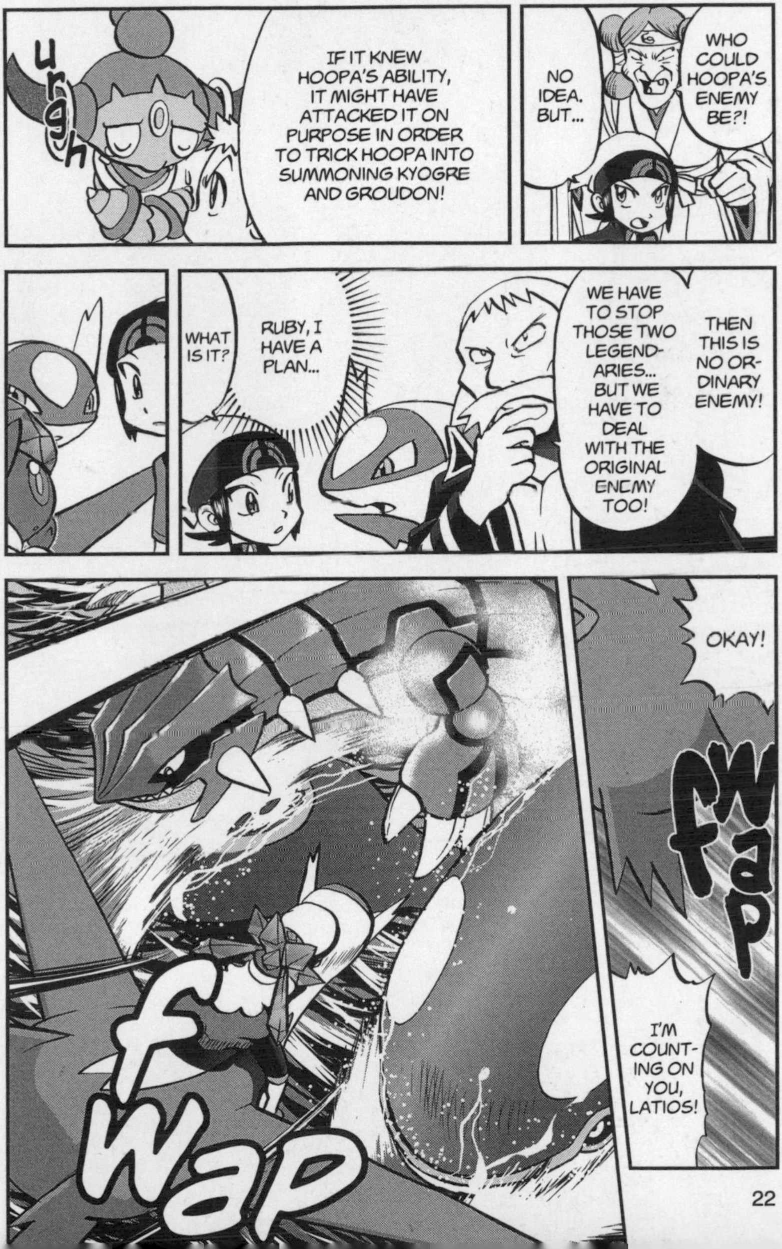
WHO COULD HOOPA'S ENEMY BE?!
NO IDEA. BUT...
IF IT KNEW HOOPA'S ABILITY, IT MIGHT HAVE ATTACKED IT ON PURPOSE IN ORDER TO TRICK HOOPA INTO SUMMONING KYOGRE AND GROUDON!
urgh
THEN THIS IS NO ORDINARY ENEMY!
WE HAVE TO STOP THOSE TWO LEGENDARIES... BUT WE HAVE TO DEAL WITH THE ORIGINAL ENEMY TOO!
RUBY, I HAVE A PLAN...
WHAT IS IT?
OKAY!
fwap
I'M COUNTING ON YOU, LATIOS!
fwap

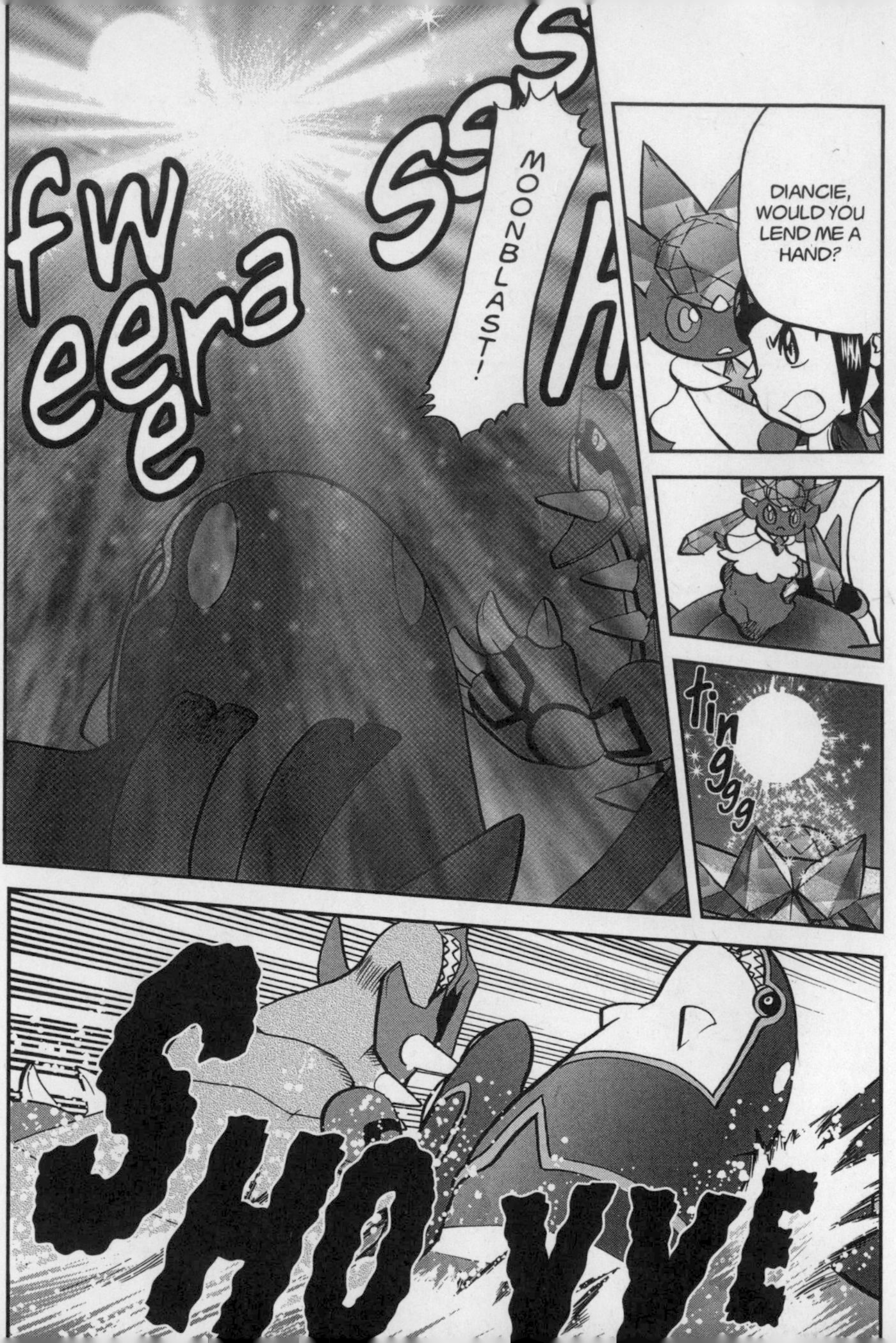

DIANCIE, WOULD YOU LEND ME A HAND?
tinggg
MOONBLAST!
fweeeera
sssssh
SHOVVE

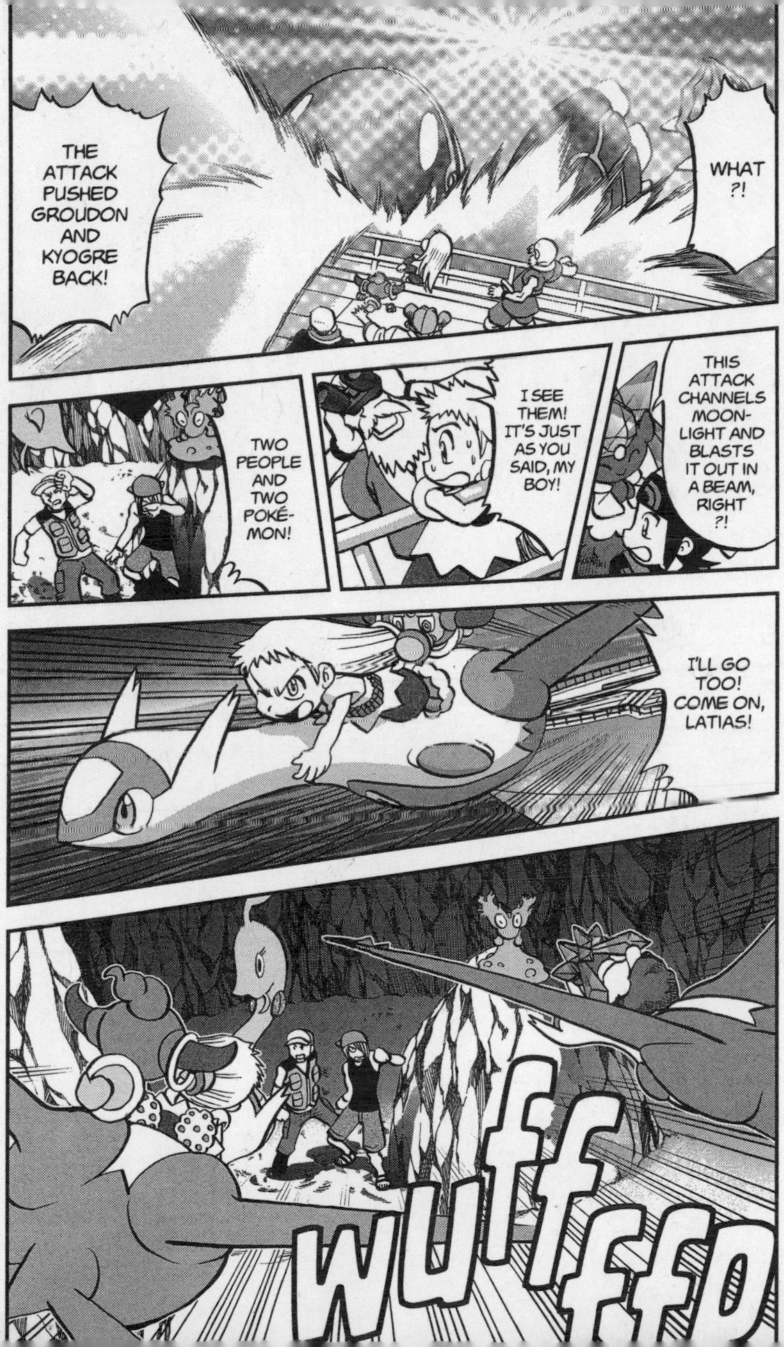
WHAT ?!
THE ATTACK PUSHED GROUDON AND KYOGRE BACK!
THIS ATTACK CHANNELS MOON-LIGHT AND BLASTS IT OUT IN A BEAM, RIGHT ?!
I SEE THEM! IT'S JUST AS YOU SAID, MY BOY!
TWO PEOPLE AND TWO POKÉ-MON!
I'LL GO TOO! COME ON, LATIAS!
wuffffo

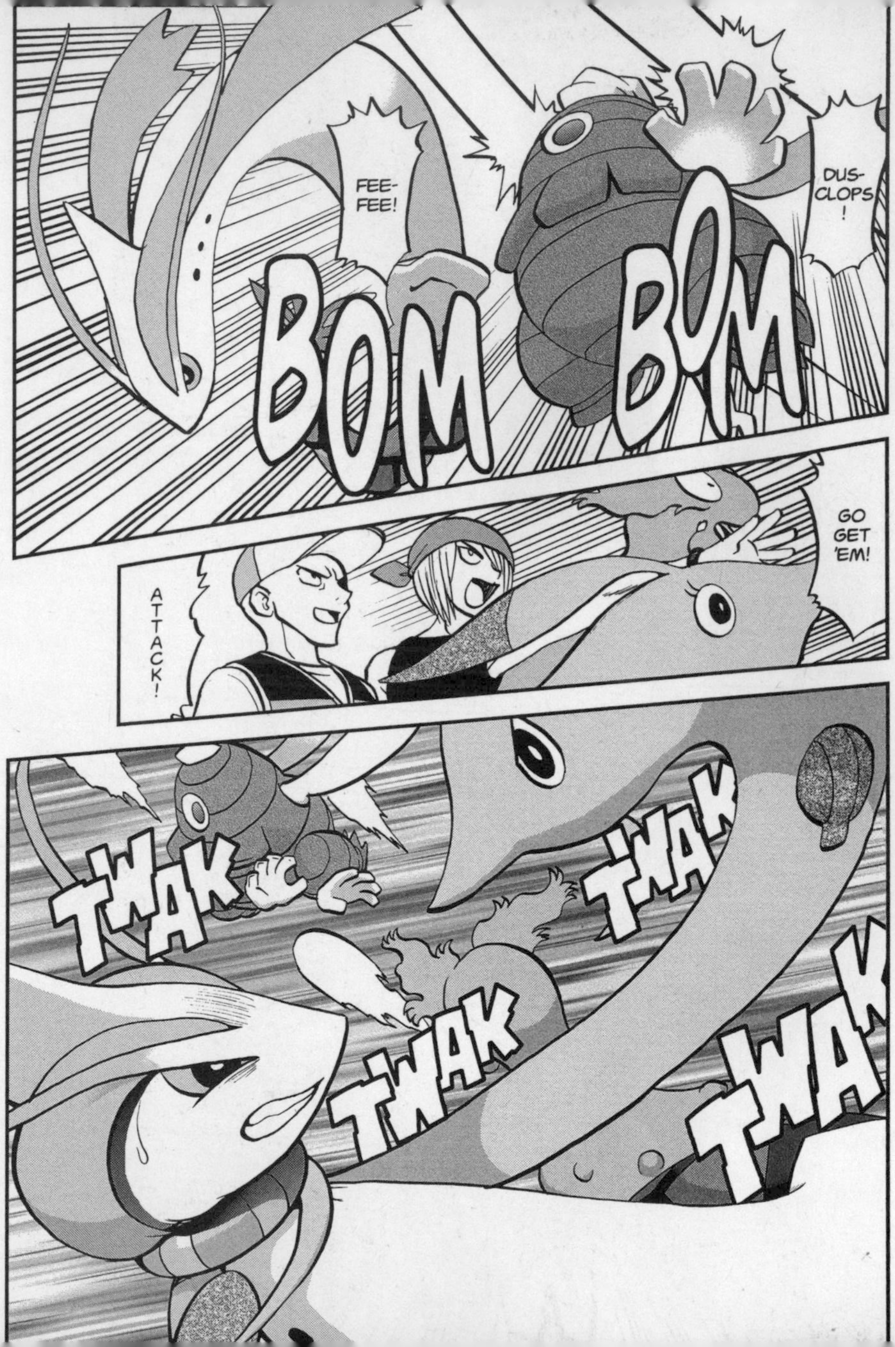
DUS-CLOPS!
FEE-FEE!
BOM
BOM
GO GET 'EM!
ATTACK!
TWAK
TWAK
TWAK
TWAK

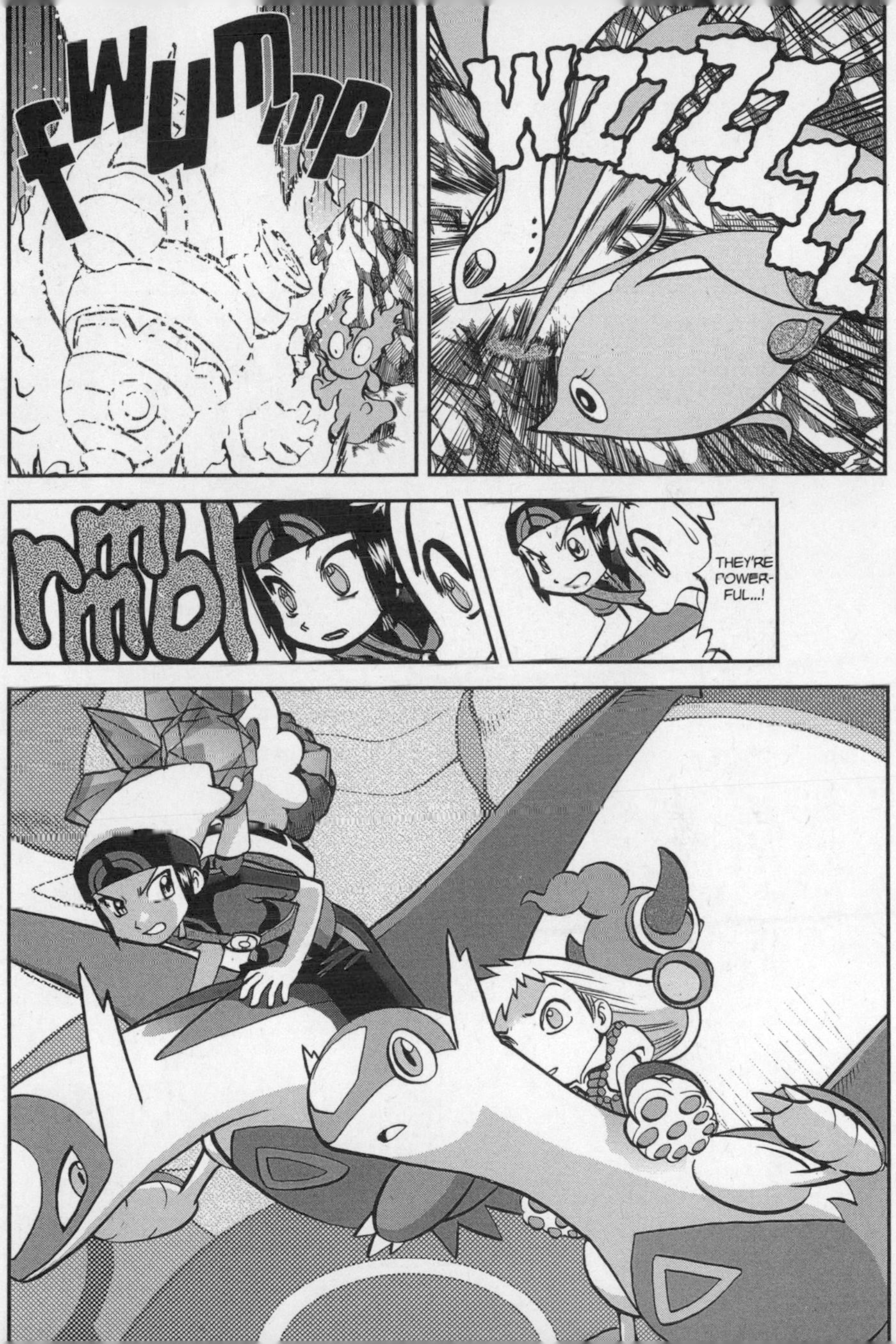
fwummp
THEY'RE POWER-FUL...!
rmmbl

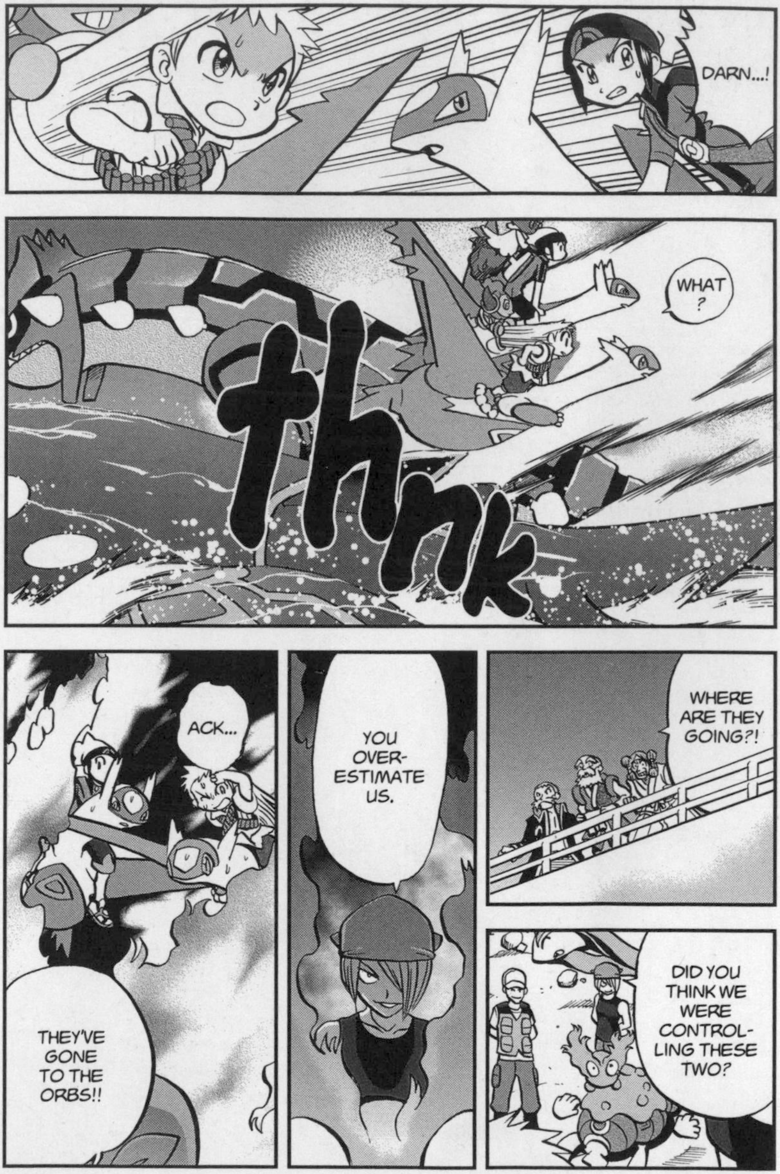
DARN...!
WHAT?
thnk
WHERE ARE THEY GOING?!
DID YOU THINK WE WERE CONTROL-LING THESE TWO?
YOU OVER-ESTIMATE US.
ACK...
THEY'VE GONE TO THE ORBS!!

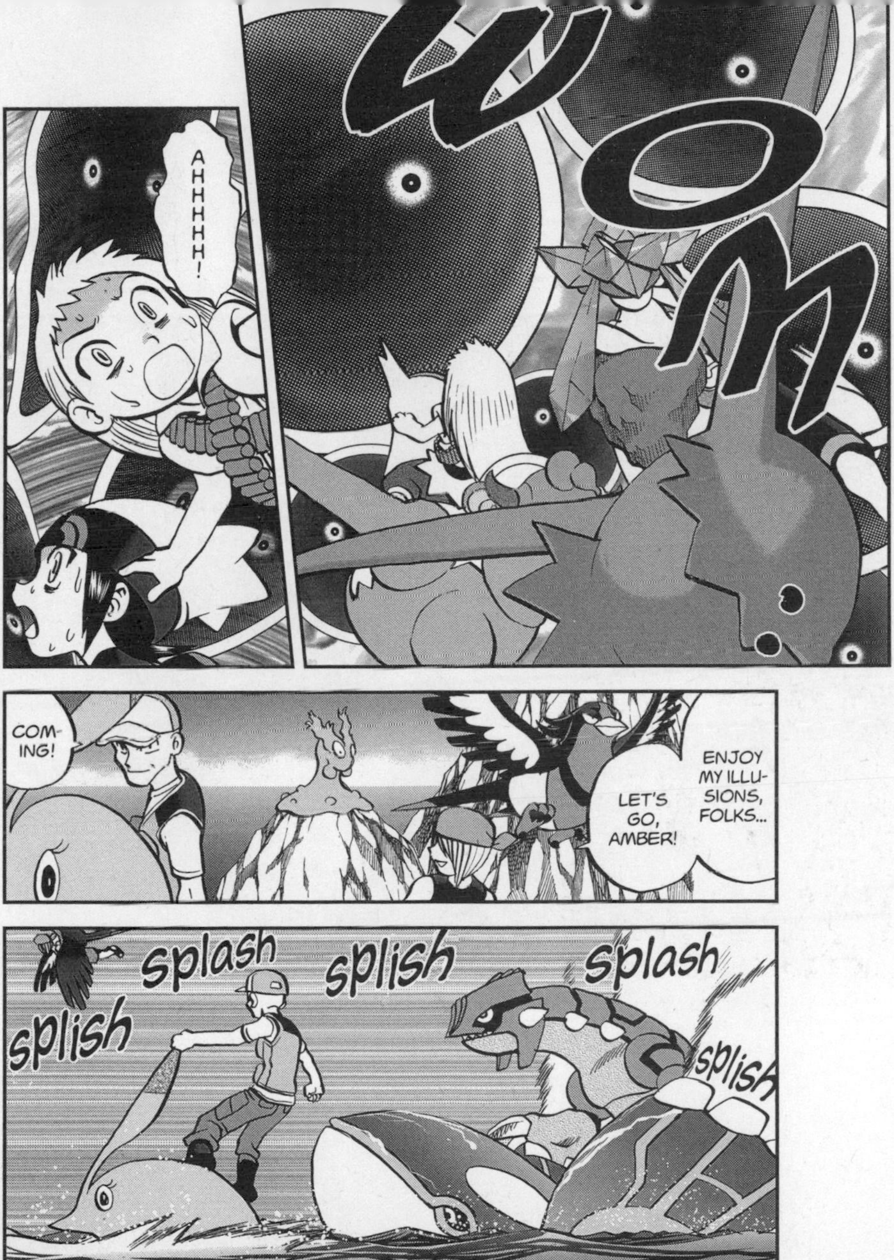
WOM
AHHHHH!
ENJOY MY ILLUSIONS, FOLKS...
LET'S GO, AMBER!
COMING!
splash
splish
splish
splash
splish

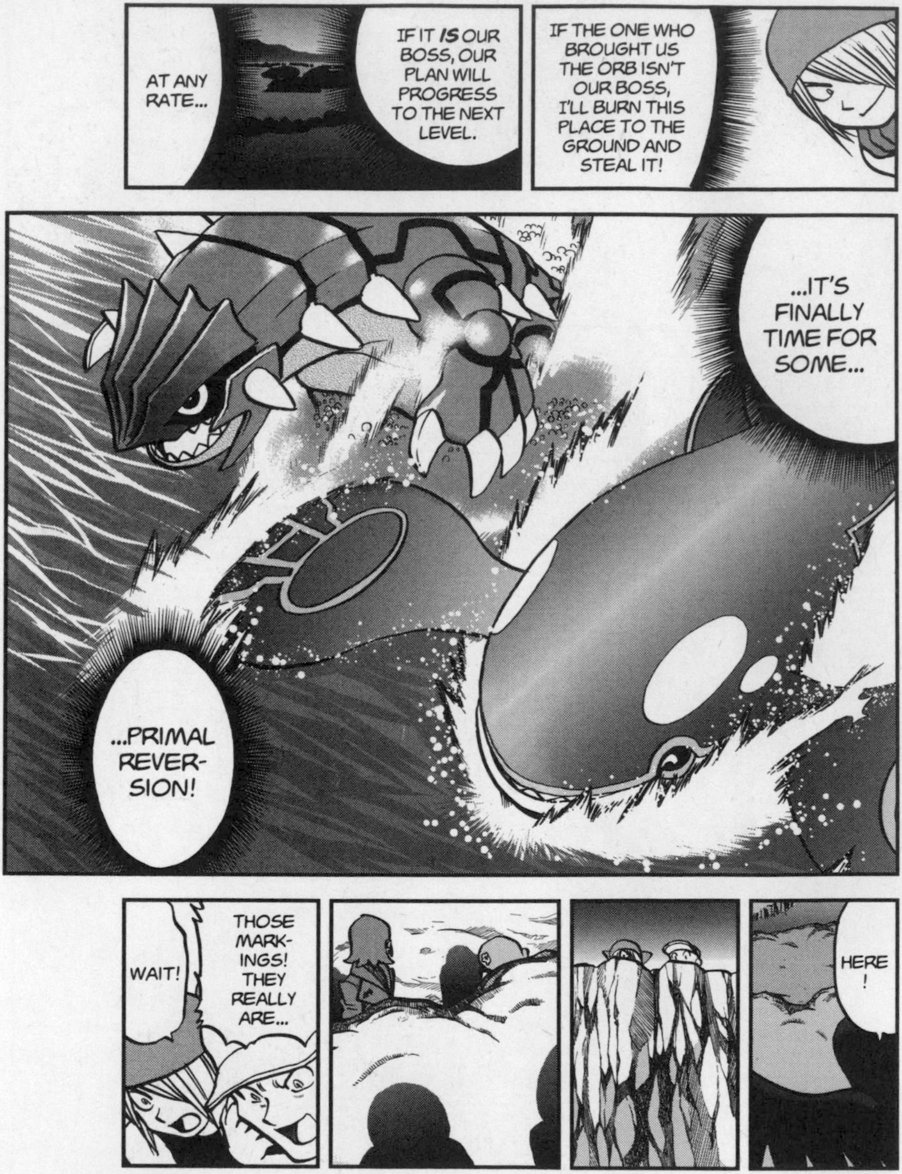
AT ANY RATE...
IF IT IS OUR BOSS, OUR PLAN WILL PROGRESS TO THE NEXT LEVEL.
IF THE ONE WHO BROUGHT US THE ORB ISN'T OUR BOSS, I'LL BURN THIS PLACE TO THE GROUND AND STEAL IT!
...IT'S FINALLY TIME FOR SOME...
...PRIMAL REVER-SION!
WAIT!
THOSE MARK-INGS! THEY REALLY ARE...
HERE!

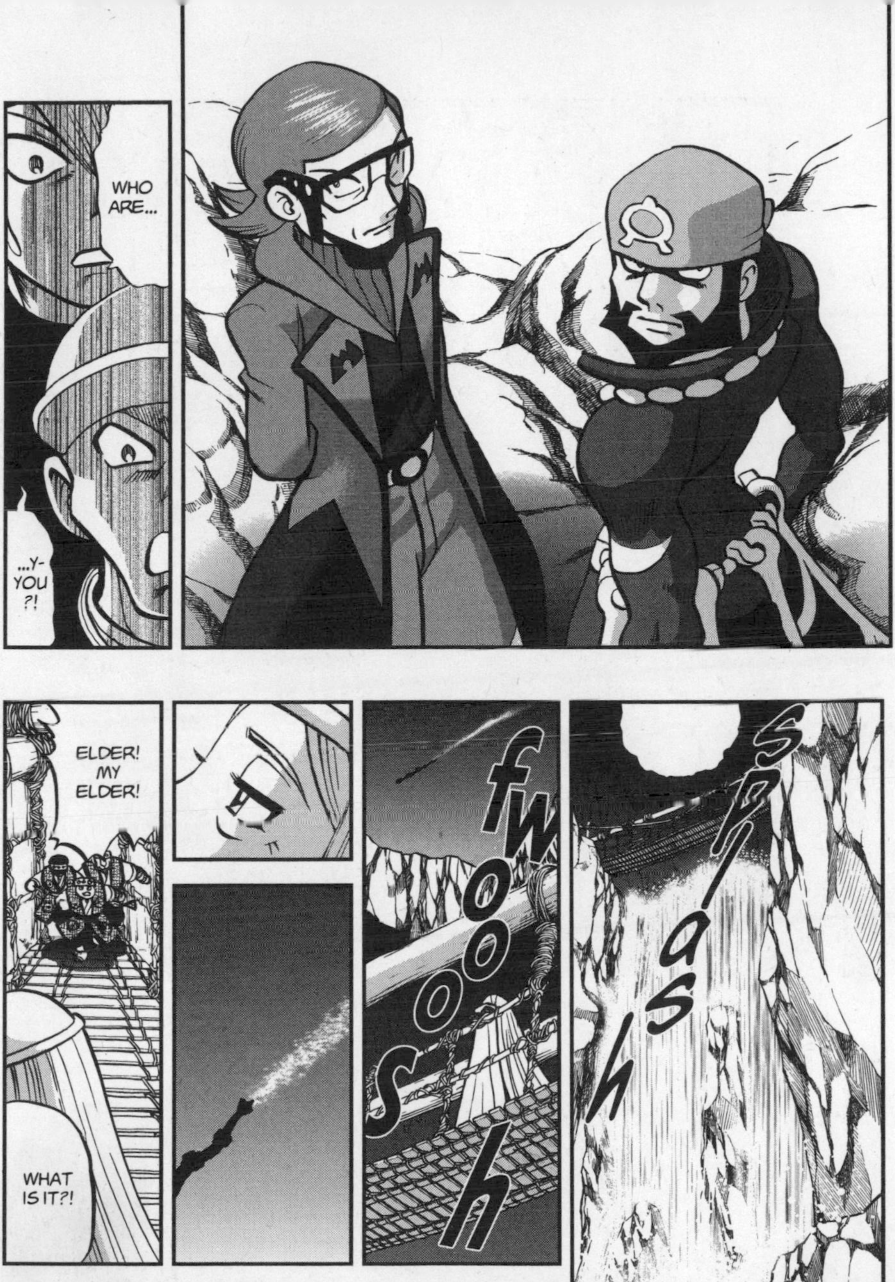
WHO ARE...
...Y-YOU?!
splash
fwoooosh
ELDER! MY ELDER!
WHAT IS IT?!

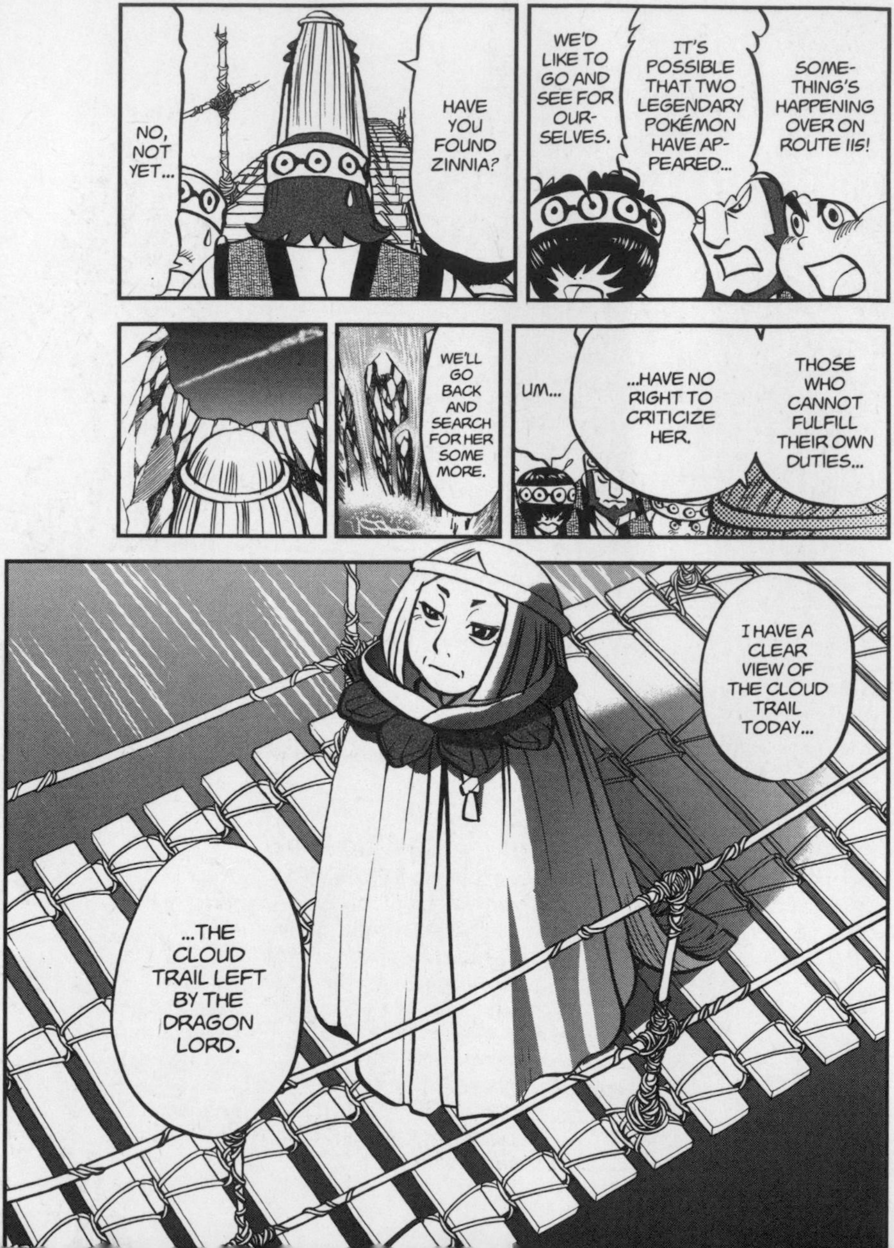
SOMETHING'S HAPPENING OVER ON ROUTE 115!
IT'S POSSIBLE THAT TWO LEGENDARY POKÉMON HAVE APPEARED...
WE'D LIKE TO GO AND SEE FOR OURSELVES.
HAVE YOU FOUND ZINNIA?
NO, NOT YET...
THOSE WHO CANNOT FULFILL THEIR OWN DUTIES...
...HAVE NO RIGHT TO CRITICIZE HER.
UM...
WE'LL GO BACK AND SEARCH FOR HER SOME MORE.
I HAVE A CLEAR VIEW OF THE CLOUD TRAIL TODAY...
...THE CLOUD TRAIL LEFT BY THE DRAGON LORD.

METEOR FALLS

The place where the Draconid live. It can be entered from Route 114 and Route 115. Many Trainers train their Dragon-type Pokémon here. One must traverse a massive mazelike route to reach the Draconid's village. Rumor has it that a huge open space exists behind a waterfall there...

THE DRACONID PEOPLE

For a thousand years, this tribe has passed down the lore of how to stop a large meteor from striking the planet. The name Draconid is closely related to "Dragon," so, as you've probably guessed, they are specialists in Dragon-type Pokémon. The Draconid live in a secluded village without modern technology, so few know of their existence. The member of the tribe who takes on the role of passing down the lore is called the Lorekeeper and has a special high status in the tribe.

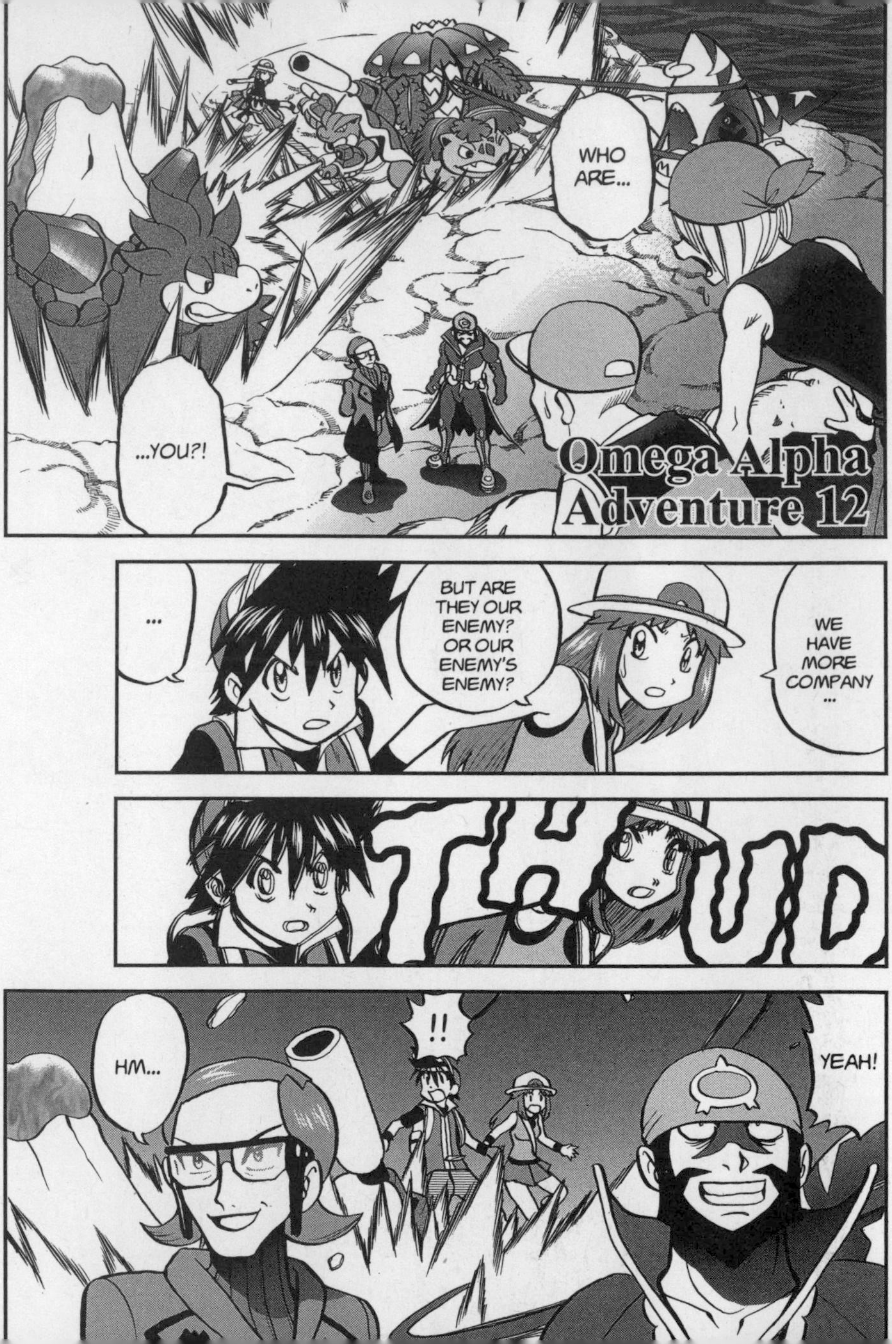
WHO ARE...
...YOU?!
Omega Alpha Adventure 12
WE HAVE MORE COMPANY ...
BUT ARE THEY OUR ENEMY? OR OUR ENEMY'S ENEMY?
...
THUD
YEAH!
!!
HM...

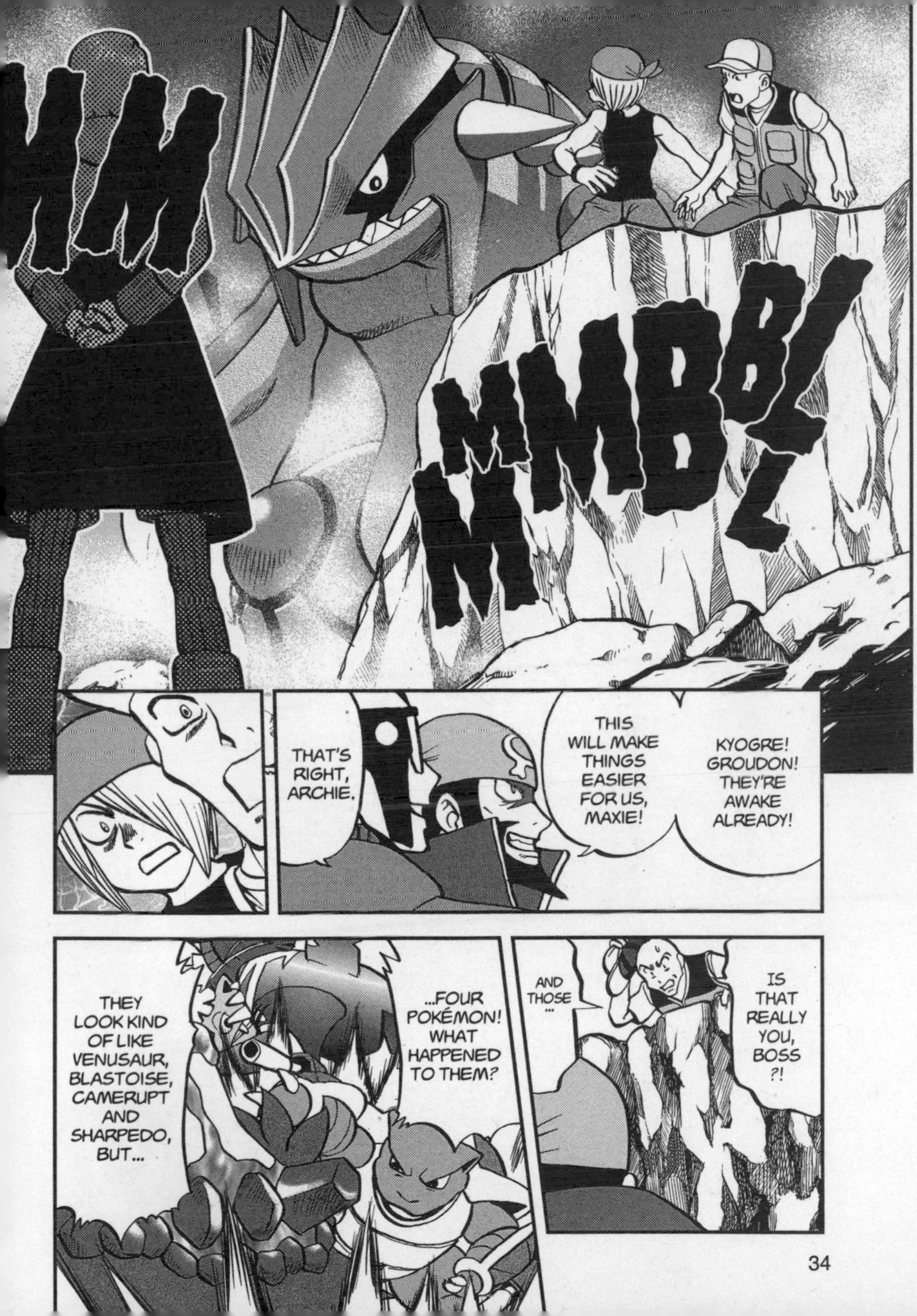

MMBL
MMBL
KYOGRE! GROUDON! THEY'RE AWAKE ALREADY!
THIS WILL MAKE THINGS EASIER FOR US, MAXIE!
THAT'S RIGHT, ARCHIE.
IS THAT REALLY YOU, BOSS?!
AND THOSE ...
...FOUR POKÉMON! WHAT HAPPENED TO THEM?
THEY LOOK KIND OF LIKE VENUSAUR, BLASTOISE, CAMERUPT AND SHARPEDO, BUT...

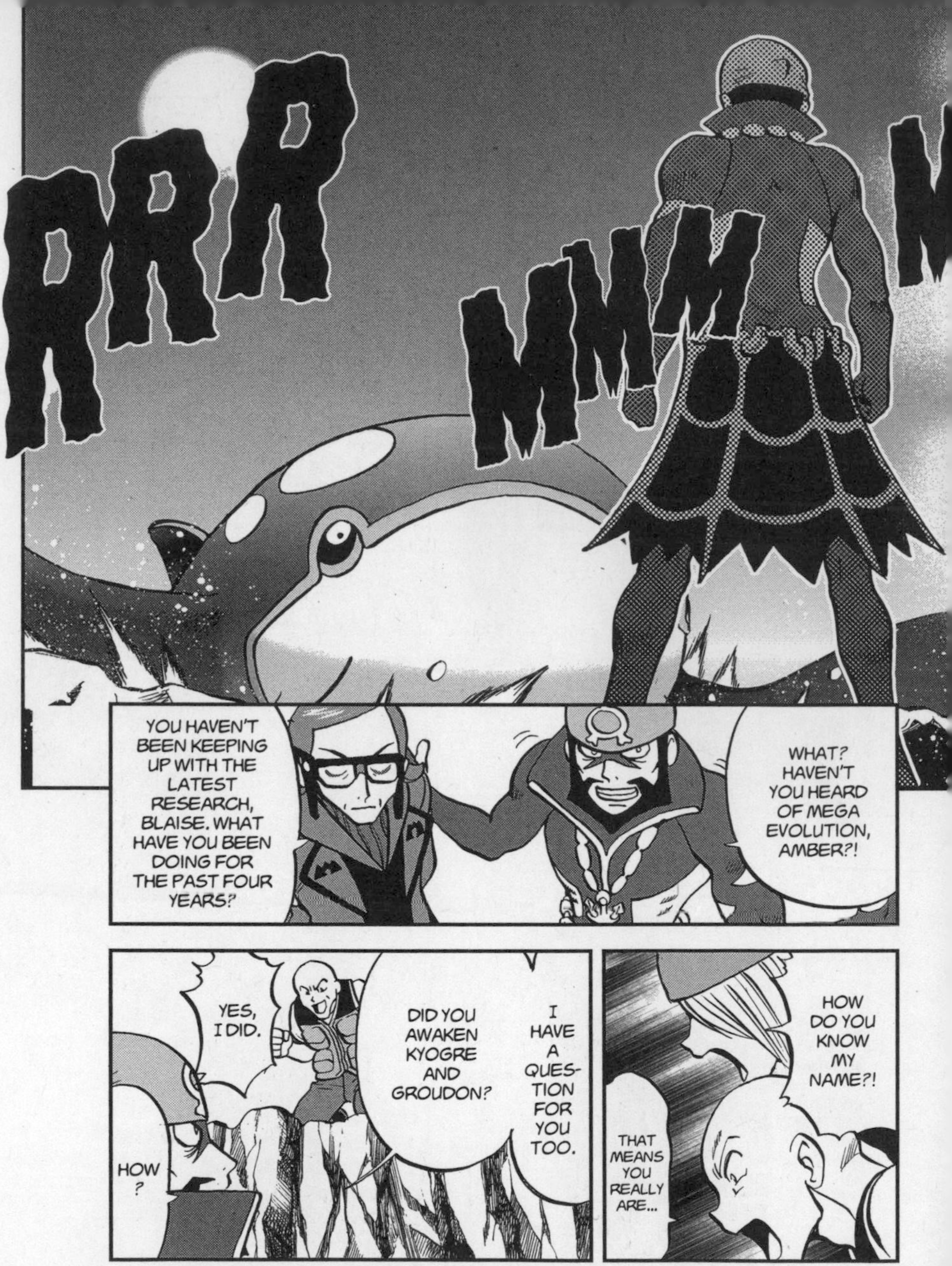

RRRMMMM
WHAT? HAVEN'T YOU HEARD OF MEGA EVOLUTION, AMBER?!
YOU HAVEN'T BEEN KEEPING UP WITH THE LATEST RESEARCH, BLAISE. WHAT HAVE YOU BEEN DOING FOR THE PAST FOUR YEARS?
HOW DO YOU KNOW MY NAME?!
THAT MEANS YOU REALLY ARE...
I HAVE A QUES-TION FOR YOU TOO.
DID YOU AWAKEN KYOGRE AND GROUDON?
YES, I DID.
HOW?

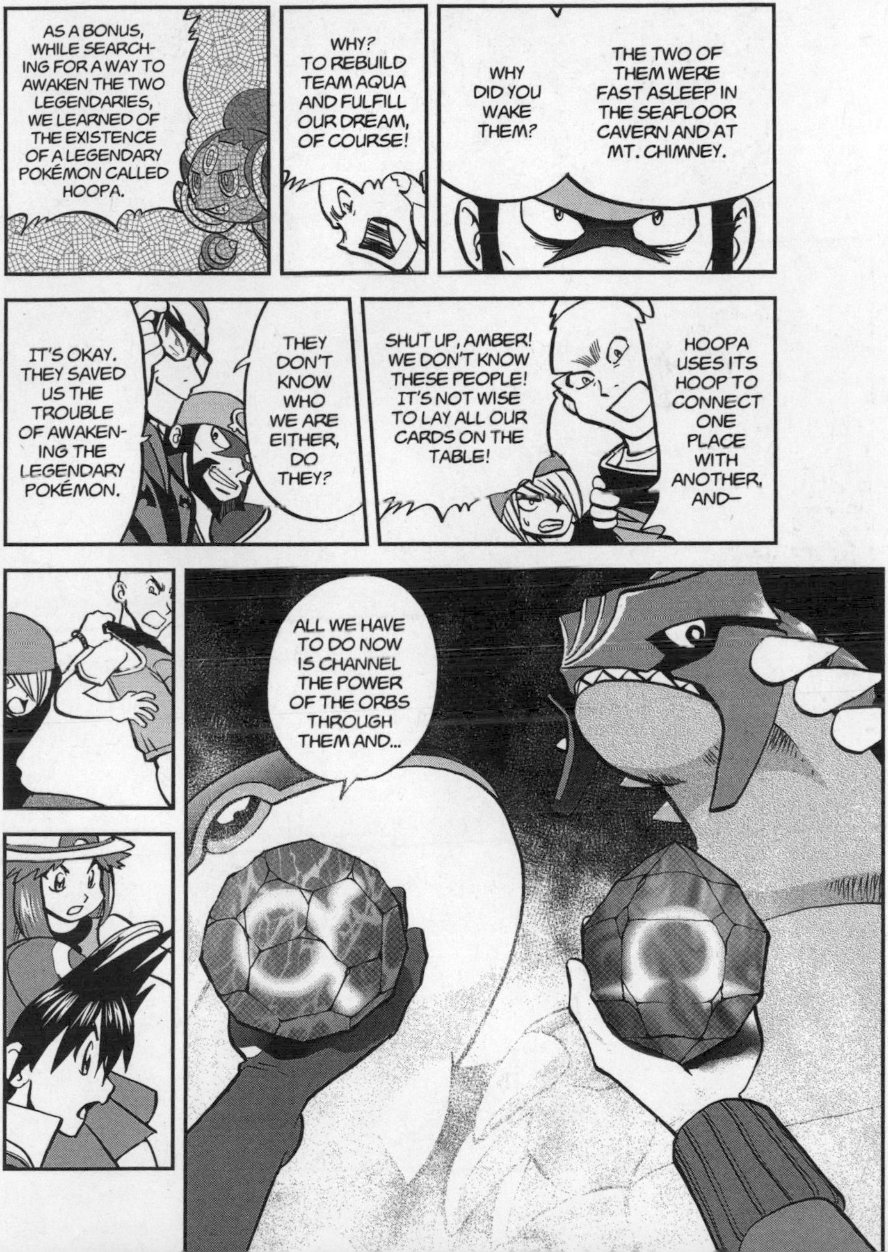
THE TWO OF THEM WERE FAST ASLEEP IN THE SEAFLOOR CAVERN AND AT MT. CHIMNEY.
WHY DID YOU WAKE THEM?
WHY? TO REBUILD TEAM AQUA AND FULFILL OUR DREAM, OF COURSE!
AS A BONUS, WHILE SEARCHING FOR A WAY TO AWAKEN THE TWO LEGENDARIES, WE LEARNED OF THE EXISTENCE OF A LEGENDARY POKÉMON CALLED HOOPA.
HOOPA USES ITS HOOP TO CONNECT ONE PLACE WITH ANOTHER, AND—
SHUT UP, AMBER! WE DON'T KNOW THESE PEOPLE! IT'S NOT WISE TO LAY ALL OUR CARDS ON THE TABLE!
THEY DON'T KNOW WHO WE ARE EITHER, DO THEY?
IT'S OKAY. THEY SAVED US THE TROUBLE OF AWAKENING THE LEGENDARY POKÉMON.
ALL WE HAVE TO DO NOW IS CHANNEL THE POWER OF THE ORBS THROUGH THEM AND...

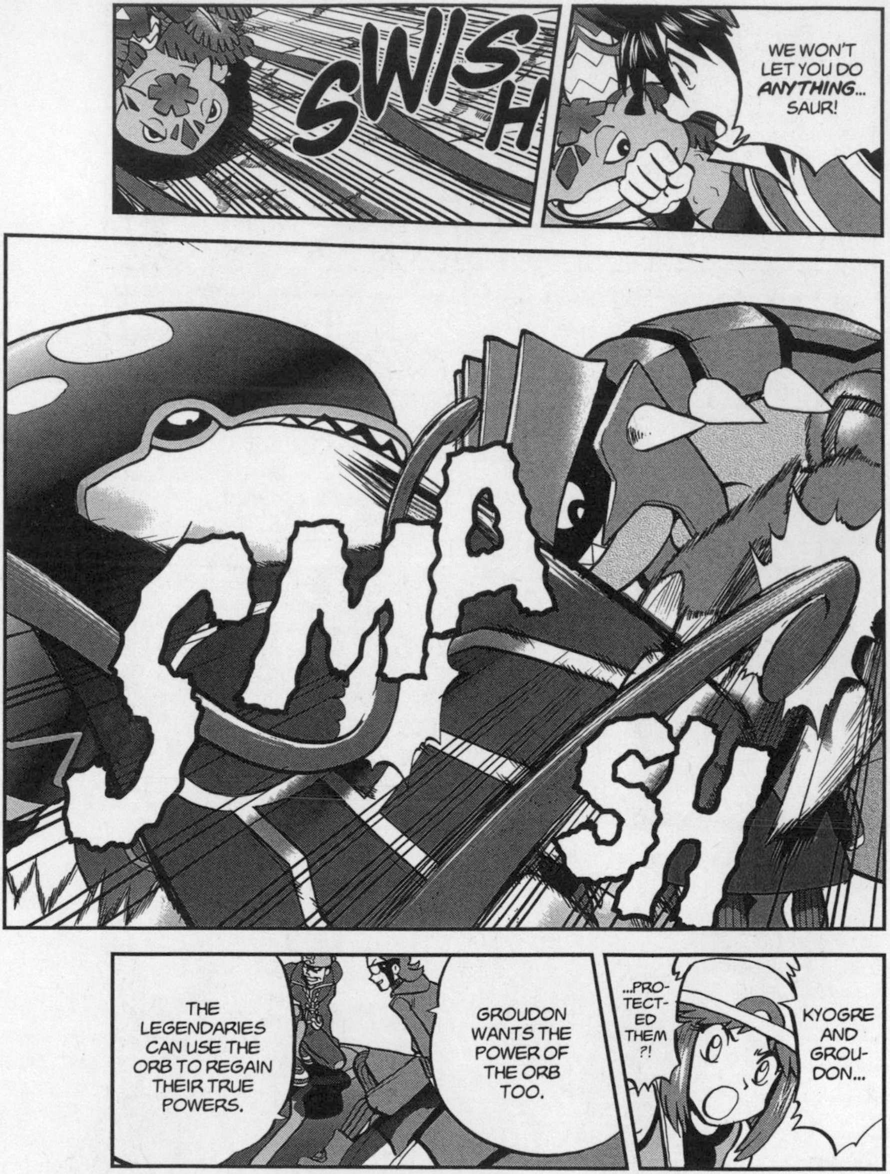
WE WON'T LET YOU DO **ANYTHING**... SAUR!
SWISH
SMASH
KYOGRE AND GROUDON...
...PROTECTED THEM?!
GROUDON WANTS THE POWER OF THE ORB TOO.
THE LEGENDARIES CAN USE THE ORB TO REGAIN THEIR TRUE POWERS.

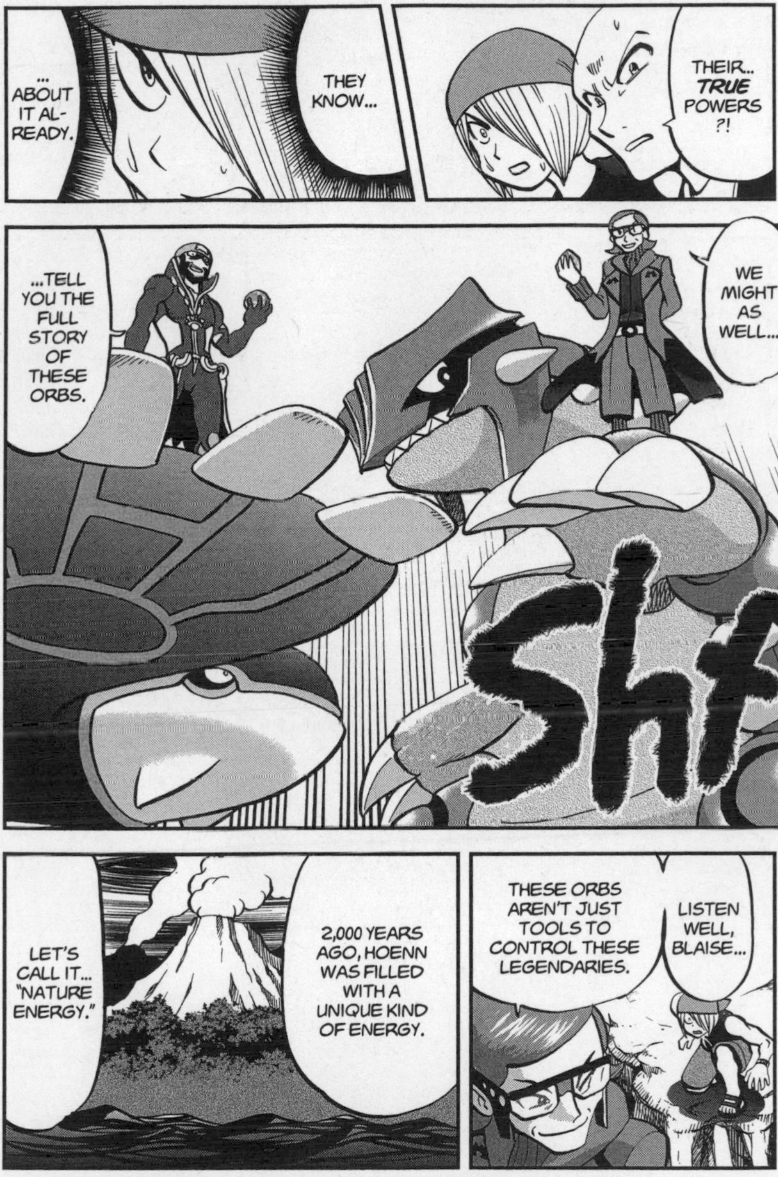
THEIR... **TRUE** POWERS?!
THEY KNOW...
... ABOUT IT AL-READY.
WE MIGHT AS WELL...
...TELL YOU THE FULL STORY OF THESE ORBS.
Shff
LISTEN WELL, BLAISE...
THESE ORBS AREN'T JUST TOOLS TO CONTROL THESE LEGENDARIES.
2,000 YEARS AGO, HOENN WAS FILLED WITH A UNIQUE KIND OF ENERGY.
LET'S CALL IT... "NATURE ENERGY."

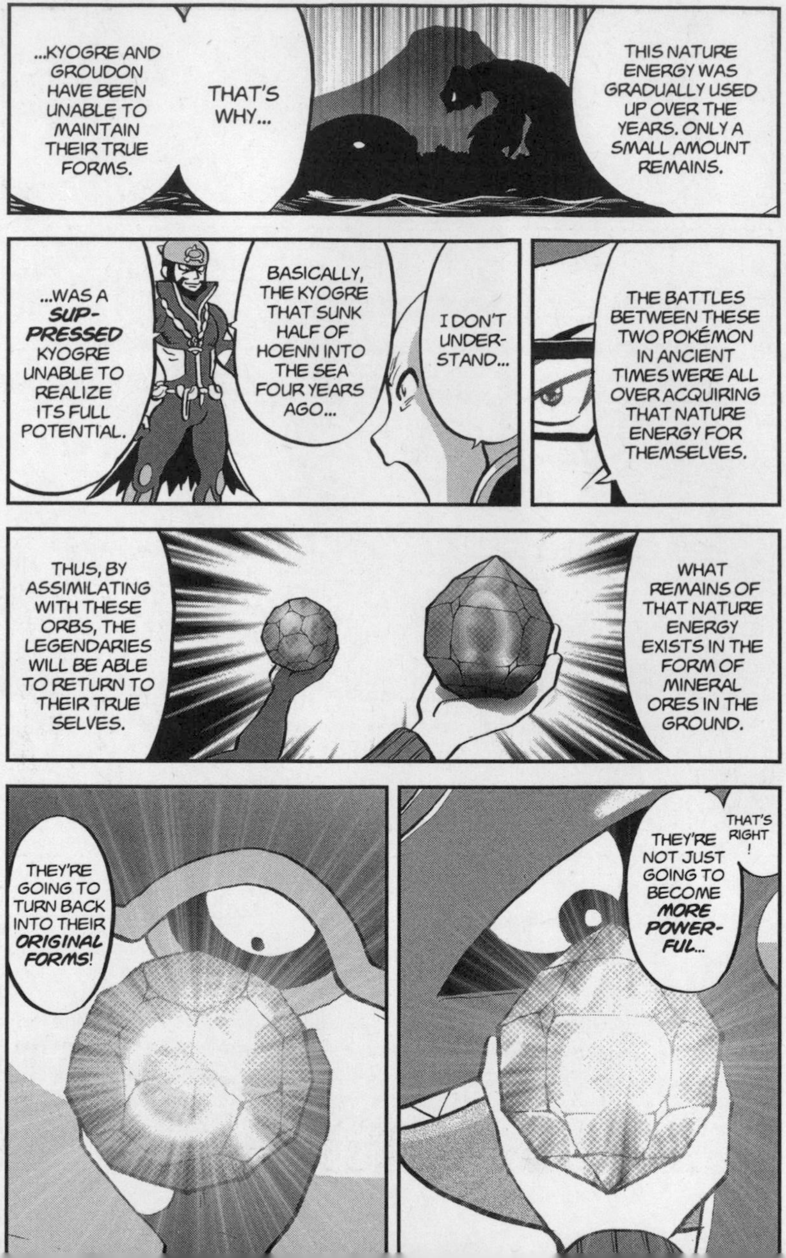
THIS NATURE ENERGY WAS GRADUALLY USED UP OVER THE YEARS. ONLY A SMALL AMOUNT REMAINS.
THAT'S WHY...
...KYOGRE AND GROUDON HAVE BEEN UNABLE TO MAINTAIN THEIR TRUE FORMS.
THE BATTLES BETWEEN THESE TWO POKÉMON IN ANCIENT TIMES WERE ALL OVER ACQUIRING THAT NATURE ENERGY FOR THEMSELVES.
I DON'T UNDERSTAND...
BASICALLY, THE KYOGRE THAT SUNK HALF OF HOENN INTO THE SEA FOUR YEARS AGO...
...WAS A ***SUPPRESSED*** KYOGRE UNABLE TO REALIZE ITS FULL POTENTIAL.
WHAT REMAINS OF THAT NATURE ENERGY EXISTS IN THE FORM OF MINERAL ORES IN THE GROUND.
THUS, BY ASSIMILATING WITH THESE ORBS, THE LEGENDARIES WILL BE ABLE TO RETURN TO THEIR TRUE SELVES.
THAT'S RIGHT!
THEY'RE NOT JUST GOING TO BECOME ***MORE POWERFUL***...
THEY'RE GOING TO TURN BACK INTO THEIR ***ORIGINAL FORMS***!

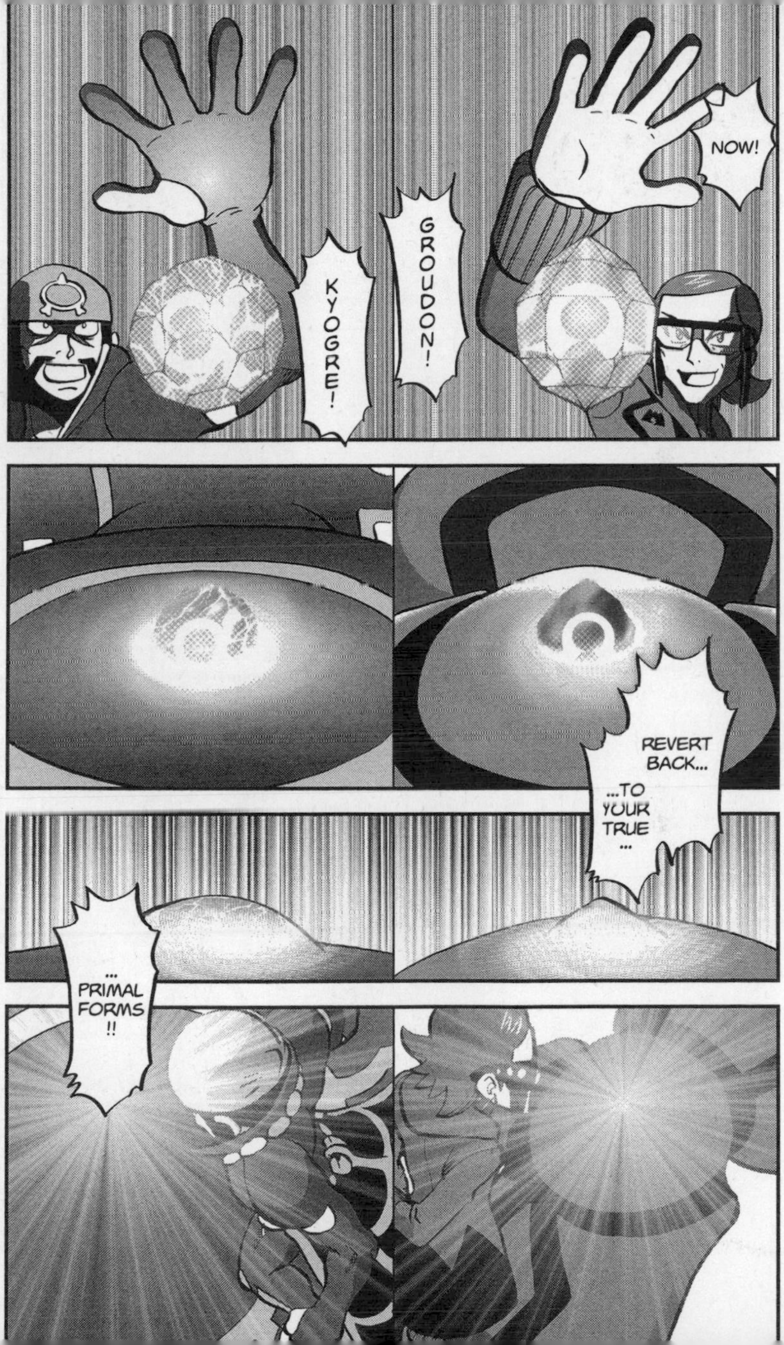
NOW!
GROUDON!
KYOGRE!
REVERT BACK...
...TO YOUR TRUE ...
... PRIMAL FORMS !!

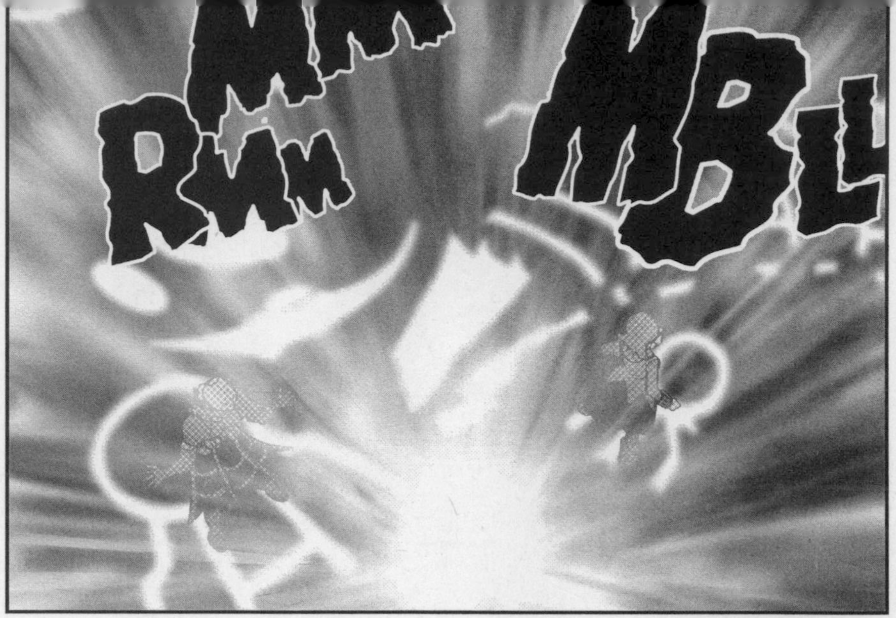
RMMMMBL

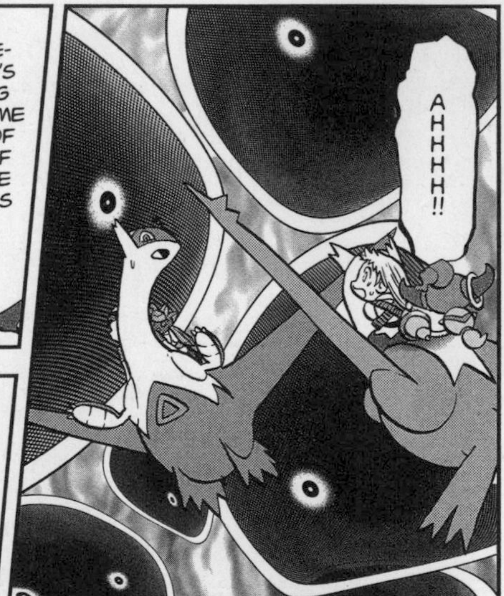
AHHHHH!!

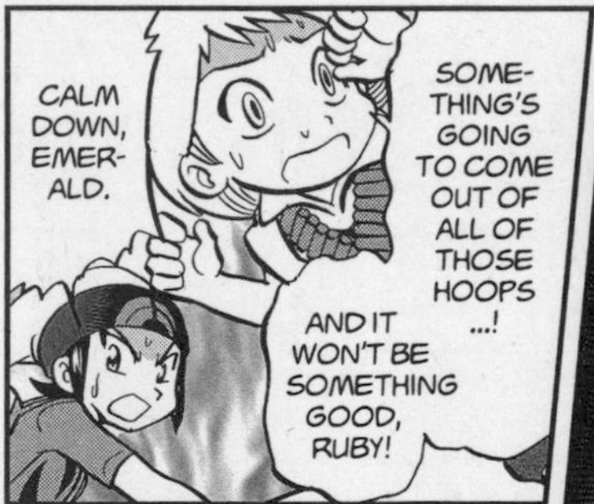
SOME-THING'S GOING TO COME OUT OF ALL OF THOSE HOOPS ...!
CALM DOWN, EMER-ALD.
AND IT WON'T BE SOMETHING GOOD, RUBY!

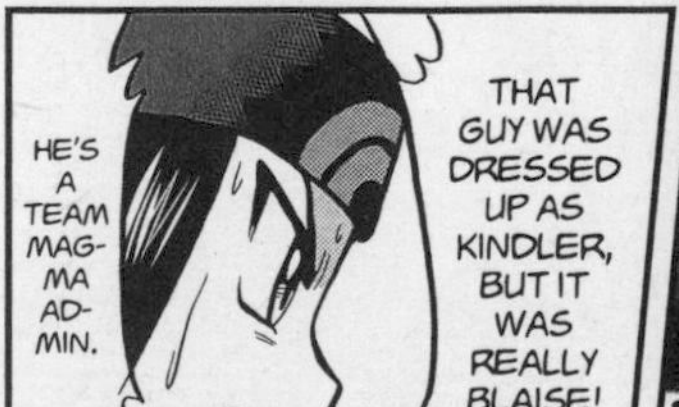
THAT GUY WAS DRESSED UP AS KINDLER, BUT IT WAS REALLY BLAISE!
HE'S A TEAM MAG-MA AD-MIN.

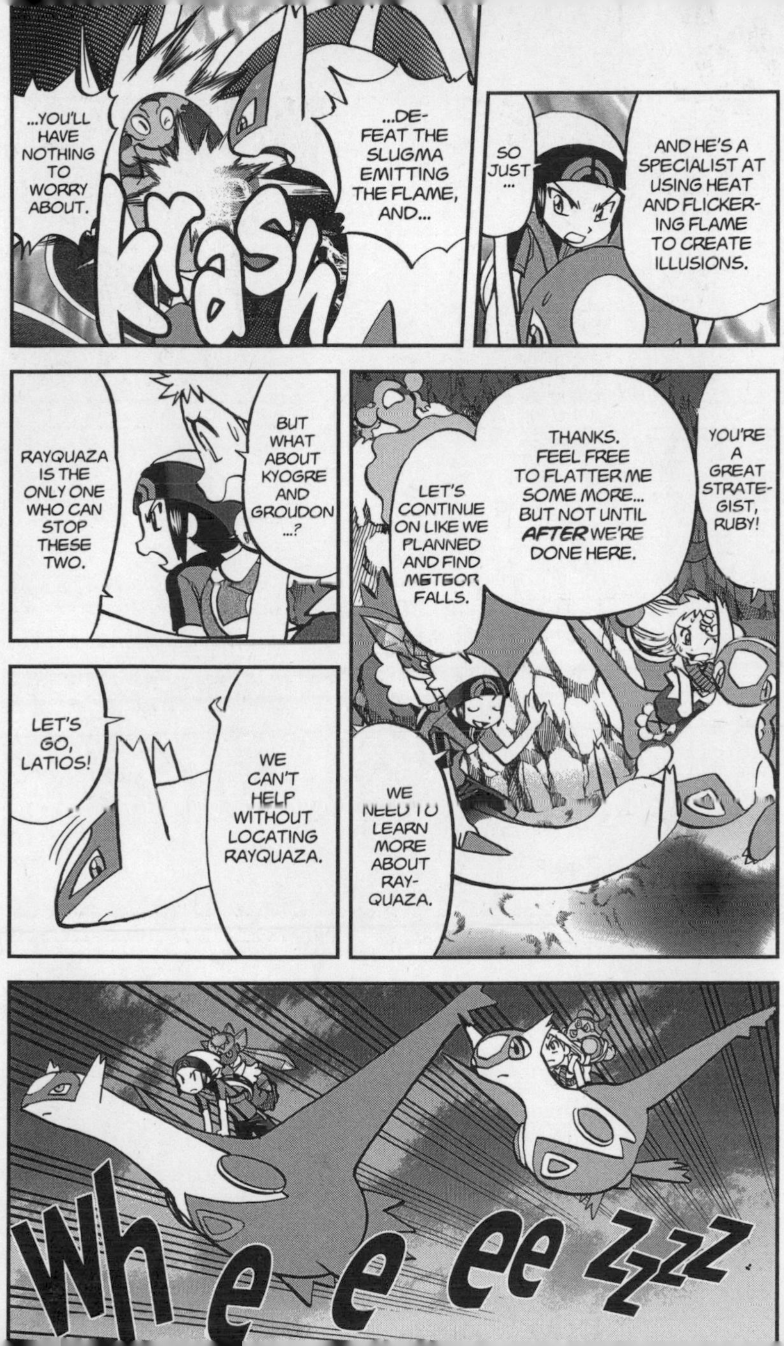
AND HE'S A SPECIALIST AT USING HEAT AND FLICKERING FLAME TO CREATE ILLUSIONS.
SO JUST...
...DEFEAT THE SLUGMA EMITTING THE FLAME, AND...
...YOU'LL HAVE NOTHING TO WORRY ABOUT.
krash
YOU'RE A GREAT STRATEGIST, RUBY!
THANKS. FEEL FREE TO FLATTER ME SOME MORE... BUT NOT UNTIL *AFTER* WE'RE DONE HERE.
LET'S CONTINUE ON LIKE WE PLANNED AND FIND METEOR FALLS.
WE NEED TO LEARN MORE ABOUT RAYQUAZA.
BUT WHAT ABOUT KYOGRE AND GROUDON...?
RAYQUAZA IS THE ONLY ONE WHO CAN STOP THESE TWO.
WE CAN'T HELP WITHOUT LOCATING RAYQUAZA.
LET'S GO, LATIOS!
Wheeeeezzzz

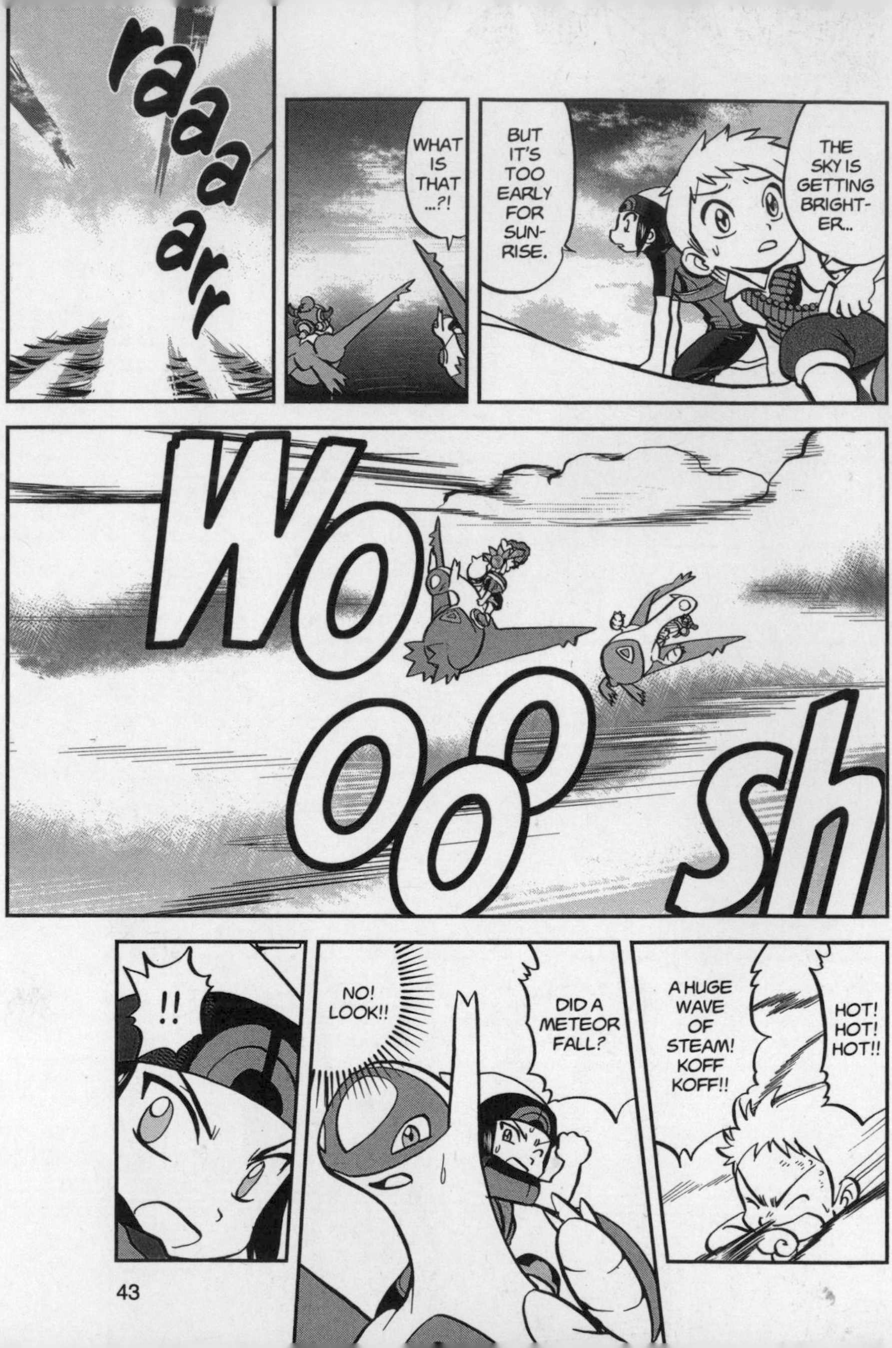
THE SKY IS GETTING BRIGHT-ER..
BUT IT'S TOO EARLY FOR SUN-RISE.
WHAT IS THAT ...?!
raaaarr
Wooosh
HOT! HOT! HOT!!
A HUGE WAVE OF STEAM! KOFF KOFF!!
DID A METEOR FALL?
NO! LOOK!!
!!

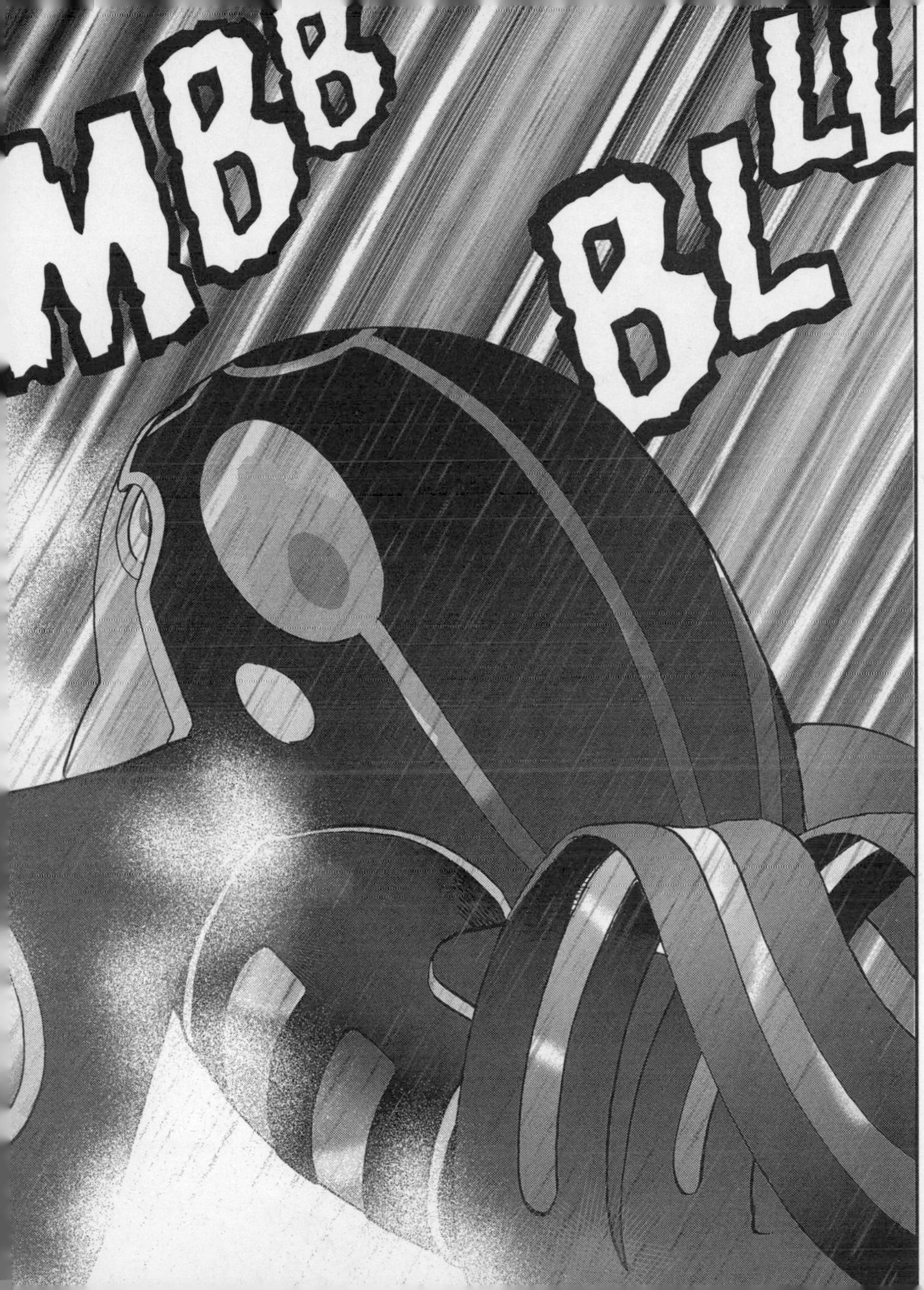
MBB BLL

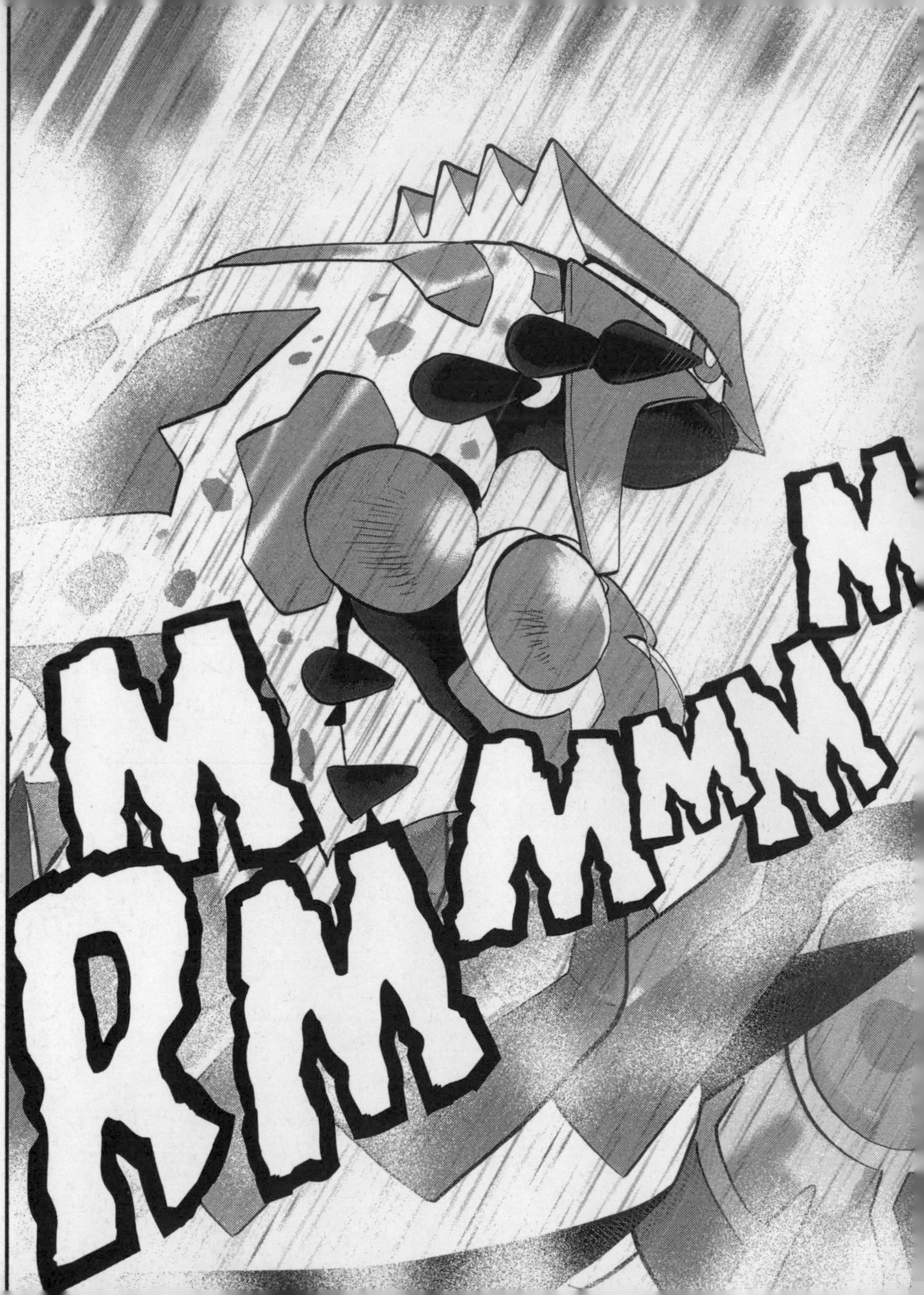
RMMMMMMM

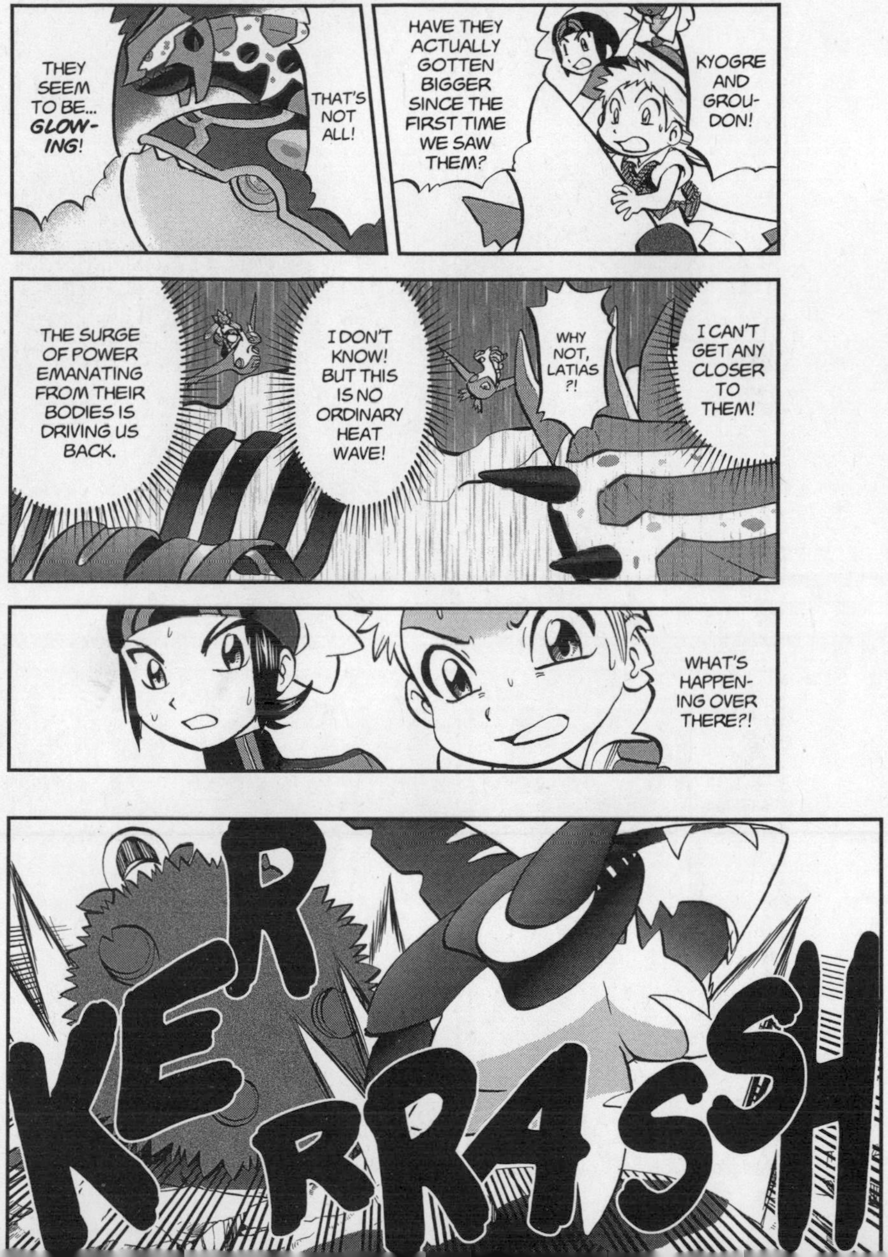
KYOGRE AND GROUDON!
HAVE THEY ACTUALLY GOTTEN BIGGER SINCE THE FIRST TIME WE SAW THEM?
THAT'S NOT ALL!
THEY SEEM TO BE... *GLOWING*!
I CAN'T GET ANY CLOSER TO THEM!
WHY NOT, LATIAS?!
I DON'T KNOW! BUT THIS IS NO ORDINARY HEAT WAVE!
THE SURGE OF POWER EMANATING FROM THEIR BODIES IS DRIVING US BACK.
WHAT'S HAPPENING OVER THERE?!
KERRRASSH!!

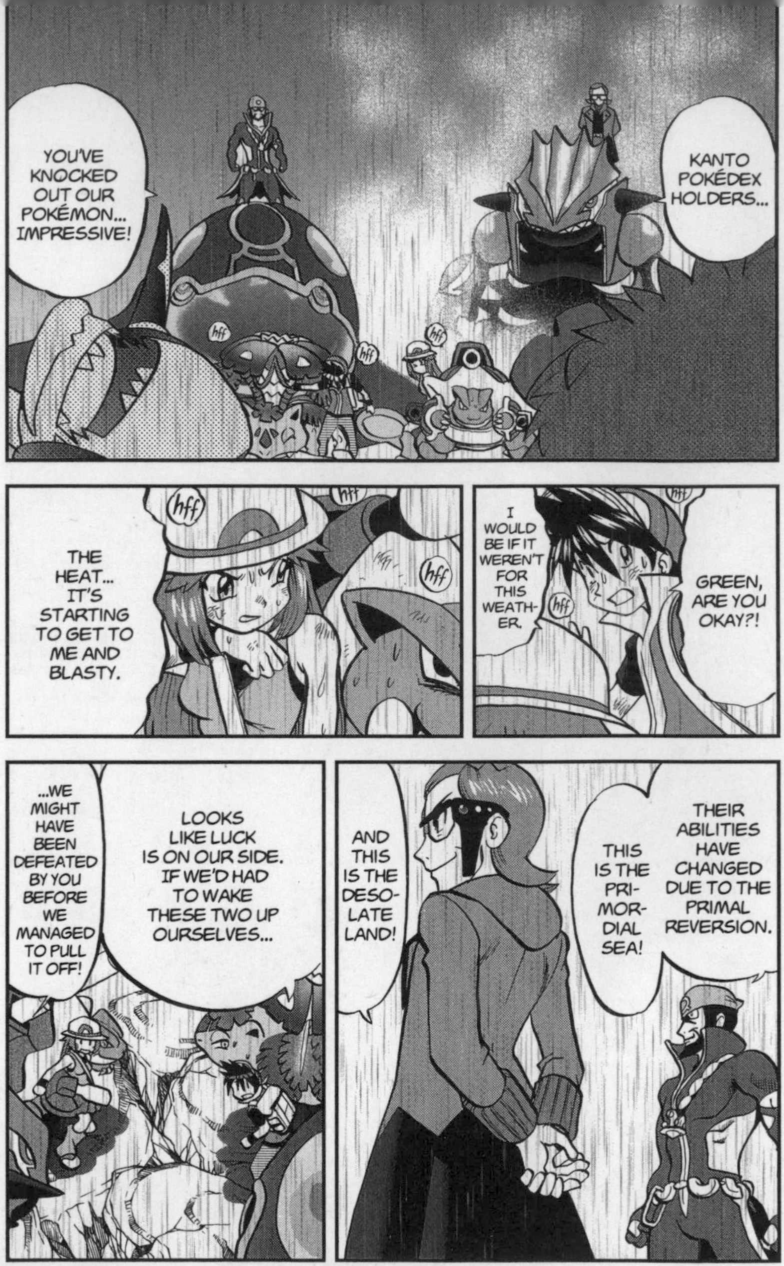
KANTO POKÉDEX HOLDERS...
YOU'VE KNOCKED OUT OUR POKÉMON... IMPRESSIVE!
hff
hff
hff
GREEN, ARE YOU OKAY?!
I WOULD BE IF IT WEREN'T FOR THIS WEATH-ER.
hff
hff
hff
THE HEAT... IT'S STARTING TO GET TO ME AND BLASTY.
hff
THEIR ABILITIES HAVE CHANGED DUE TO THE PRIMAL REVERSION.
THIS IS THE PRI-MOR-DIAL SEA!
AND THIS IS THE DESO-LATE LAND!
LOOKS LIKE LUCK IS ON OUR SIDE. IF WE'D HAD TO WAKE THESE TWO UP OURSELVES...
...WE MIGHT HAVE BEEN DEFEATED BY YOU BEFORE WE MANAGED TO PULL IT OFF!

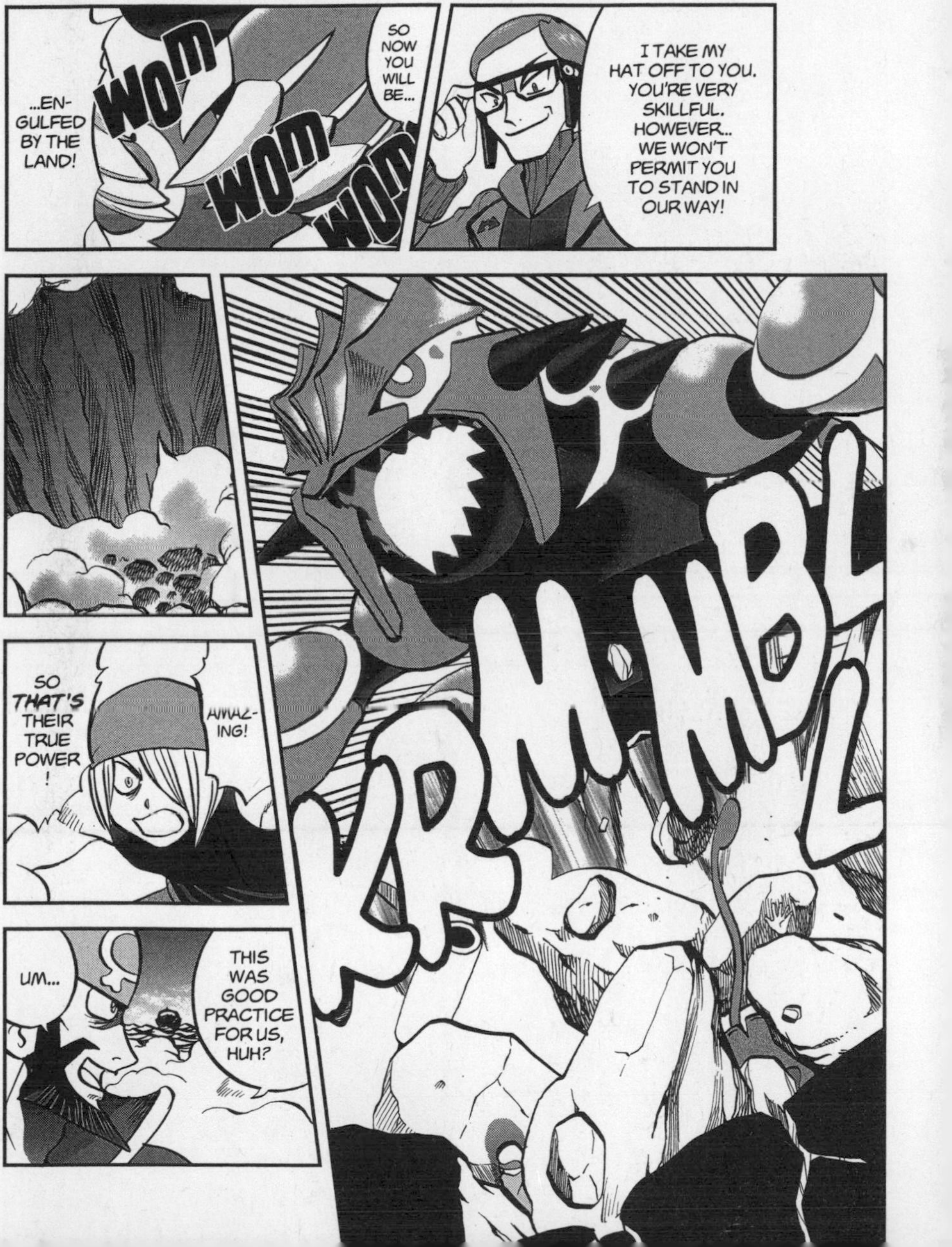
I TAKE MY HAT OFF TO YOU. YOU'RE VERY SKILLFUL. HOWEVER... WE WON'T PERMIT YOU TO STAND IN OUR WAY!
SO NOW YOU WILL BE...
WOM WOM WOM
...EN-GULFED BY THE LAND!
KRMMBL
AMAZ-ING!
SO THAT'S THEIR TRUE POWER!
THIS WAS GOOD PRACTICE FOR US, HUH?
UM...

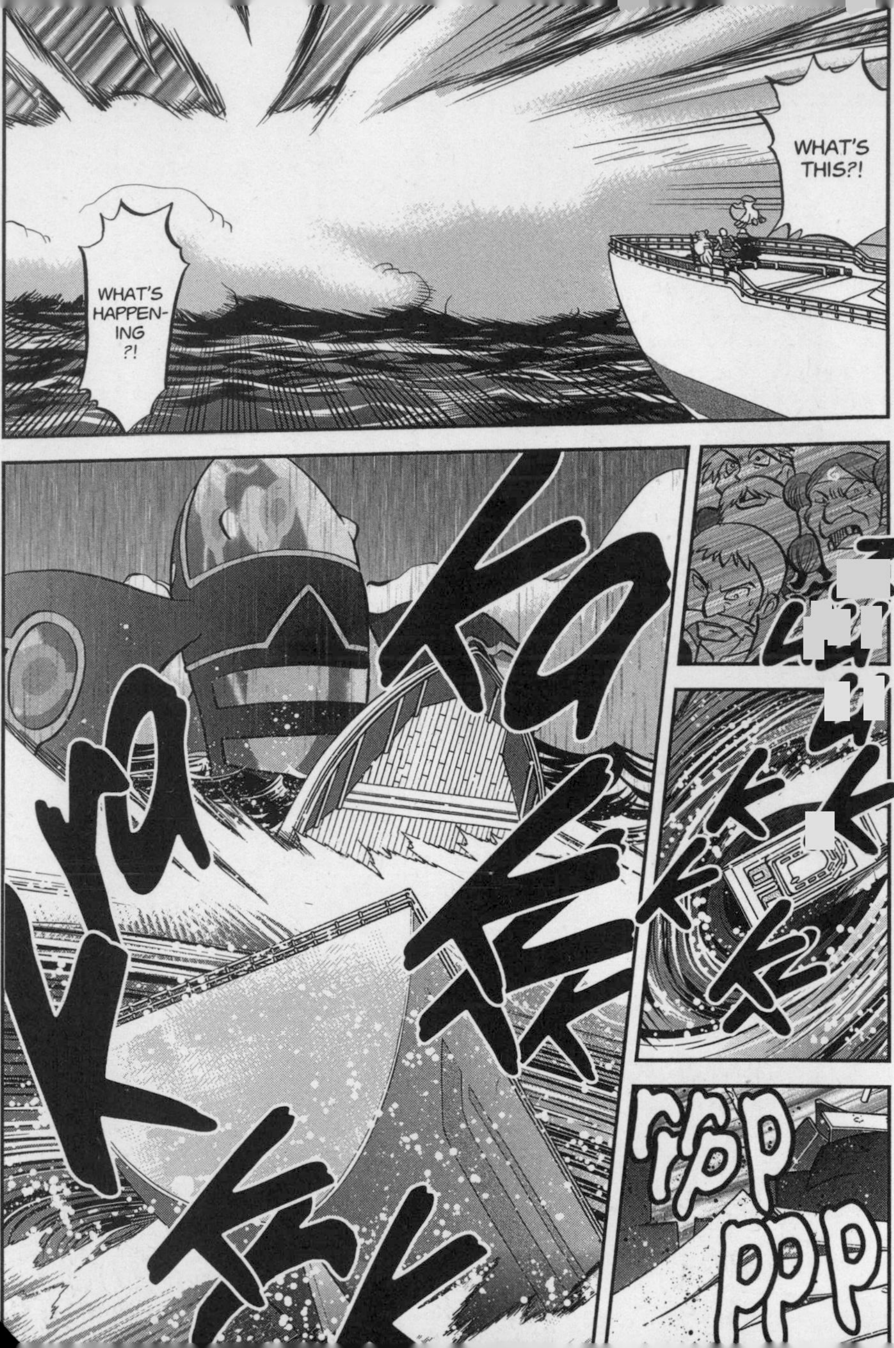
WHAT'S THIS?!
WHAT'S HAPPEN-ING ?!

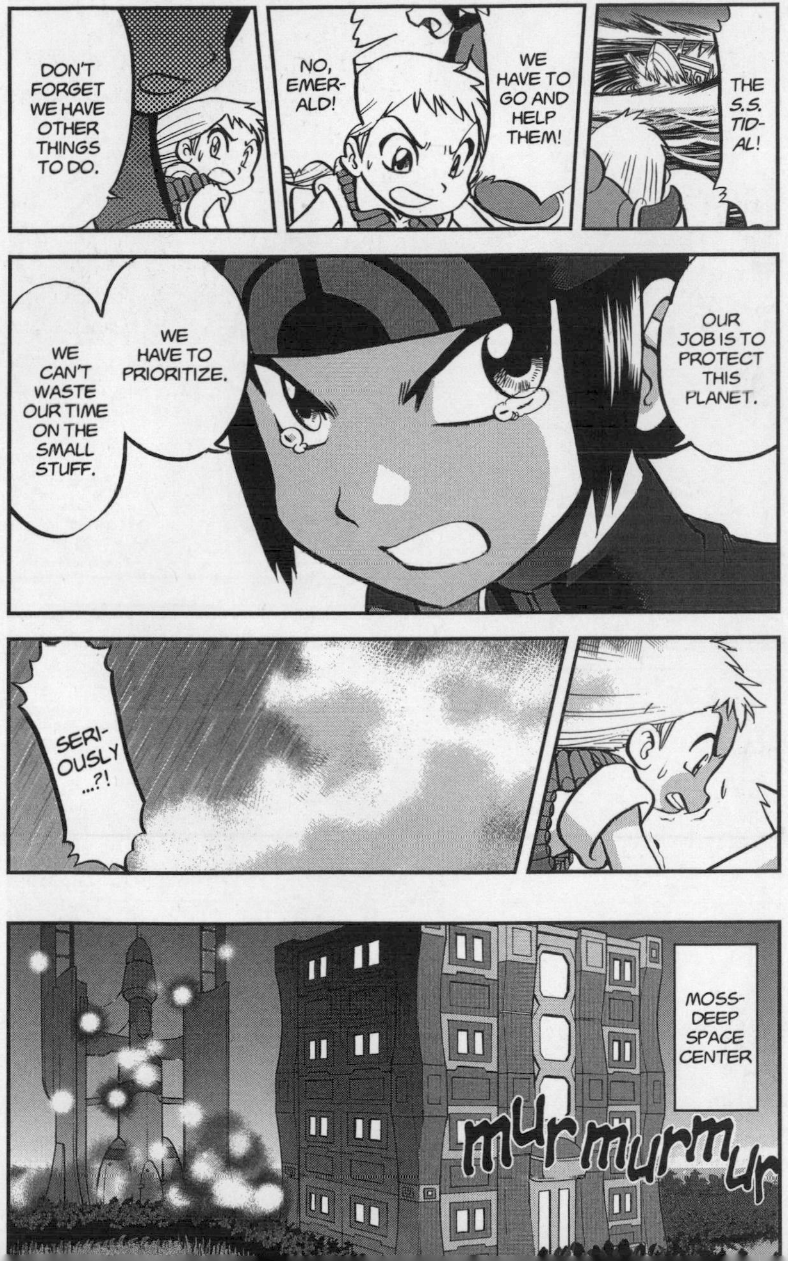
THE S.S. TIDAL!
WE HAVE TO GO AND HELP THEM!
NO, EMERALD!
DON'T FORGET WE HAVE OTHER THINGS TO DO.
OUR JOB IS TO PROTECT THIS PLANET.
WE HAVE TO PRIORITIZE.
WE CAN'T WASTE OUR TIME ON THE SMALL STUFF.
SERIOUSLY...?!
MOSSDEEP SPACE CENTER
murmurmurmur

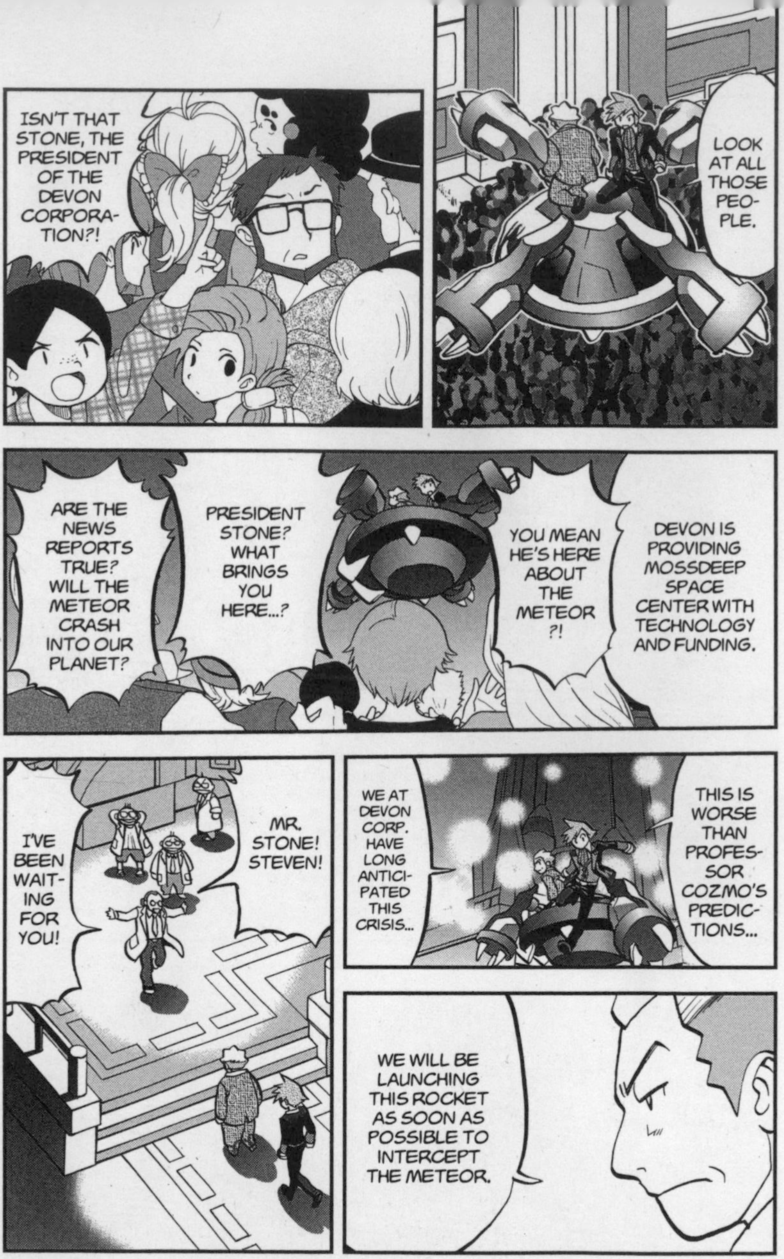
LOOK AT ALL THOSE PEO-PLE.
ISN'T THAT STONE, THE PRESIDENT OF THE DEVON CORPORA-TION?!
DEVON IS PROVIDING MOSSDEEP SPACE CENTER WITH TECHNOLOGY AND FUNDING.
YOU MEAN HE'S HERE ABOUT THE METEOR ?!
PRESIDENT STONE? WHAT BRINGS YOU HERE...?
ARE THE NEWS REPORTS TRUE? WILL THE METEOR CRASH INTO OUR PLANET?
THIS IS WORSE THAN PROFES-SOR COZMO'S PREDIC-TIONS...
WE AT DEVON CORP. HAVE LONG ANTICI-PATED THIS CRISIS...
WE WILL BE LAUNCHING THIS ROCKET AS SOON AS POSSIBLE TO INTERCEPT THE METEOR.
MR. STONE! STEVEN!
I'VE BEEN WAIT-ING FOR YOU!

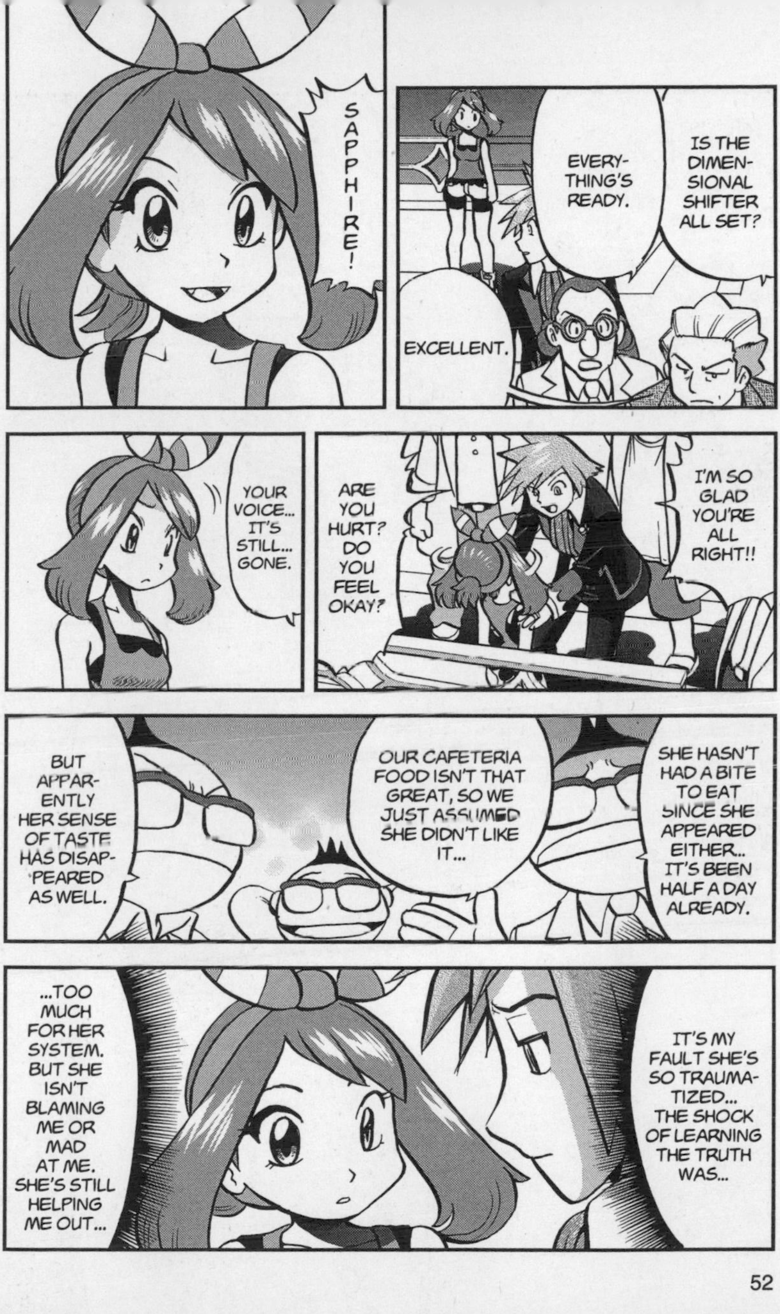
IS THE DIMENSIONAL SHIFTER ALL SET?
EVERYTHING'S READY.
EXCELLENT.
SAPPHIRE!
I'M SO GLAD YOU'RE ALL RIGHT!!
ARE YOU HURT? DO YOU FEEL OKAY?
YOUR VOICE... IT'S STILL... GONE.
SHE HASN'T HAD A BITE TO EAT SINCE SHE APPEARED EITHER... IT'S BEEN HALF A DAY ALREADY.
OUR CAFETERIA FOOD ISN'T THAT GREAT, SO WE JUST ASSUMED SHE DIDN'T LIKE IT...
BUT APPARENTLY HER SENSE OF TASTE HAS DISAPPEARED AS WELL.
IT'S MY FAULT SHE'S SO TRAUMATIZED... THE SHOCK OF LEARNING THE TRUTH WAS...
...TOO MUCH FOR HER SYSTEM. BUT SHE ISN'T BLAMING ME OR MAD AT ME. SHE'S STILL HELPING ME OUT...

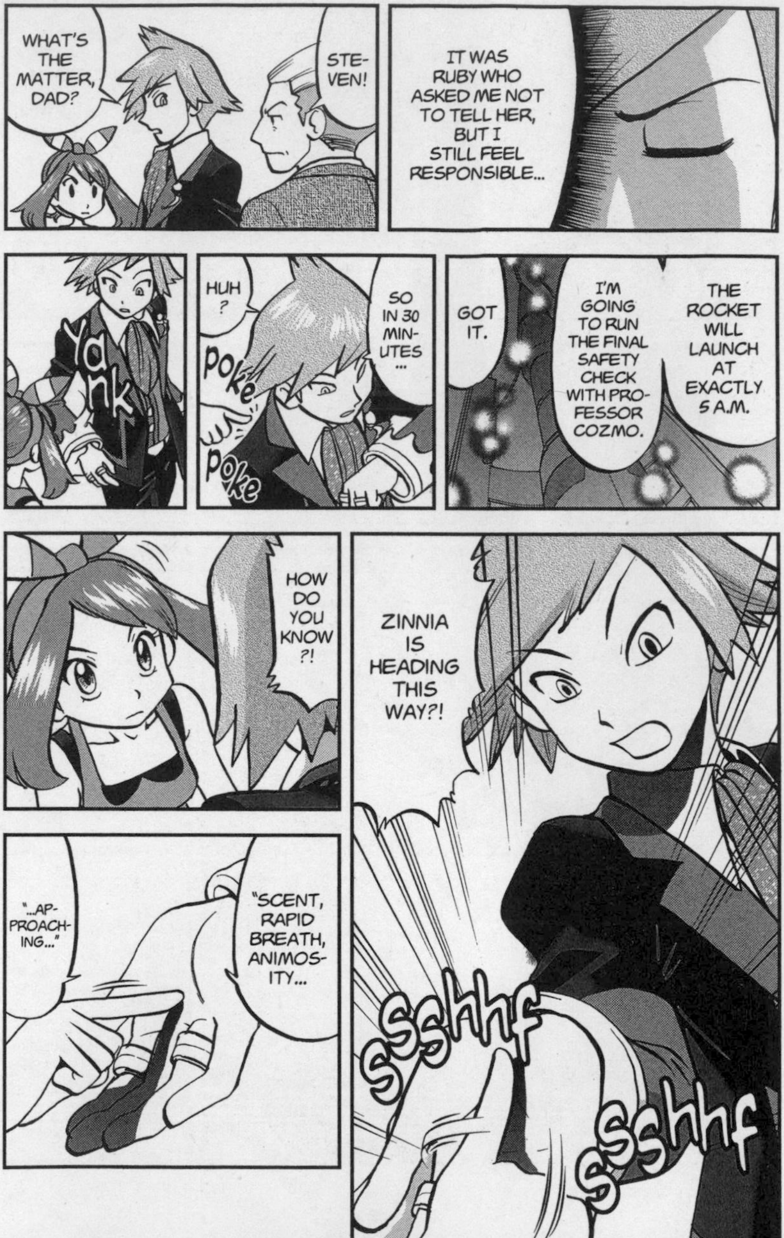
IT WAS RUBY WHO ASKED ME NOT TO TELL HER, BUT I STILL FEEL RESPONSIBLE...
STEVEN!
WHAT'S THE MATTER, DAD?
THE ROCKET WILL LAUNCH AT EXACTLY 5 A.M.
I'M GOING TO RUN THE FINAL SAFETY CHECK WITH PROFESSOR COZMO.
GOT IT.
SO IN 30 MINUTES...
HUH?
poke
poke
Yank
ZINNIA IS HEADING THIS WAY?!
ssshf
ssshf
HOW DO YOU KNOW?!
"SCENT, RAPID BREATH, ANIMOSITY...
"...APPROACHING..."

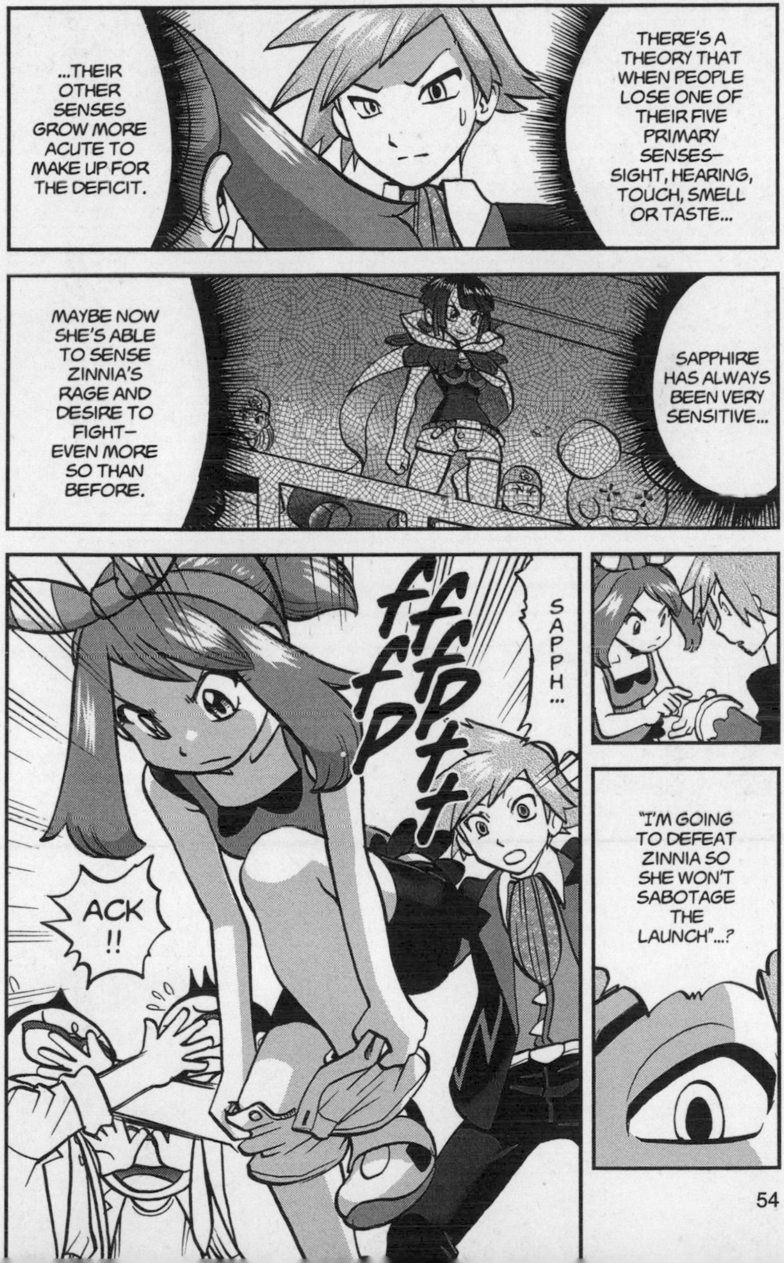
THERE'S A THEORY THAT WHEN PEOPLE LOSE ONE OF THEIR FIVE PRIMARY SENSES—SIGHT, HEARING, TOUCH, SMELL OR TASTE...
...THEIR OTHER SENSES GROW MORE ACUTE TO MAKE UP FOR THE DEFICIT.
SAPPHIRE HAS ALWAYS BEEN VERY SENSITIVE...
MAYBE NOW SHE'S ABLE TO SENSE ZINNIA'S RAGE AND DESIRE TO FIGHT—EVEN MORE SO THAN BEFORE.
"I'M GOING TO DEFEAT ZINNIA SO SHE WON'T SABOTAGE THE LAUNCH"...?
SAPPH...
fffffpptttt
ACK!!

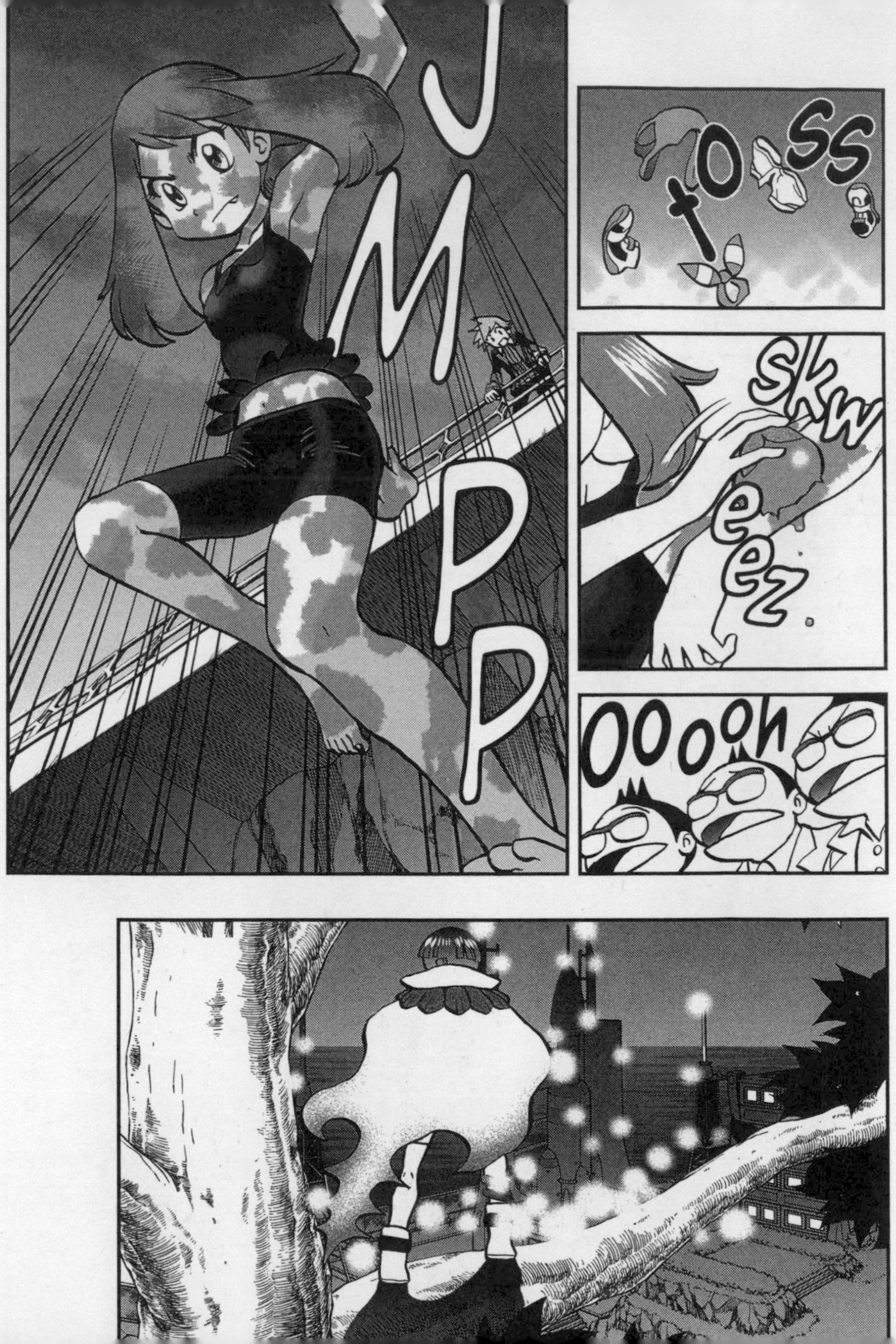
toss
skweez.
Ooooh
JUMPP

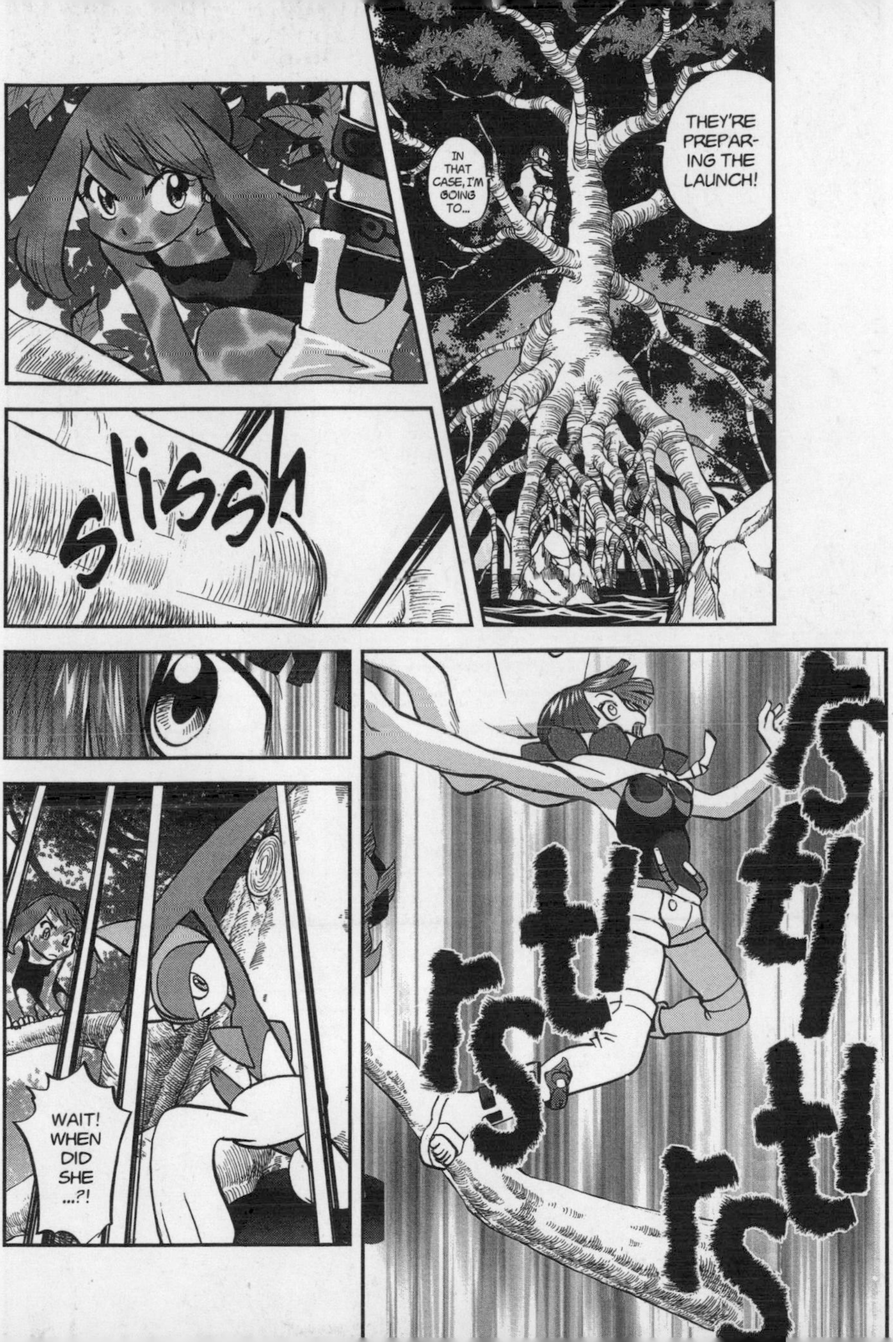
THEY'RE PREPAR-ING THE LAUNCH!
IN THAT CASE, I'M GOING TO...
slissh
rstl
rstl
rstl
rstl
WAIT! WHEN DID SHE ...?!

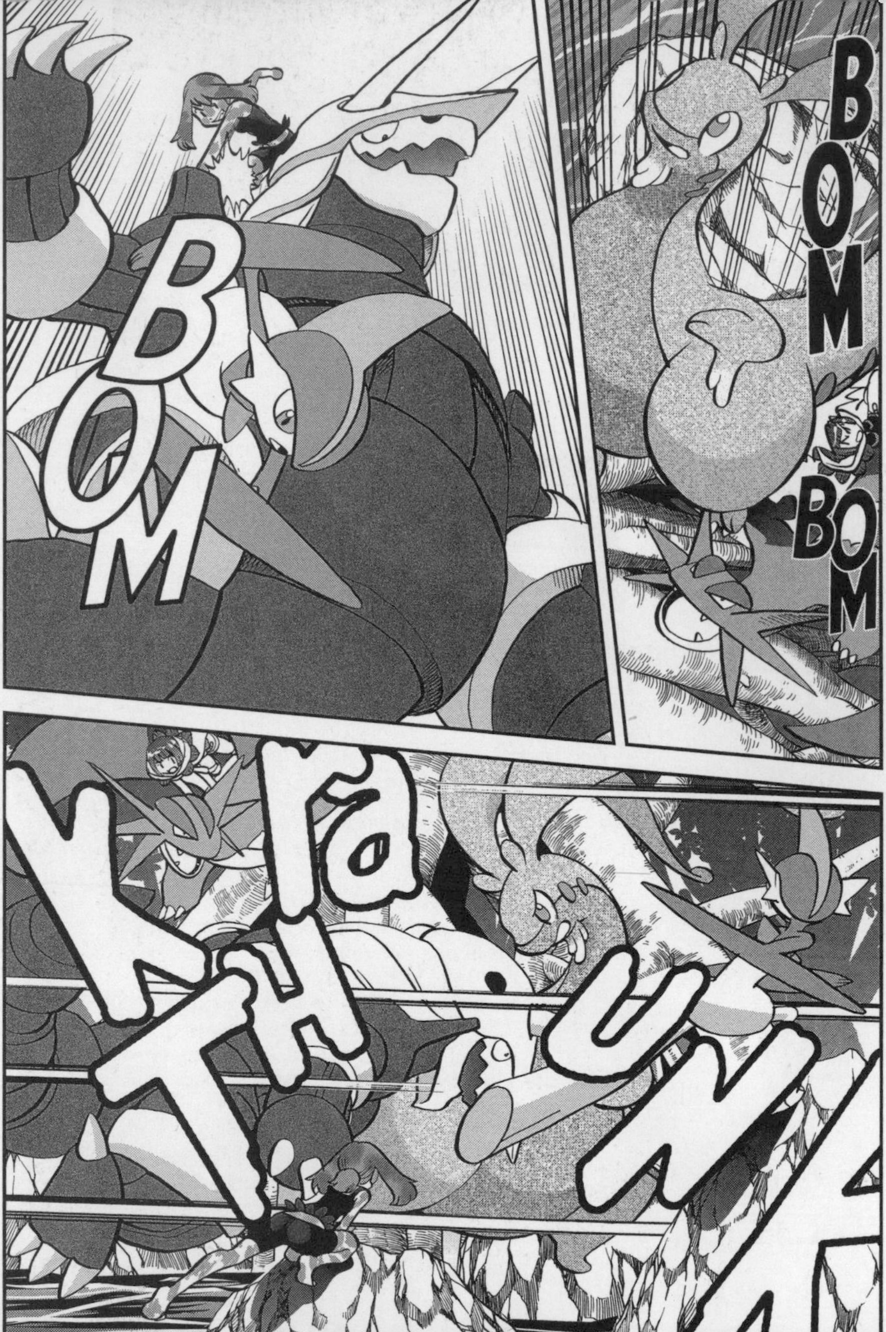
BOM
BOM
BOM
KRATHUNK

PRIMAL REVERSION

Primal Reversion is a process by which ancient Pokémon retrieve their lost powers and revert to their true original forms. Kyogre and Groudon have just gone through this change. Primal Reversion is an entirely different phenomenon from Form Change, Evolution or Mega Evolution. Specialists have yet to decipher the secret behind it, but the key seems to be Nature Energy. In the ancient past, the entire Hoenn region was filled with Nature Energy, but now most of it is gone. All that remains are crystalized fragments and orbs (such as the Blue and Red Orbs) containing concentrated masses of Nature Energy. By assimilating with the orbs, Kyogre and Groudon have achieved Primal Reversion.

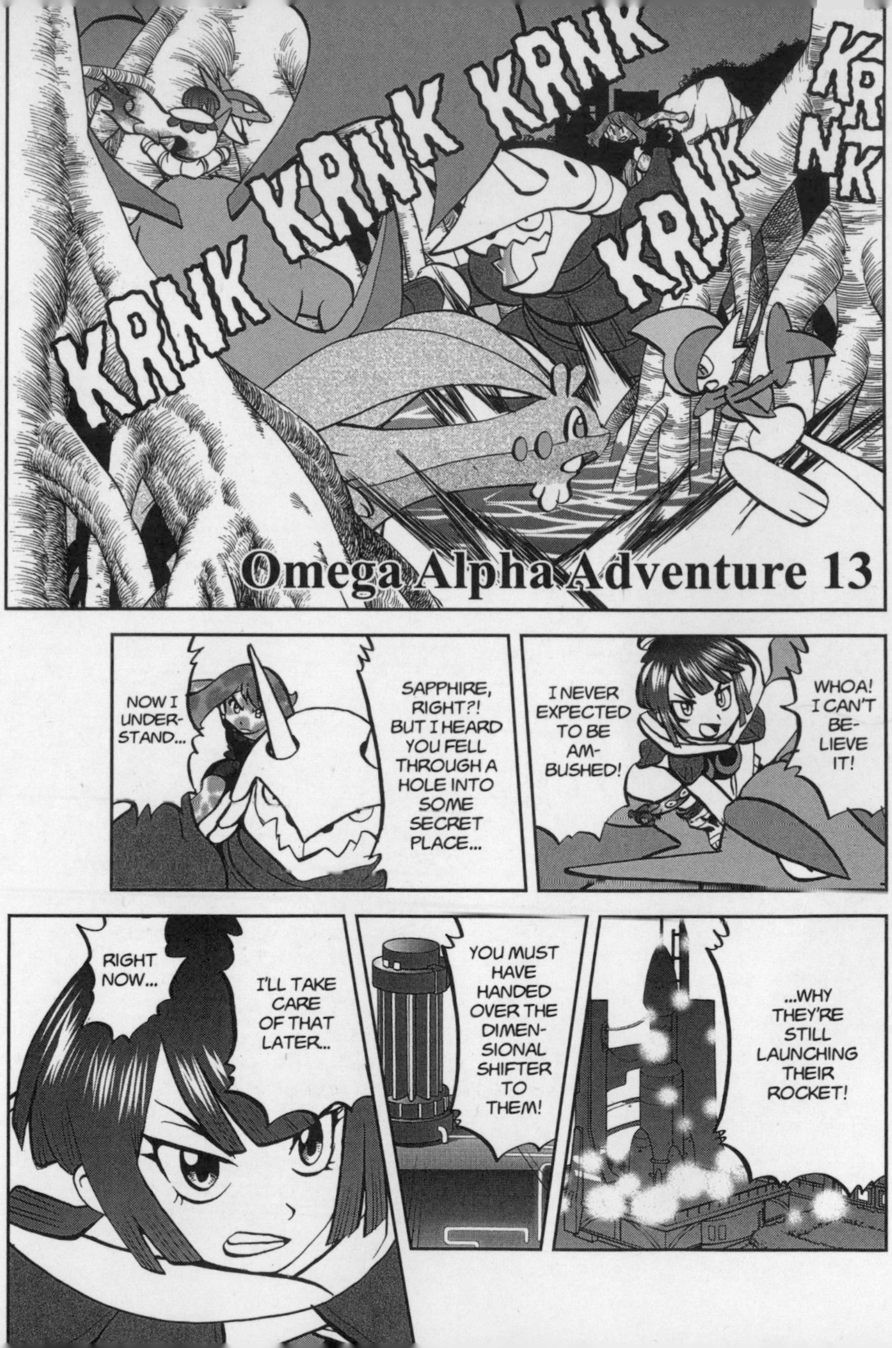
KRANK
KRANK
KRANK
KRANK
KRANK
KRANK
Omega Alpha Adventure 13
WHOA! I CAN'T BE-LIEVE IT!
I NEVER EXPECTED TO BE AM-BUSHED!
SAPPHIRE, RIGHT?! BUT I HEARD YOU FELL THROUGH A HOLE INTO SOME SECRET PLACE...
NOW I UNDER-STAND...
...WHY THEY'RE STILL LAUNCHING THEIR ROCKET!
YOU MUST HAVE HANDED OVER THE DIMEN-SIONAL SHIFTER TO THEM!
I'LL TAKE CARE OF THAT LATER..
RIGHT NOW...

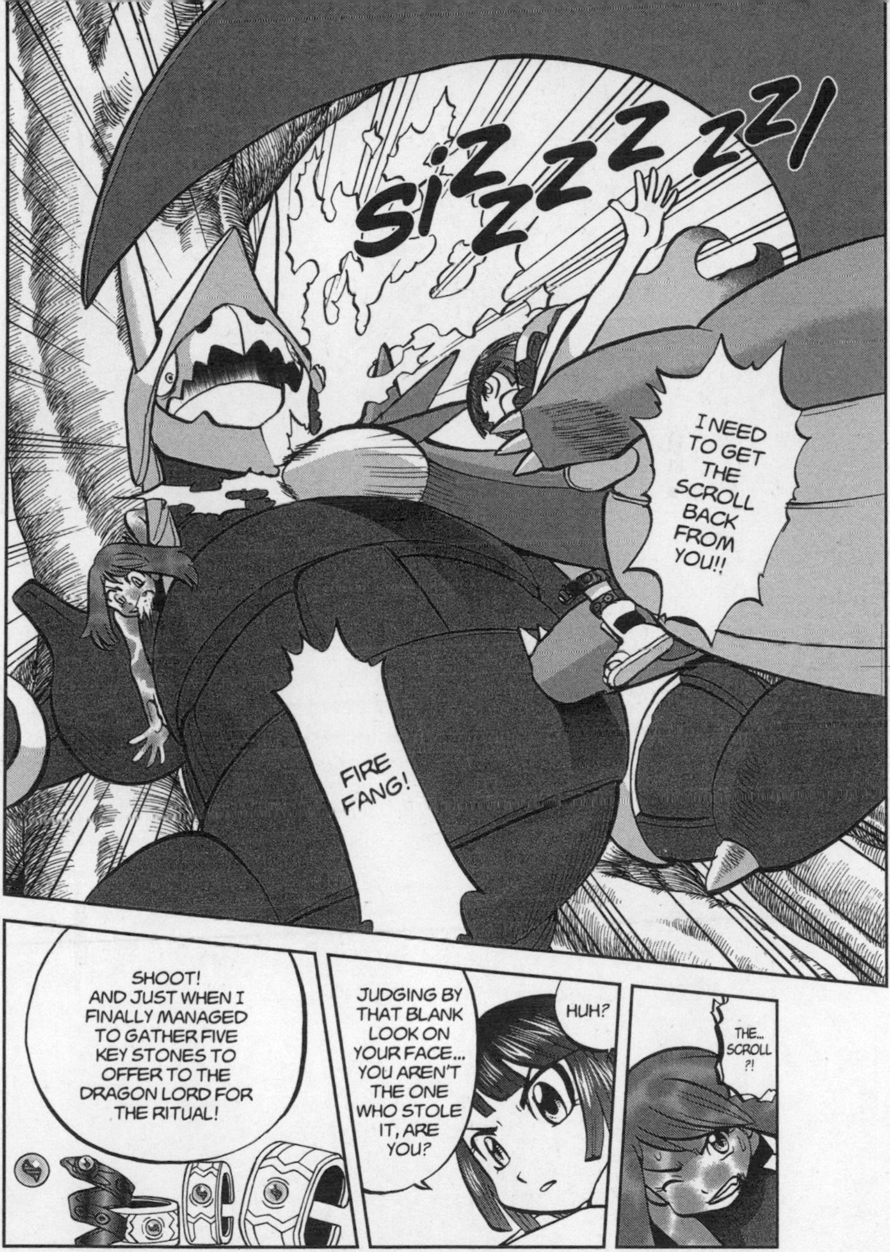

SIZZZZZZ!
I NEED TO GET THE SCROLL BACK FROM YOU!!
FIRE FANG!
THE... SCROLL ?!
HUH?
JUDGING BY THAT BLANK LOOK ON YOUR FACE... YOU AREN'T THE ONE WHO STOLE IT, ARE YOU?
SHOOT! AND JUST WHEN I FINALLY MANAGED TO GATHER FIVE KEY STONES TO OFFER TO THE DRAGON LORD FOR THE RITUAL!

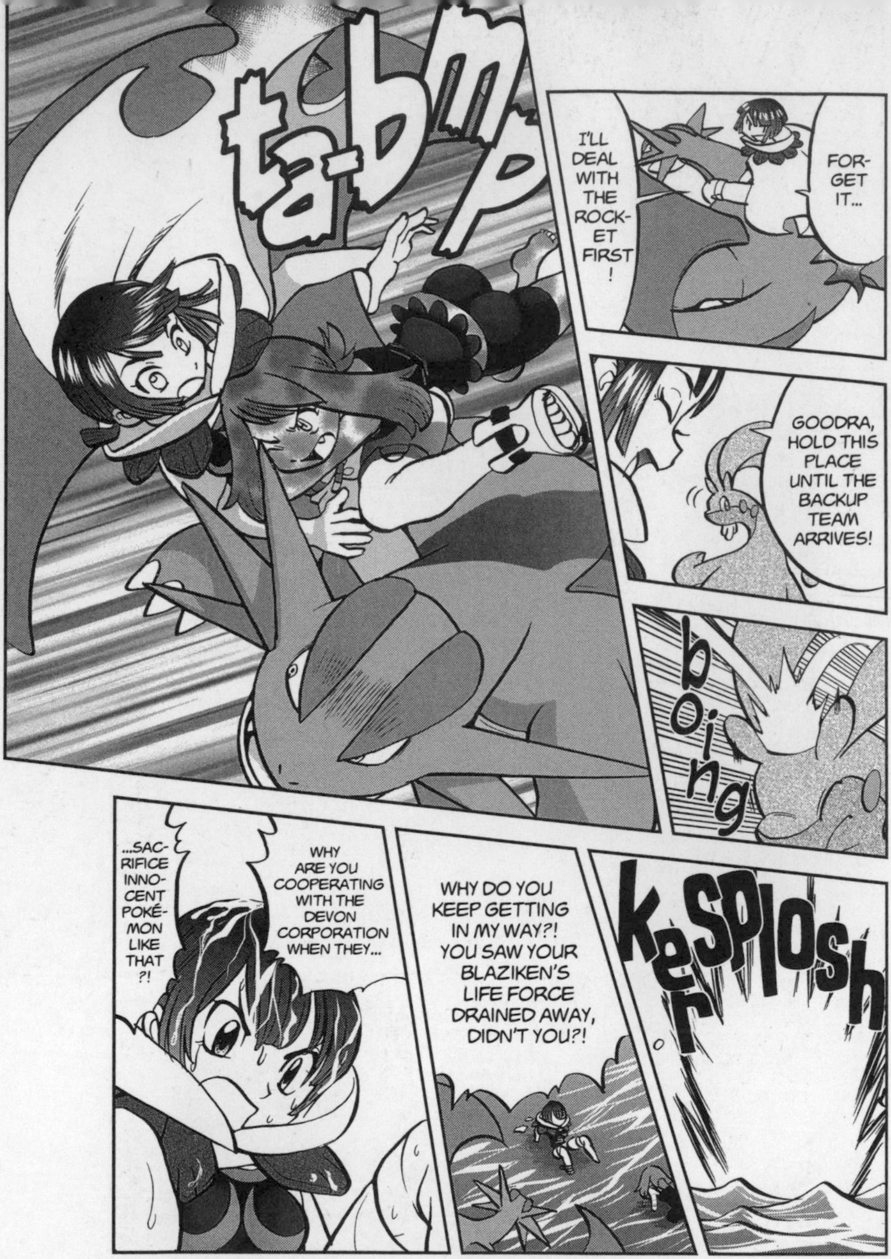
FOR-GET IT...
I'LL DEAL WITH THE ROCK-ET FIRST!
GOODRA, HOLD THIS PLACE UNTIL THE BACKUP TEAM ARRIVES!
boing
ta-bmp
kersplosh
WHY DO YOU KEEP GETTING IN MY WAY?! YOU SAW YOUR BLAZIKEN'S LIFE FORCE DRAINED AWAY, DIDN'T YOU?!
WHY ARE YOU COOPERATING WITH THE DEVON CORPORATION WHEN THEY...
...SAC-RIFICE INNO-CENT POKÉ-MON LIKE THAT?!

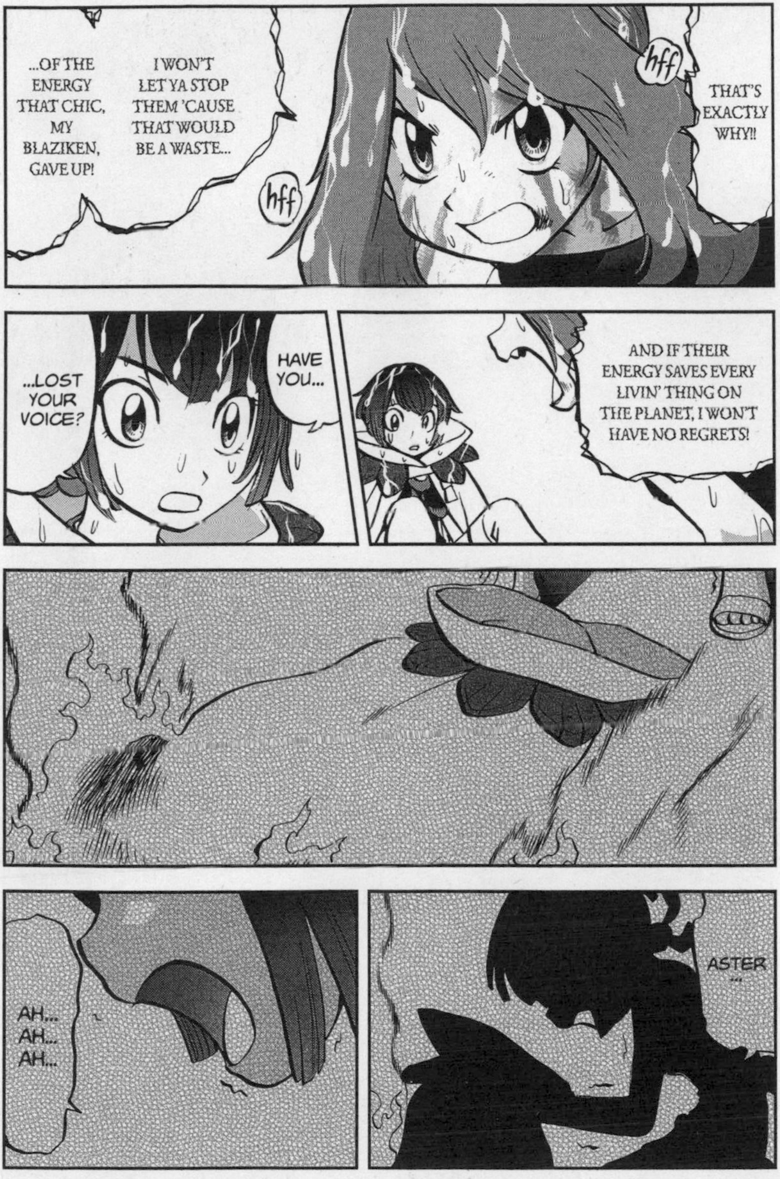
THAT'S EXACTLY WHY!!
hff
I WON'T LET YA STOP THEM 'CAUSE THAT WOULD BE A WASTE...
...OF THE ENERGY THAT CHIC, MY BLAZIKEN, GAVE UP!
hff
AND IF THEIR ENERGY SAVES EVERY LIVIN' THING ON THE PLANET, I WON'T HAVE NO REGRETS!
HAVE YOU...
...LOST YOUR VOICE?
ASTER...
AH... AH... AH...

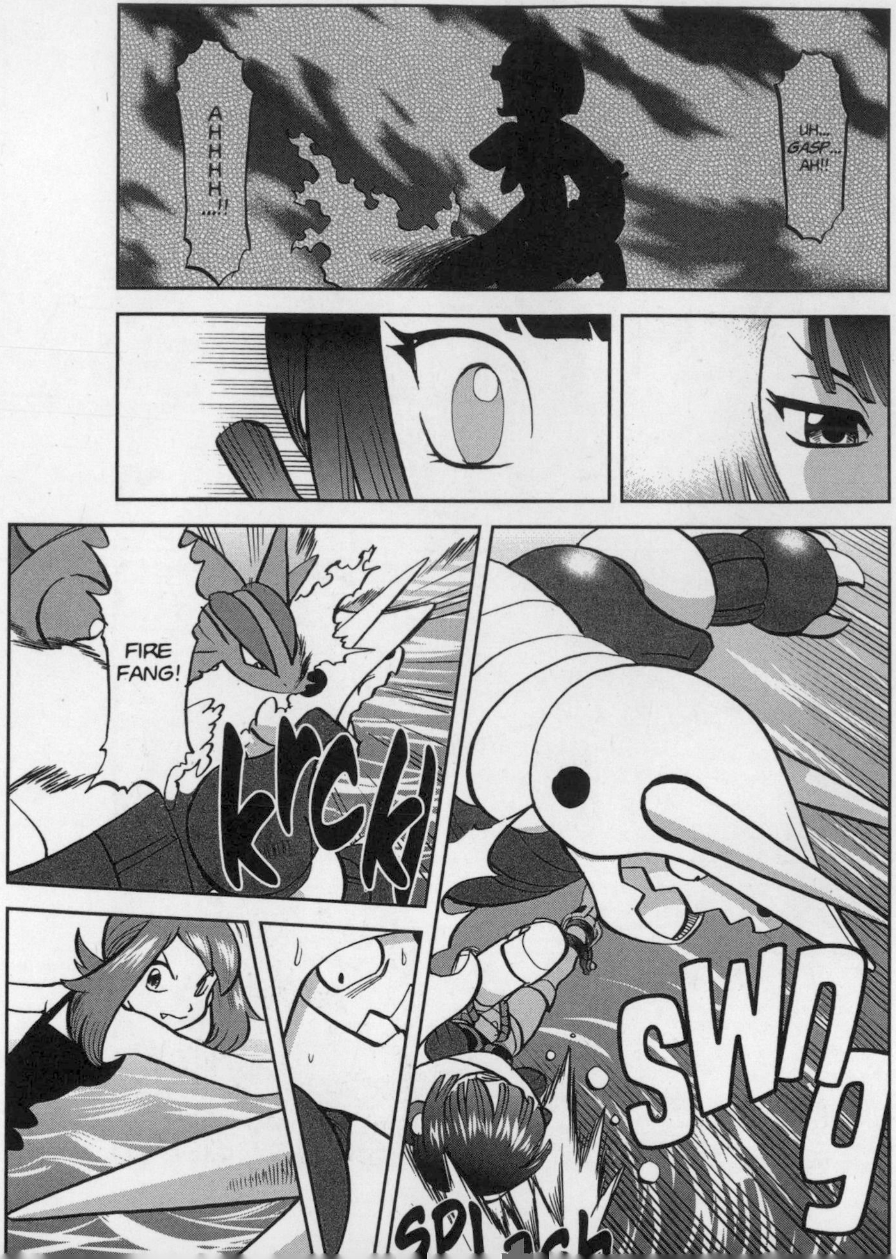
UH... GASP... AH!!
AHHHHH.....!!
FIRE FANG!
KRCK
SWNG

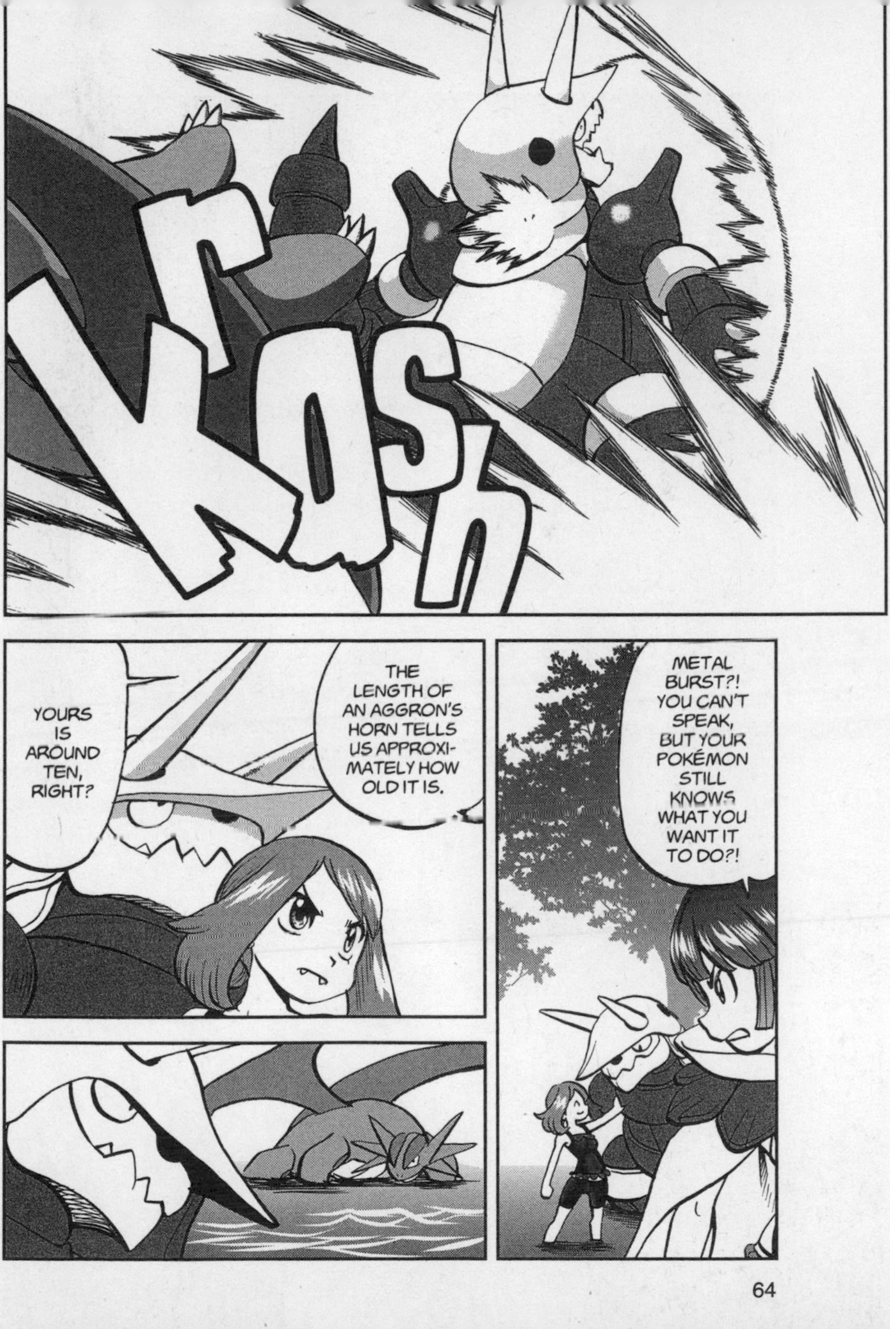
METAL BURST?! YOU CAN'T SPEAK, BUT YOUR POKÉMON STILL KNOWS WHAT YOU WANT IT TO DO?!
THE LENGTH OF AN AGGRON'S HORN TELLS US APPROXI-MATELY HOW OLD IT IS.
YOURS IS AROUND TEN, RIGHT?

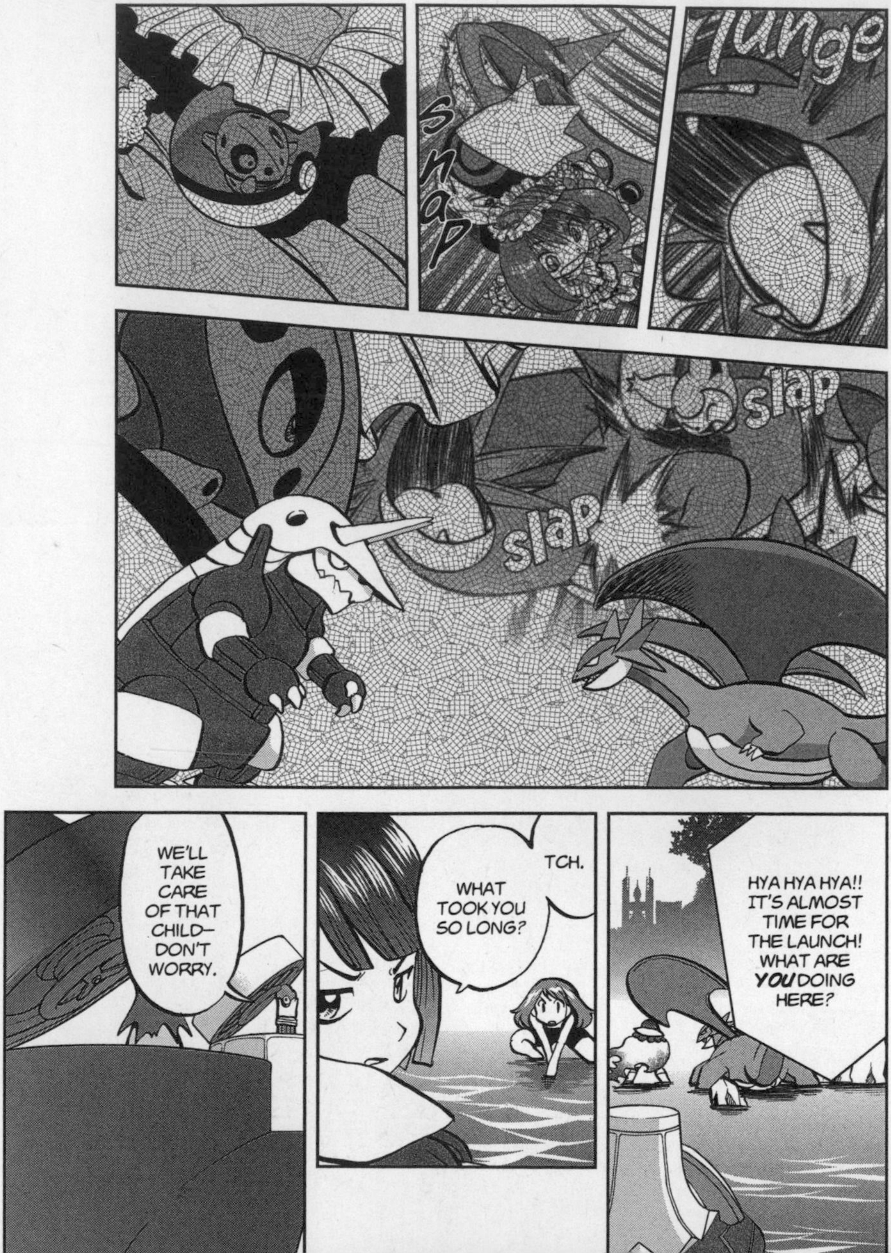
lunge
snap
slap
slap
HYA HYA HYA!! IT'S ALMOST TIME FOR THE LAUNCH! WHAT ARE ***YOU*** DOING HERE?
TCH.
WHAT TOOK YOU SO LONG?
WE'LL TAKE CARE OF THAT CHILD— DON'T WORRY.

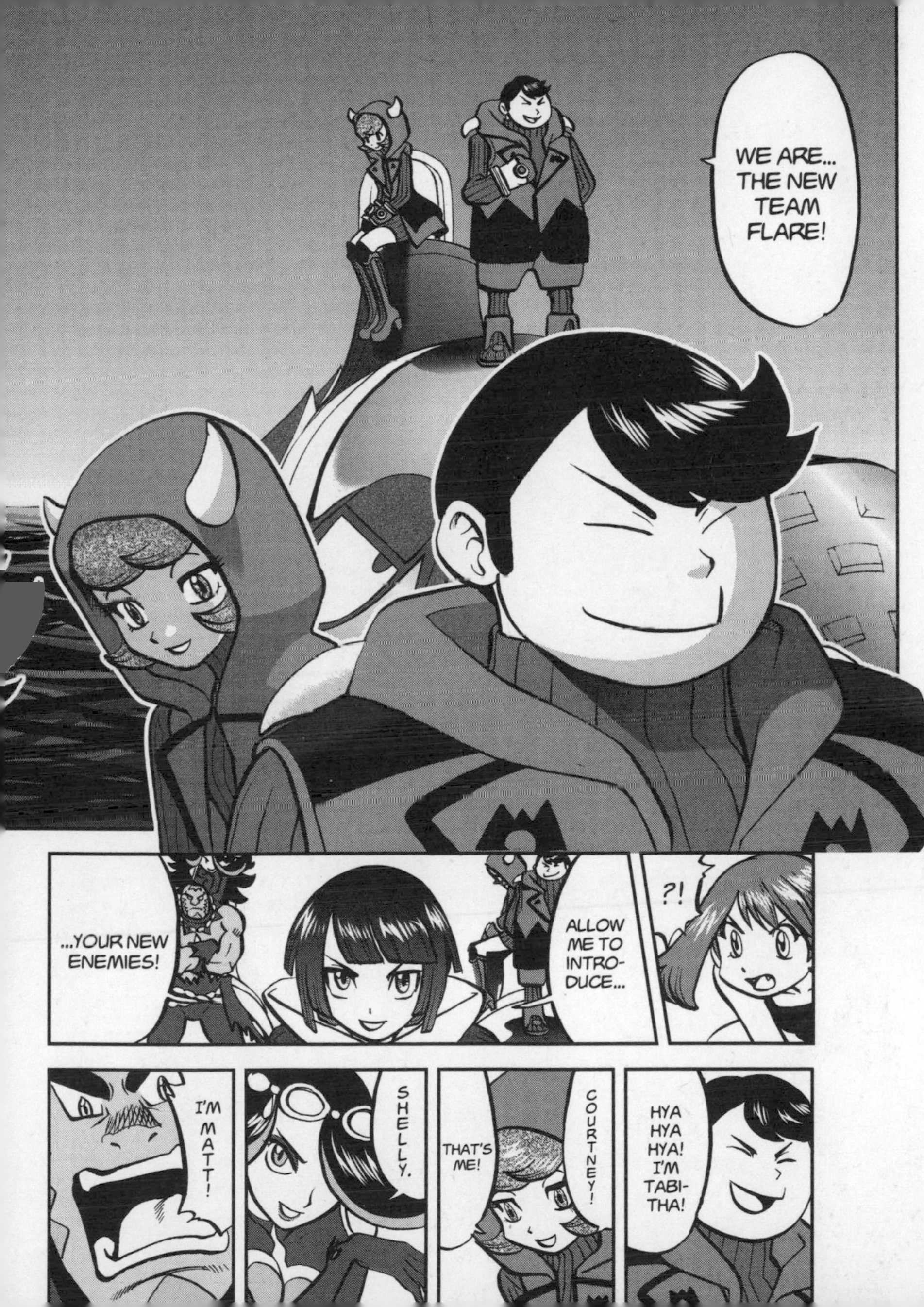
WE ARE... THE NEW TEAM FLARE!
?!
ALLOW ME TO INTRO-DUCE...
...YOUR NEW ENEMIES!
HYA HYA HYA! I'M TABI-THA!
COURTNEY!
THAT'S ME!
SHELLY.
I'M MATT!

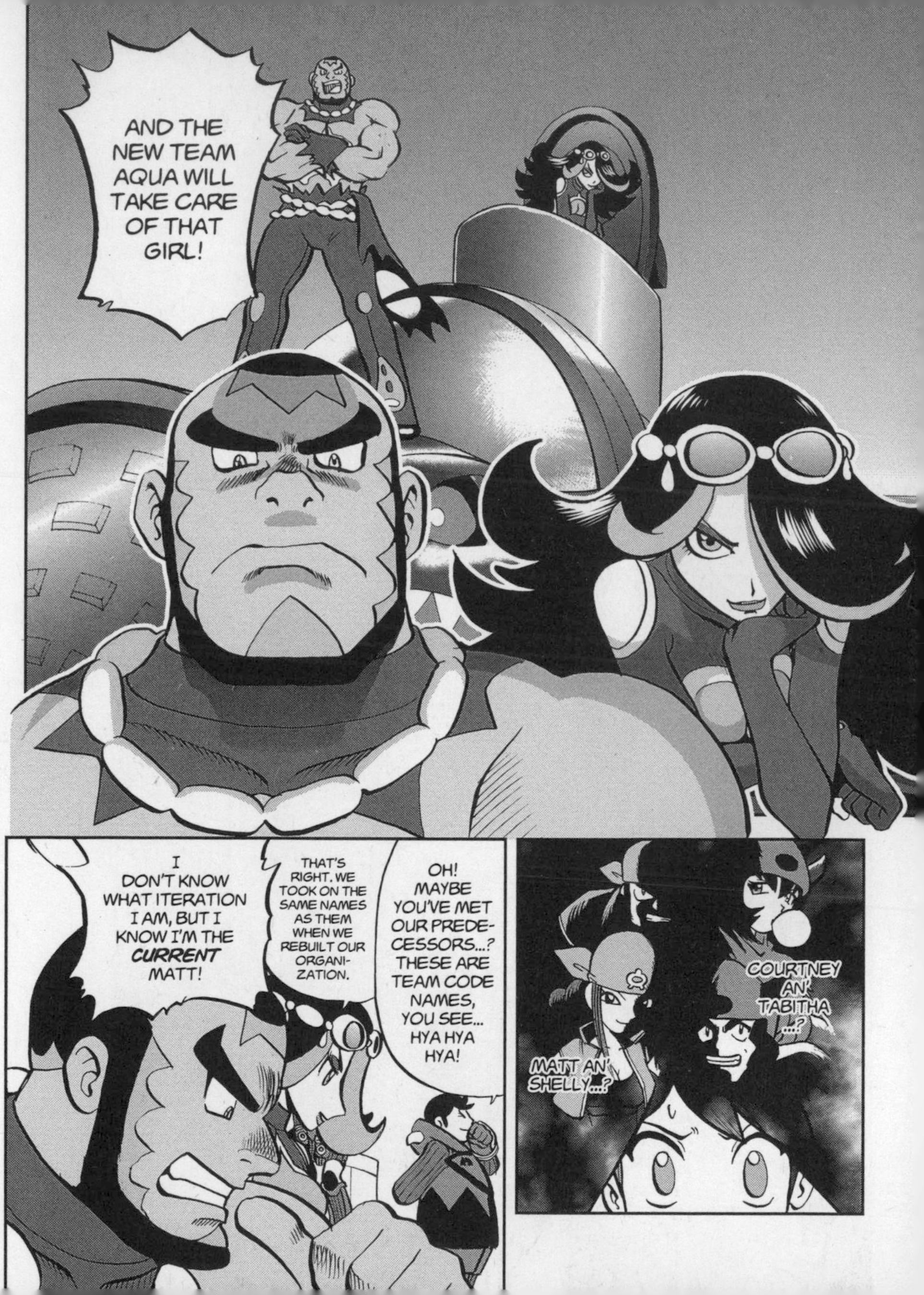
AND THE NEW TEAM AQUA WILL TAKE CARE OF THAT GIRL!
COURTNEY AN' TABITHA ...?
MATT AN' SHELLY...?
OH! MAYBE YOU'VE MET OUR PREDE-CESSORS...? THESE ARE TEAM CODE NAMES, YOU SEE... HYA HYA HYA!
THAT'S RIGHT. WE TOOK ON THE SAME NAMES AS THEM WHEN WE REBUILT OUR ORGANI-ZATION.
I DON'T KNOW WHAT ITERATION I AM, BUT I KNOW I'M THE *CURRENT* MATT!

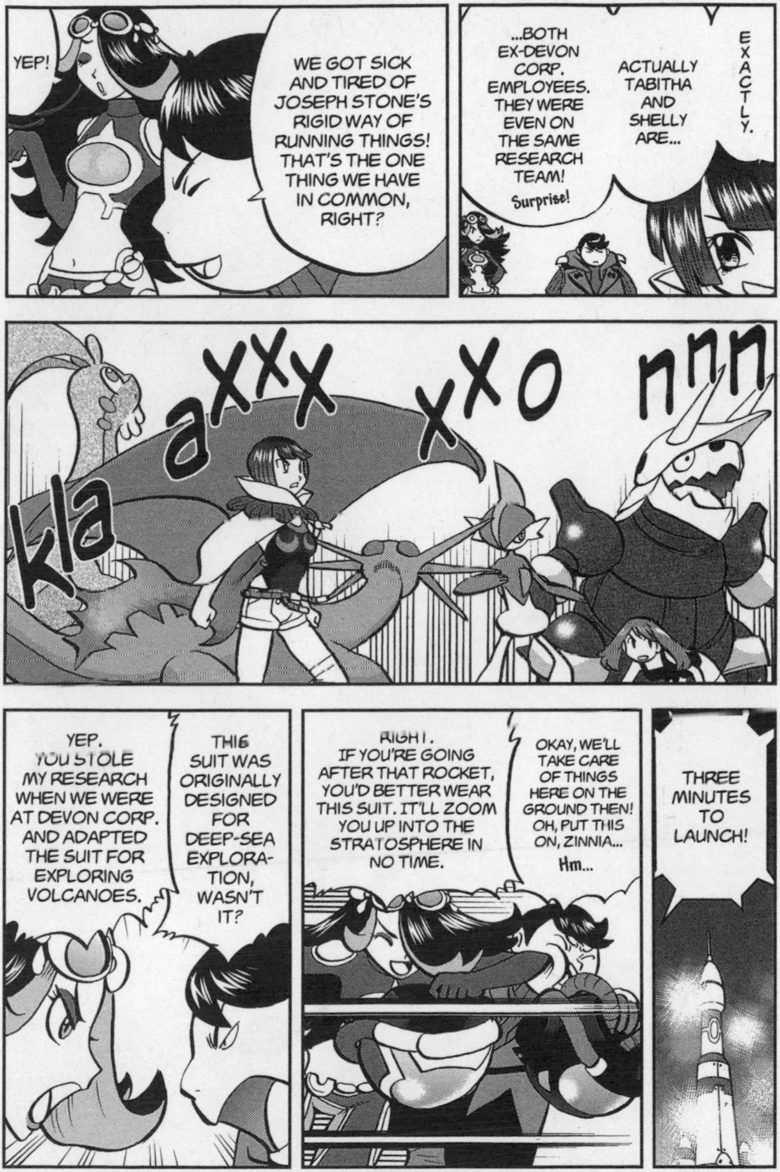
EXACTLY.
ACTUALLY TABITHA AND SHELLY ARE...
...BOTH EX-DEVON CORP. EMPLOYEES. THEY WERE EVEN ON THE SAME RESEARCH TEAM!
Surprise!
WE GOT SICK AND TIRED OF JOSEPH STONE'S RIGID WAY OF RUNNING THINGS! THAT'S THE ONE THING WE HAVE IN COMMON, RIGHT?
YEP!
kla axxx xxo nnn
THREE MINUTES TO LAUNCH!
OKAY, WE'LL TAKE CARE OF THINGS HERE ON THE GROUND THEN! OH, PUT THIS ON, ZINNIA...
Hm...
RIGHT. IF YOU'RE GOING AFTER THAT ROCKET, YOU'D BETTER WEAR THIS SUIT. IT'LL ZOOM YOU UP INTO THE STRATOSPHERE IN NO TIME.
THIS SUIT WAS ORIGINALLY DESIGNED FOR DEEP-SEA EXPLORATION, WASN'T IT?
YEP. YOU STOLE MY RESEARCH WHEN WE WERE AT DEVON CORP. AND ADAPTED THE SUIT FOR EXPLORING VOLCANOES.

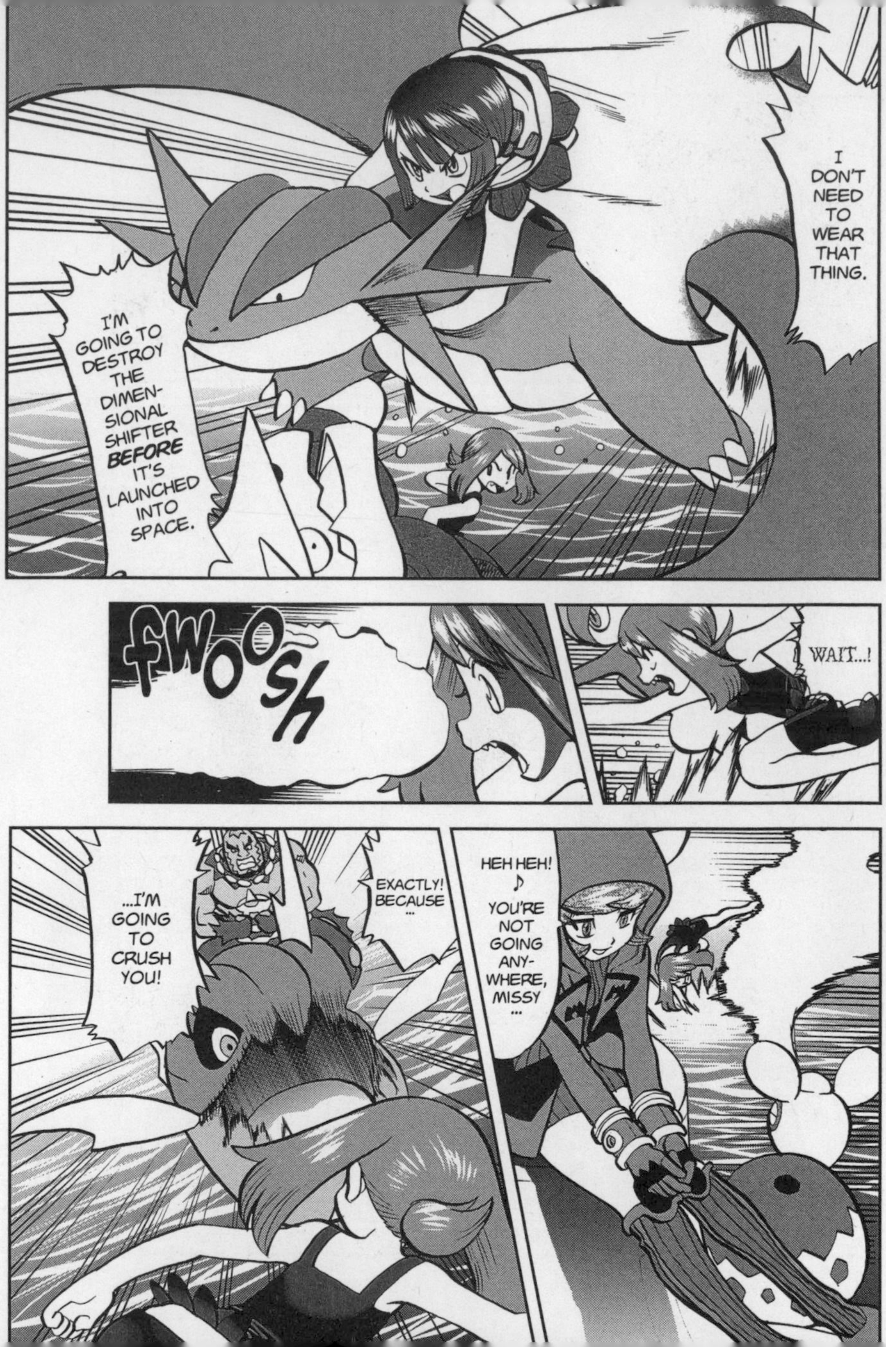
I DON'T NEED TO WEAR THAT THING.
I'M GOING TO DESTROY THE DIMENSIONAL SHIFTER **BEFORE** IT'S LAUNCHED INTO SPACE.
WAIT...!
FWOOSH
HEH HEH! ♪
YOU'RE NOT GOING ANYWHERE, MISSY...
EXACTLY! BECAUSE...
...I'M GOING TO CRUSH YOU!

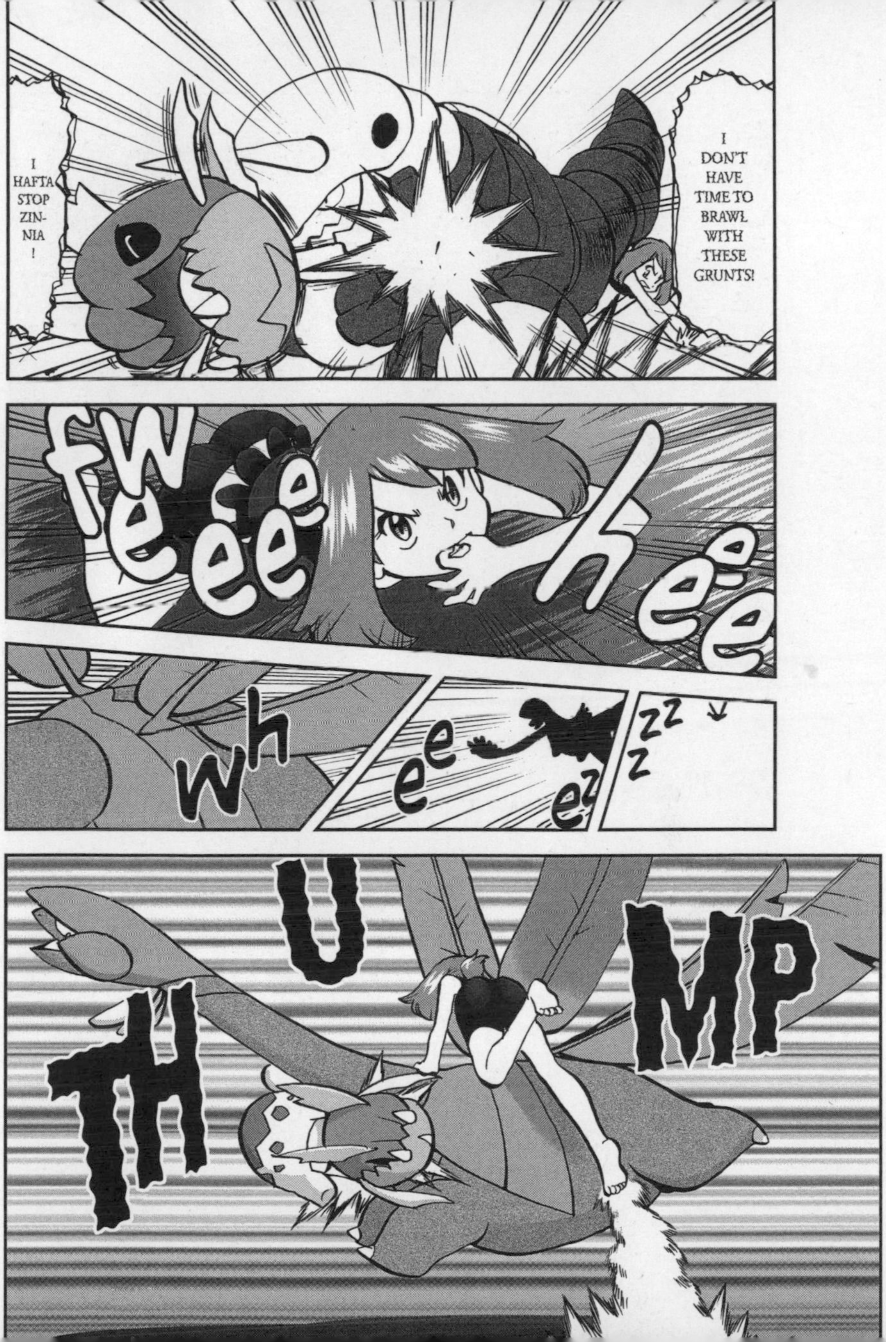
I DON'T HAVE TIME TO BRAWL WITH THESE GRUNTS!
I HAFTA STOP ZIN-NIA!
fweee
heee
wheee
zzz
THUMP

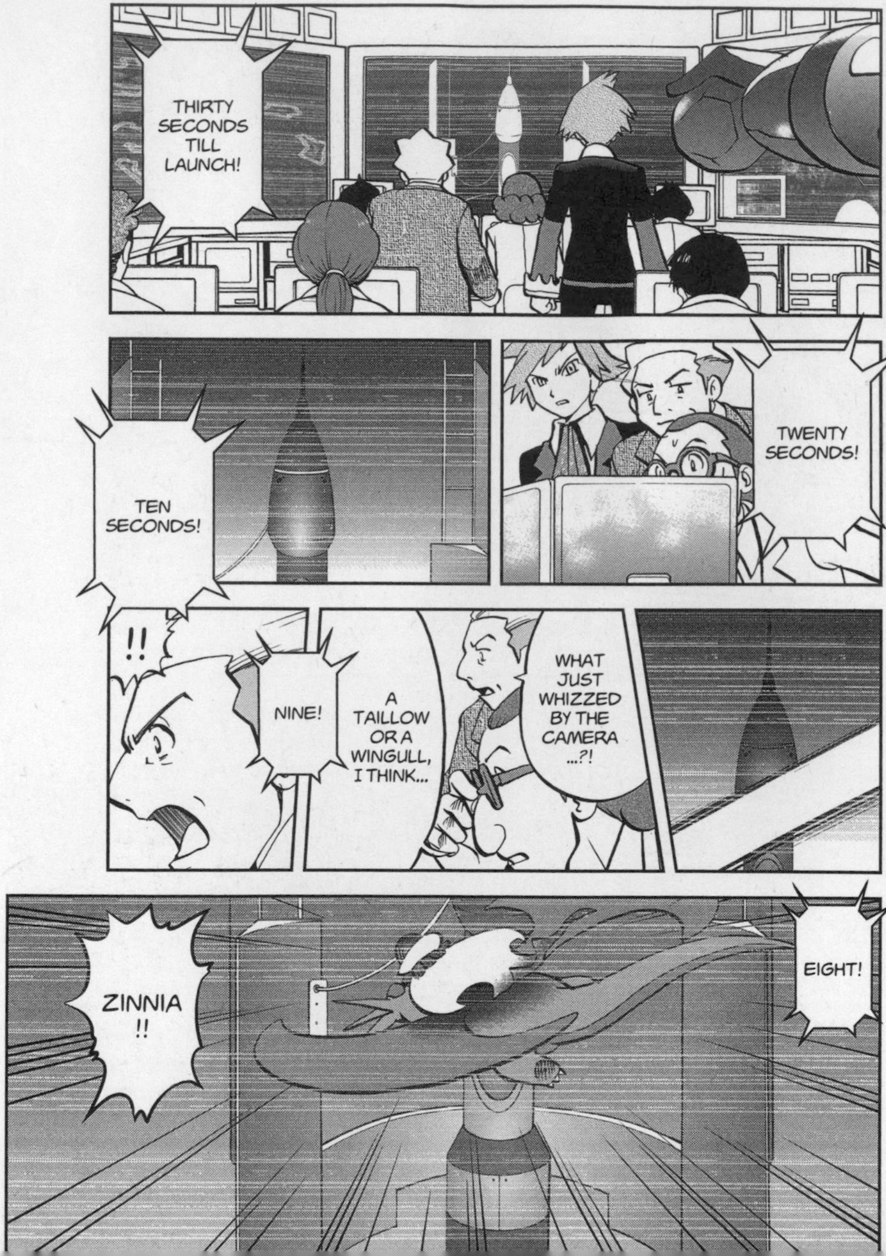
THIRTY SECONDS TILL LAUNCH!
TWENTY SECONDS!
TEN SECONDS!
WHAT JUST WHIZZED BY THE CAMERA ...?!
A TAILLOW OR A WINGULL, I THINK...
NINE!
!!
EIGHT!
ZINNIA !!

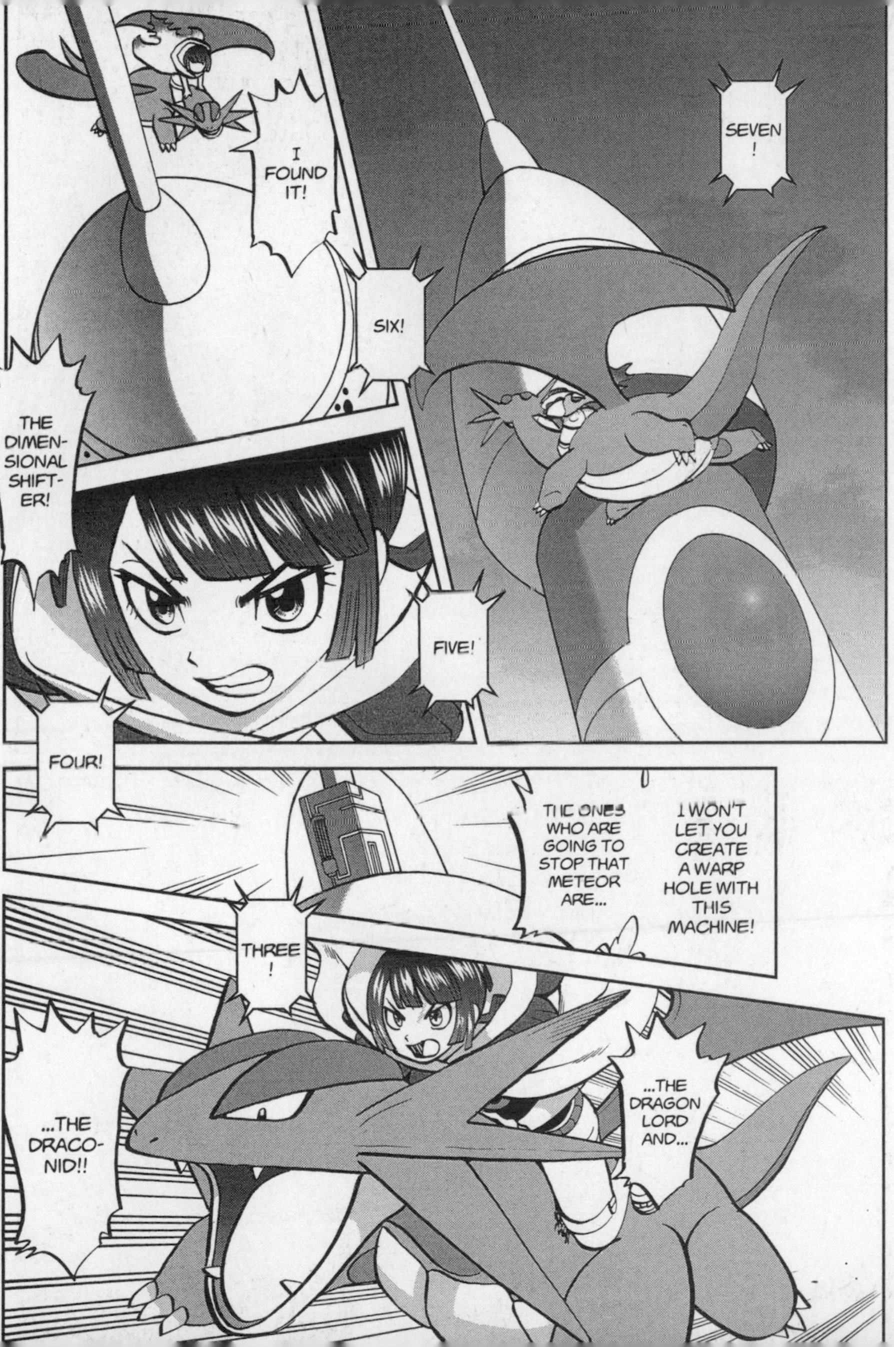
SEVEN!
I FOUND IT!
SIX!
THE DIMENSIONAL SHIFTER!
FIVE!
FOUR!
I WON'T LET YOU CREATE A WARP HOLE WITH THIS MACHINE!
THE ONES WHO ARE GOING TO STOP THAT METEOR ARE...
THREE!
...THE DRAGON LORD AND...
...THE DRACONID!!

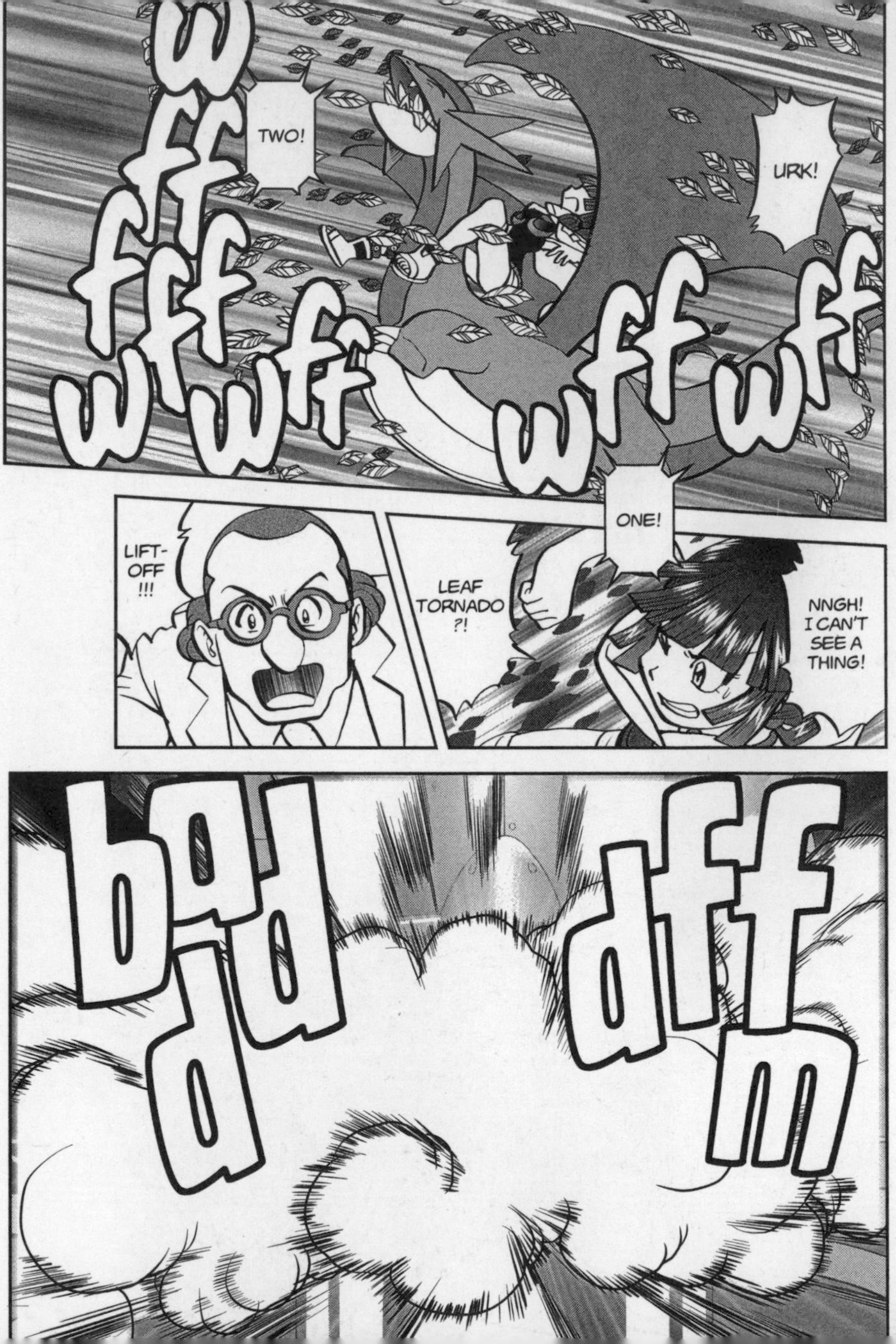
URK!
TWO!
wff wff wff
wff wff
ONE!
NNGH! I CAN'T SEE A THING!
LEAF TORNADO ?!
LIFT-OFF !!!

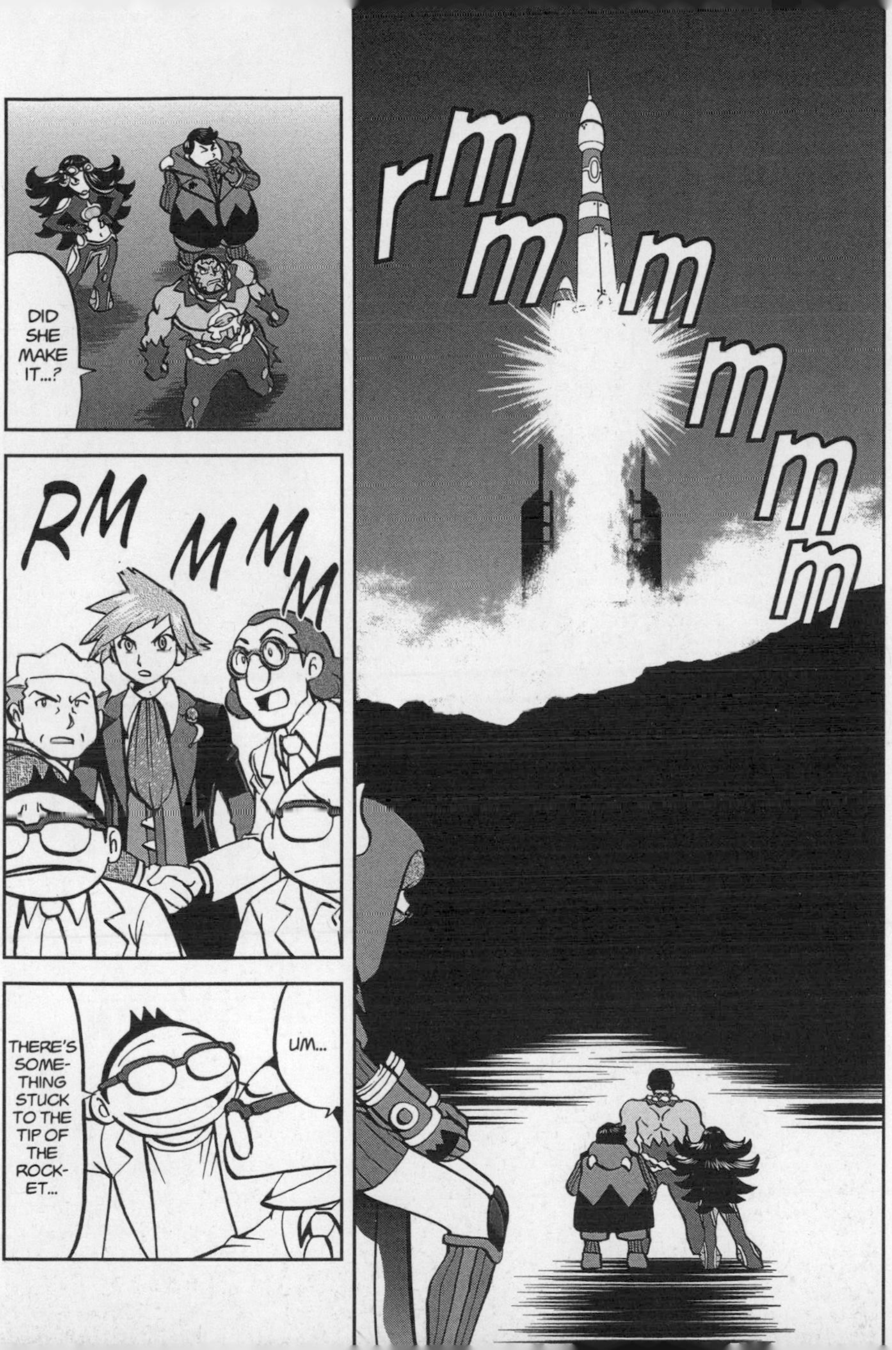

rmmmmmmmmmm
DID SHE MAKE IT...?
RMMMM
UM...
THERE'S SOME-THING STUCK TO THE TIP OF THE ROCK-ET...

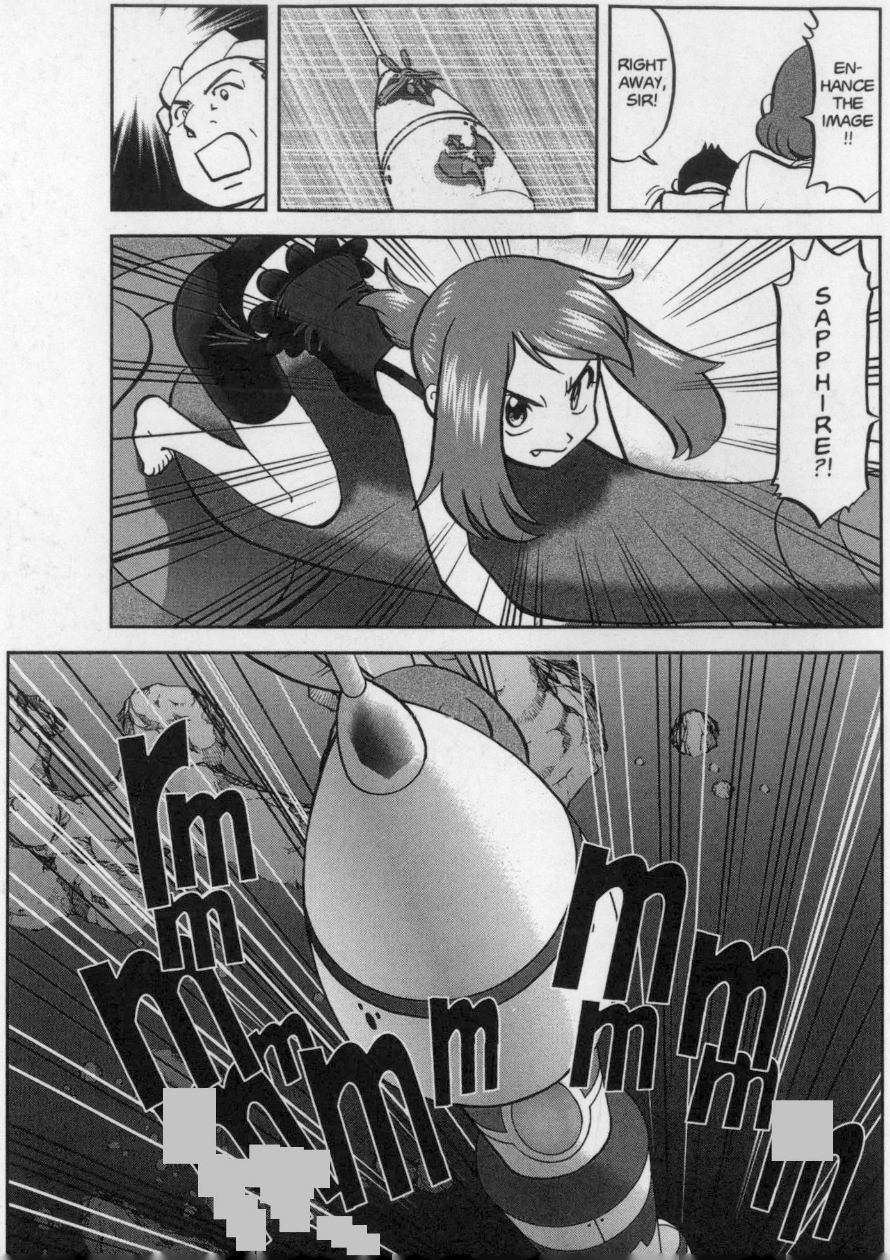
EN-HANCE THE IMAGE !!
RIGHT AWAY, SIR!
SAPPHIRE?!

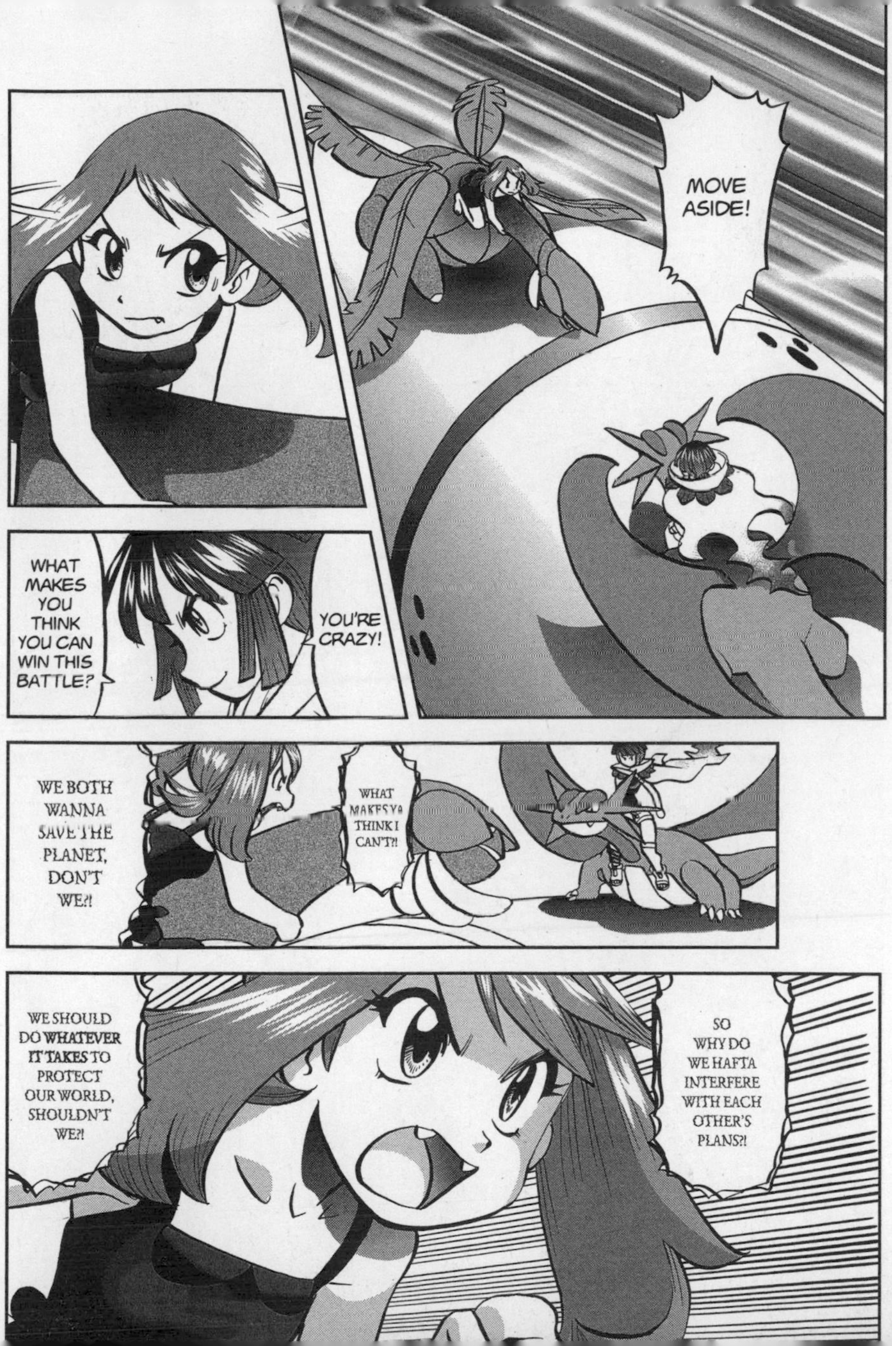
MOVE ASIDE!
YOU'RE CRAZY!
WHAT MAKES YOU THINK YOU CAN WIN THIS BATTLE?
WHAT MAKES YA THINK I CAN'T?!
WE BOTH WANNA SAVE THE PLANET, DON'T WE?!
SO WHY DO WE HAFTA INTERFERE WITH EACH OTHER'S PLANS?!
WE SHOULD DO WHATEVER IT TAKES TO PROTECT OUR WORLD, SHOULDN'T WE?!

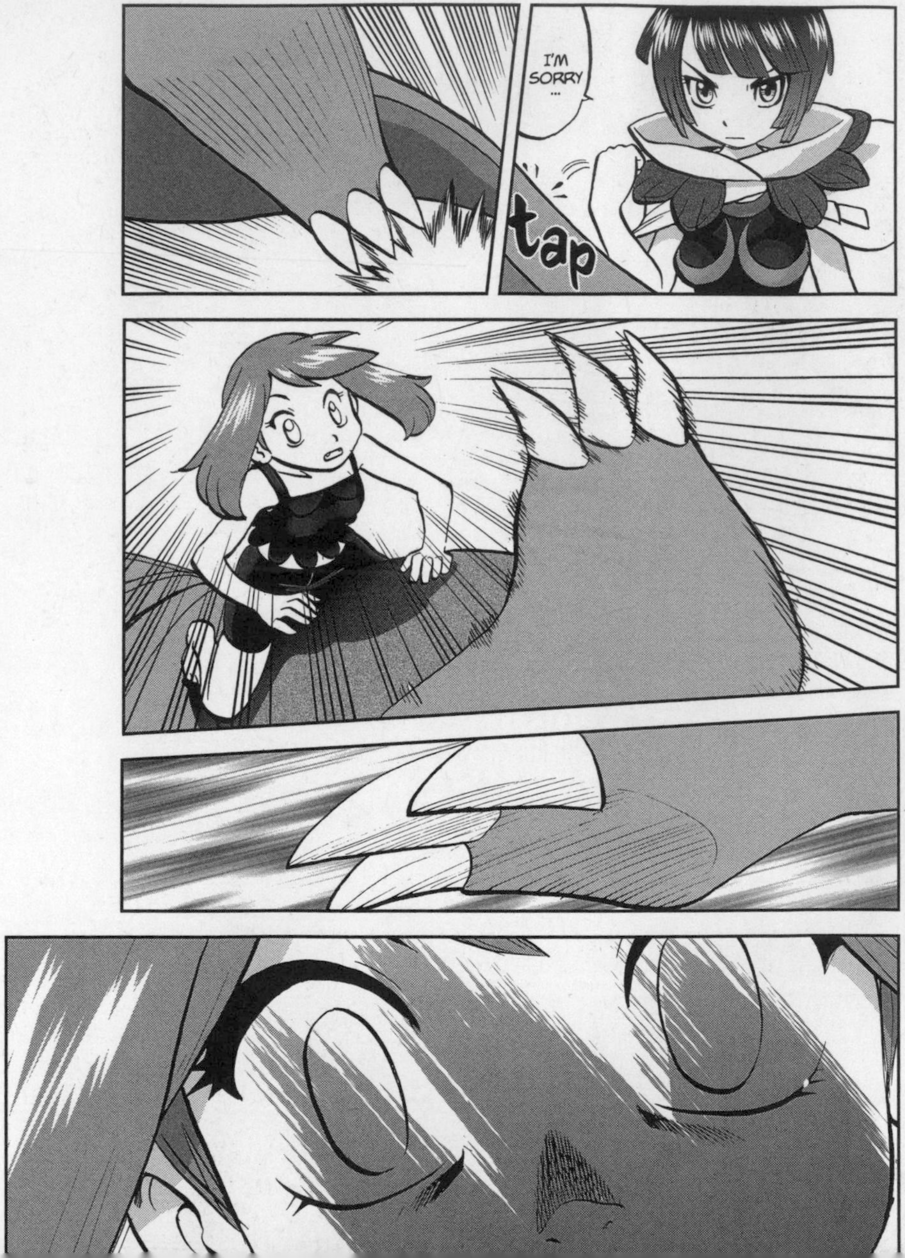
I'M SORRY ...
tap

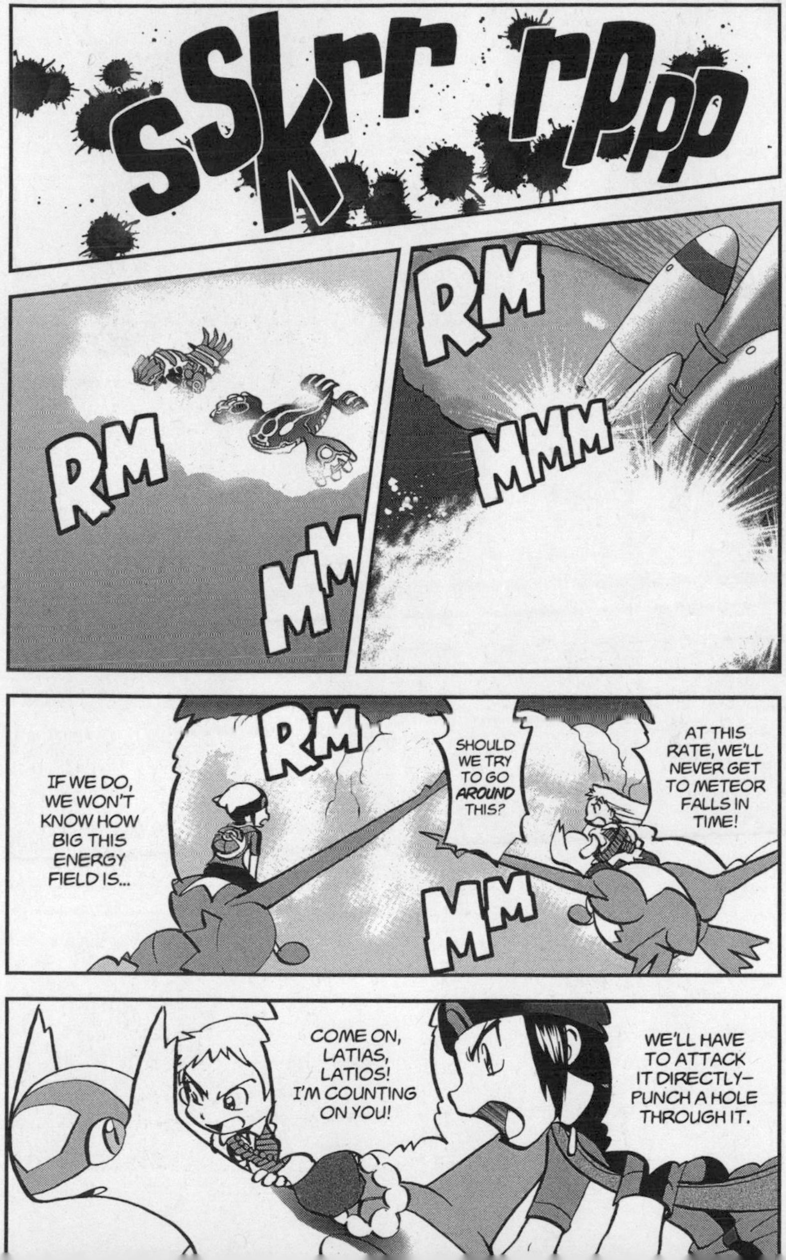
SSKRR RPPP
RM
MMM
RM
MM
AT THIS RATE, WE'LL NEVER GET TO METEOR FALLS IN TIME!
SHOULD WE TRY TO GO *AROUND* THIS?
RM
MM
IF WE DO, WE WON'T KNOW HOW BIG THIS ENERGY FIELD IS...
WE'LL HAVE TO ATTACK IT DIRECTLY—PUNCH A HOLE THROUGH IT.
COME ON, LATIAS, LATIOS! I'M COUNTING ON YOU!

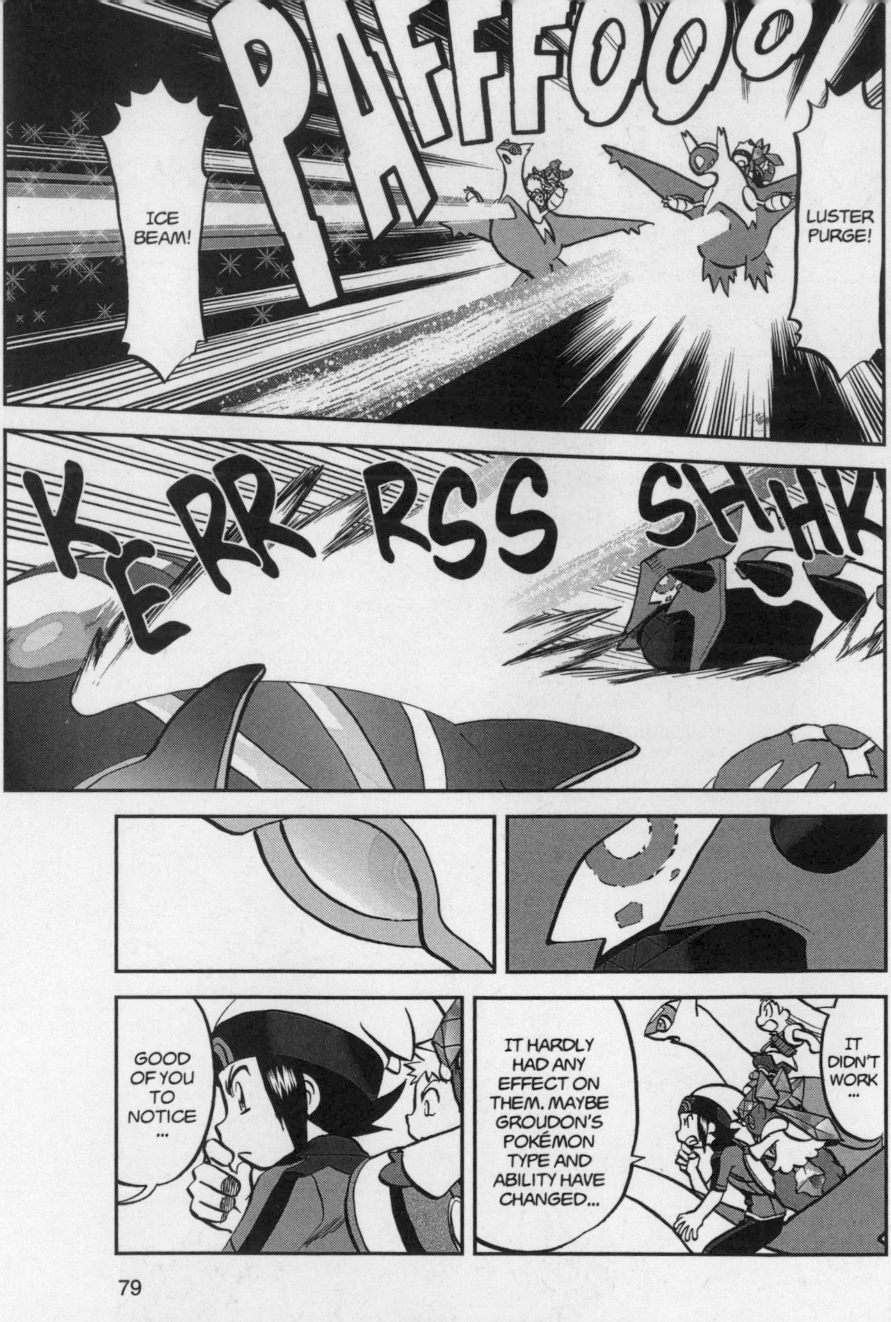
PAFFOOO!
LUSTER PURGE!
ICE BEAM!
KERR RSS SHHK
IT DIDN'T WORK ...
IT HARDLY HAD ANY EFFECT ON THEM. MAYBE GROUDON'S POKÉMON TYPE AND ABILITY HAVE CHANGED...
GOOD OF YOU TO NOTICE ...

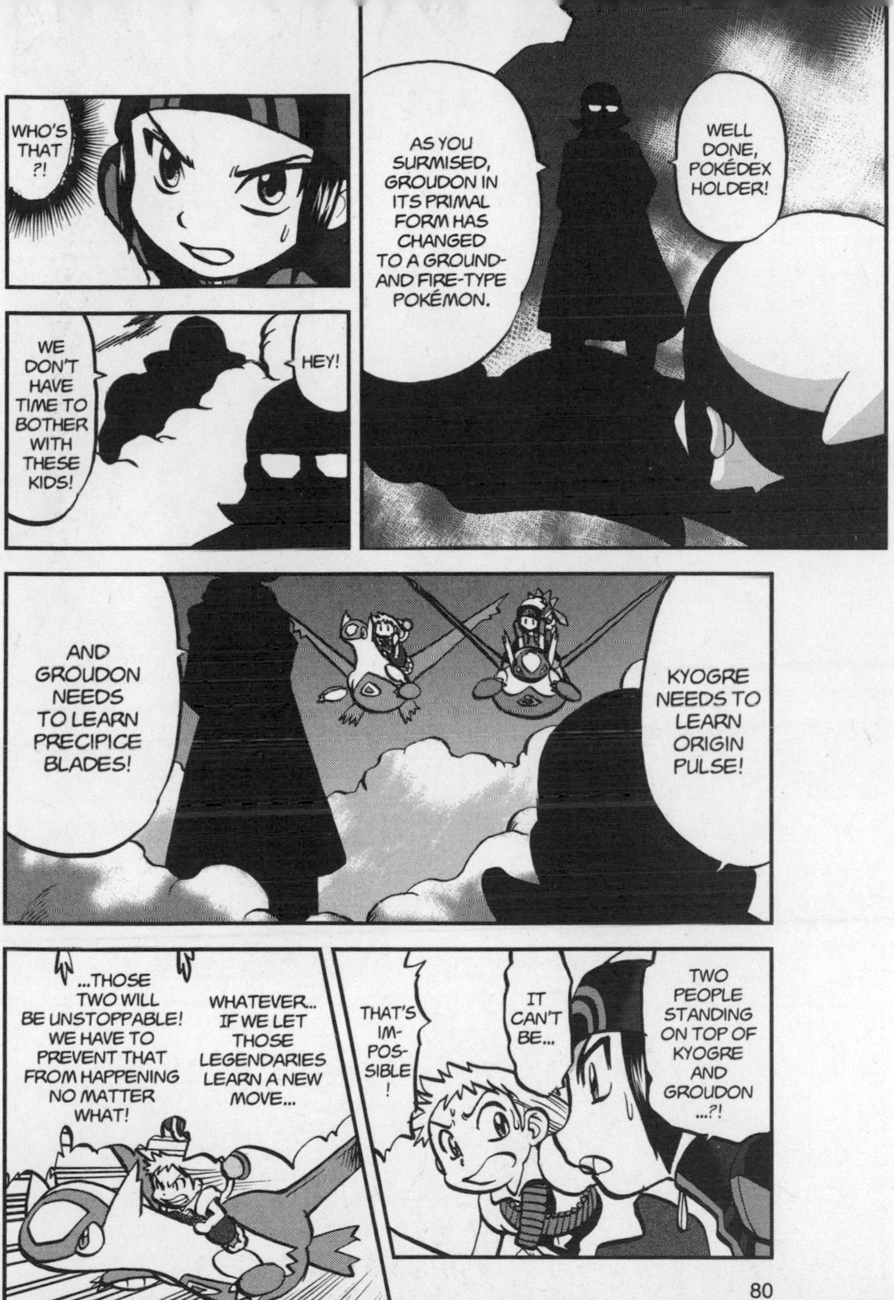
WELL DONE, POKÉDEX HOLDER!
AS YOU SURMISED, GROUDON IN ITS PRIMAL FORM HAS CHANGED TO A GROUND- AND FIRE-TYPE POKÉMON.
WHO'S THAT?!
HEY!
WE DON'T HAVE TIME TO BOTHER WITH THESE KIDS!
KYOGRE NEEDS TO LEARN ORIGIN PULSE!
AND GROUDON NEEDS TO LEARN PRECIPICE BLADES!
TWO PEOPLE STANDING ON TOP OF KYOGRE AND GROUDON ...?!
IT CAN'T BE...
THAT'S IMPOSSIBLE!
WHATEVER.. IF WE LET THOSE LEGENDARIES LEARN A NEW MOVE...
...THOSE TWO WILL BE UNSTOPPABLE! WE HAVE TO PREVENT THAT FROM HAPPENING NO MATTER WHAT!

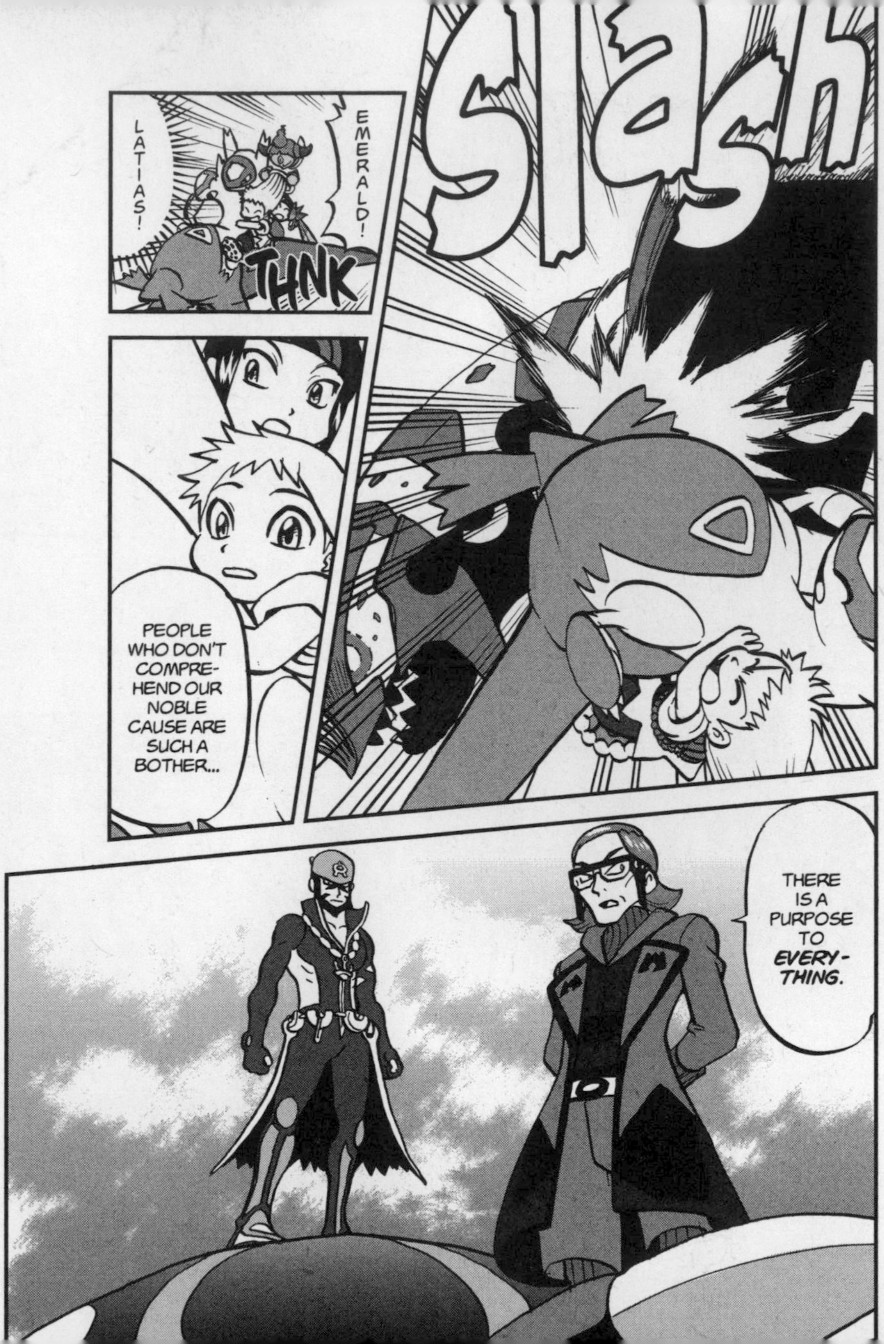
SLASH
EMERALD!
LATIAS!
THNK
PEOPLE WHO DON'T COMPREHEND OUR NOBLE CAUSE ARE SUCH A BOTHER...
THERE IS A PURPOSE TO *EVERYTHING*.

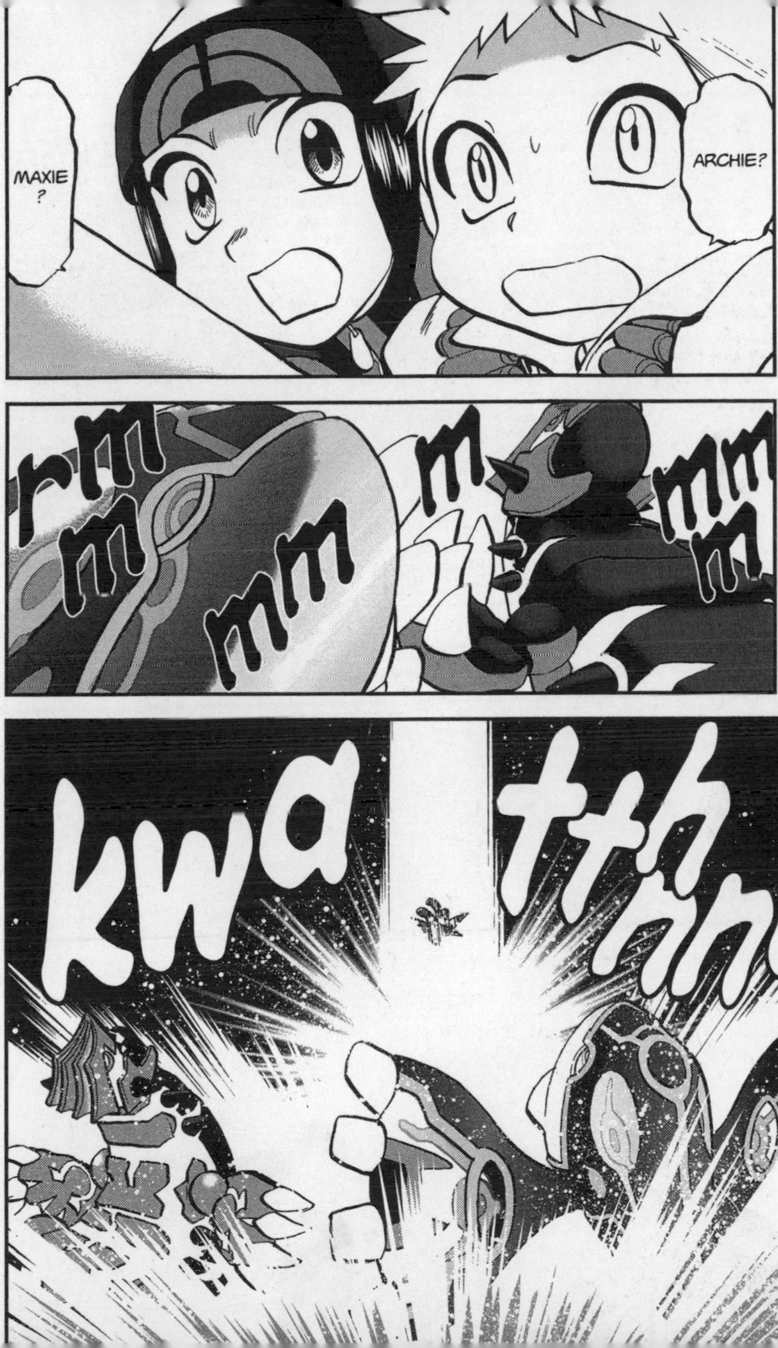
ARCHIE?
MAXIE ?
mmmm
m
rmmmmm
kwa
tthank

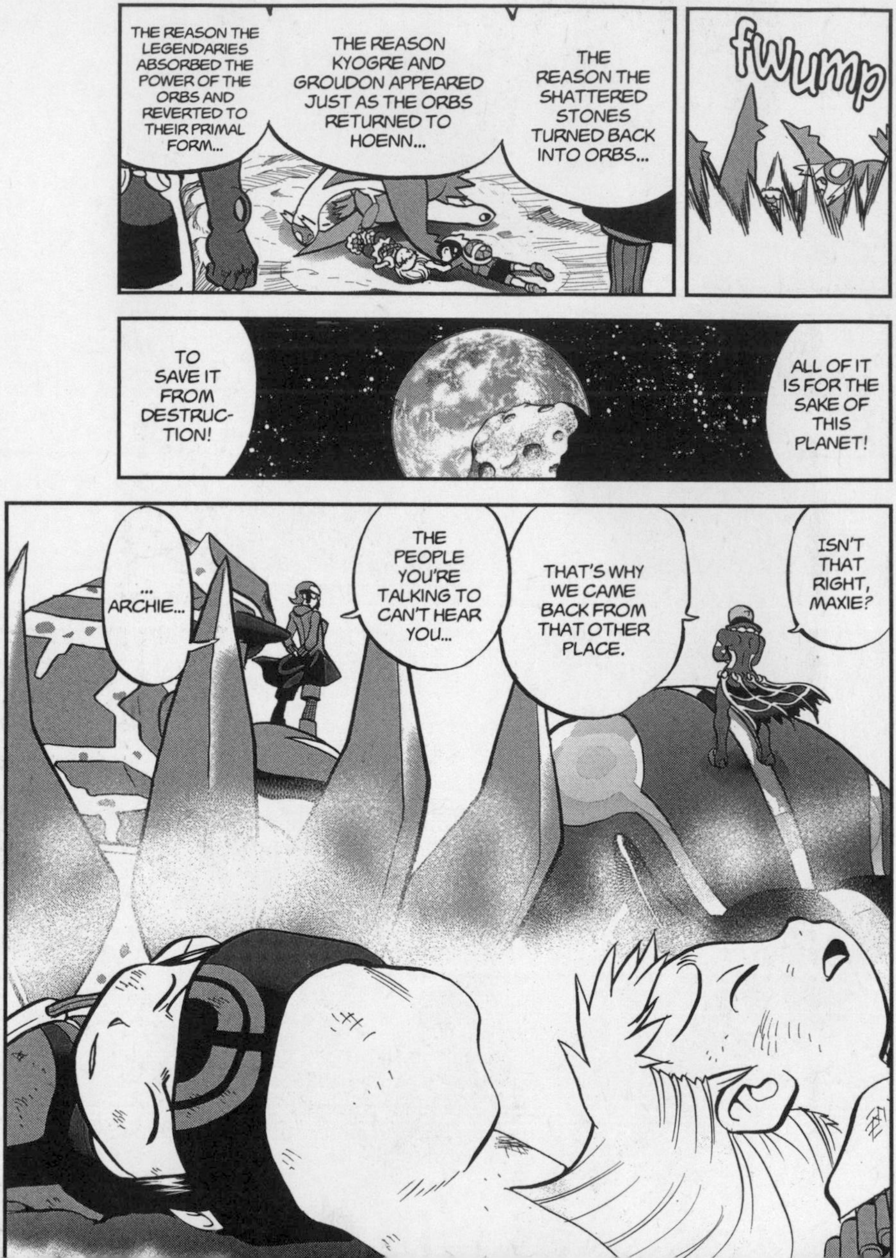
FWUMP
THE REASON THE SHATTERED STONES TURNED BACK INTO ORBS...
THE REASON KYOGRE AND GROUDON APPEARED JUST AS THE ORBS RETURNED TO HOENN...
THE REASON THE LEGENDARIES ABSORBED THE POWER OF THE ORBS AND REVERTED TO THEIR PRIMAL FORM...
ALL OF IT IS FOR THE SAKE OF THIS PLANET!
TO SAVE IT FROM DESTRUC-TION!
ISN'T THAT RIGHT, MAXIE?
THAT'S WHY WE CAME BACK FROM THAT OTHER PLACE.
THE PEOPLE YOU'RE TALKING TO CAN'T HEAR YOU...
... ARCHIE...

WARP HOLE

A ring of energy that can instantaneously transport an object (or living thing) from one place to another. The Devon Corporation had been researching this phenomenon in an attempt to artificially reproduce the stats of a certain Pokémon. Infinity Energy is shot out in the form of a ring from the Dimensional Shifter to create a warp hole. The plan devised by Devon Corporation, in cooperation with the Mossdeep Space Center, is to create a warp hole in the trajectory of the meteor to prevent it from colliding with the planet.

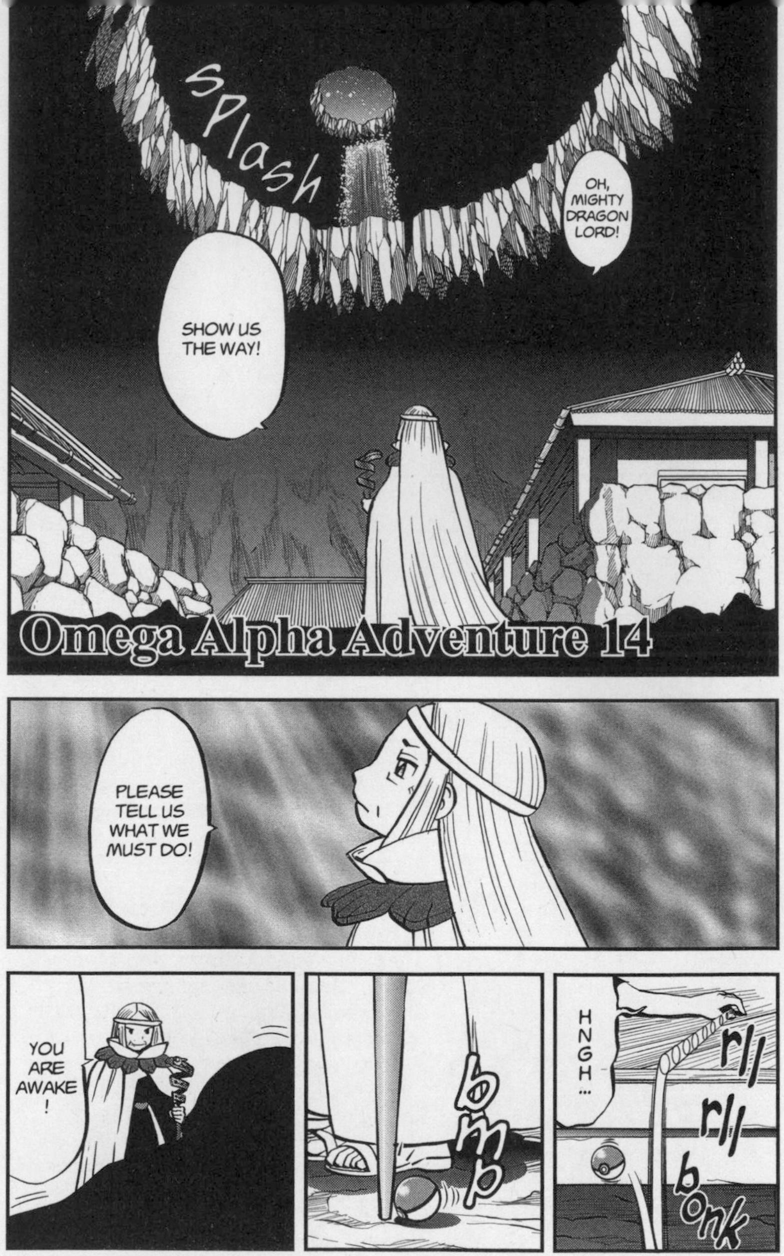
sPlash
OH, MIGHTY DRAGON LORD!
SHOW US THE WAY!
Omega Alpha Adventure 14
PLEASE TELL US WHAT WE MUST DO!
HNGH...
rl/ rl/
bonk
bmp
YOU ARE AWAKE!

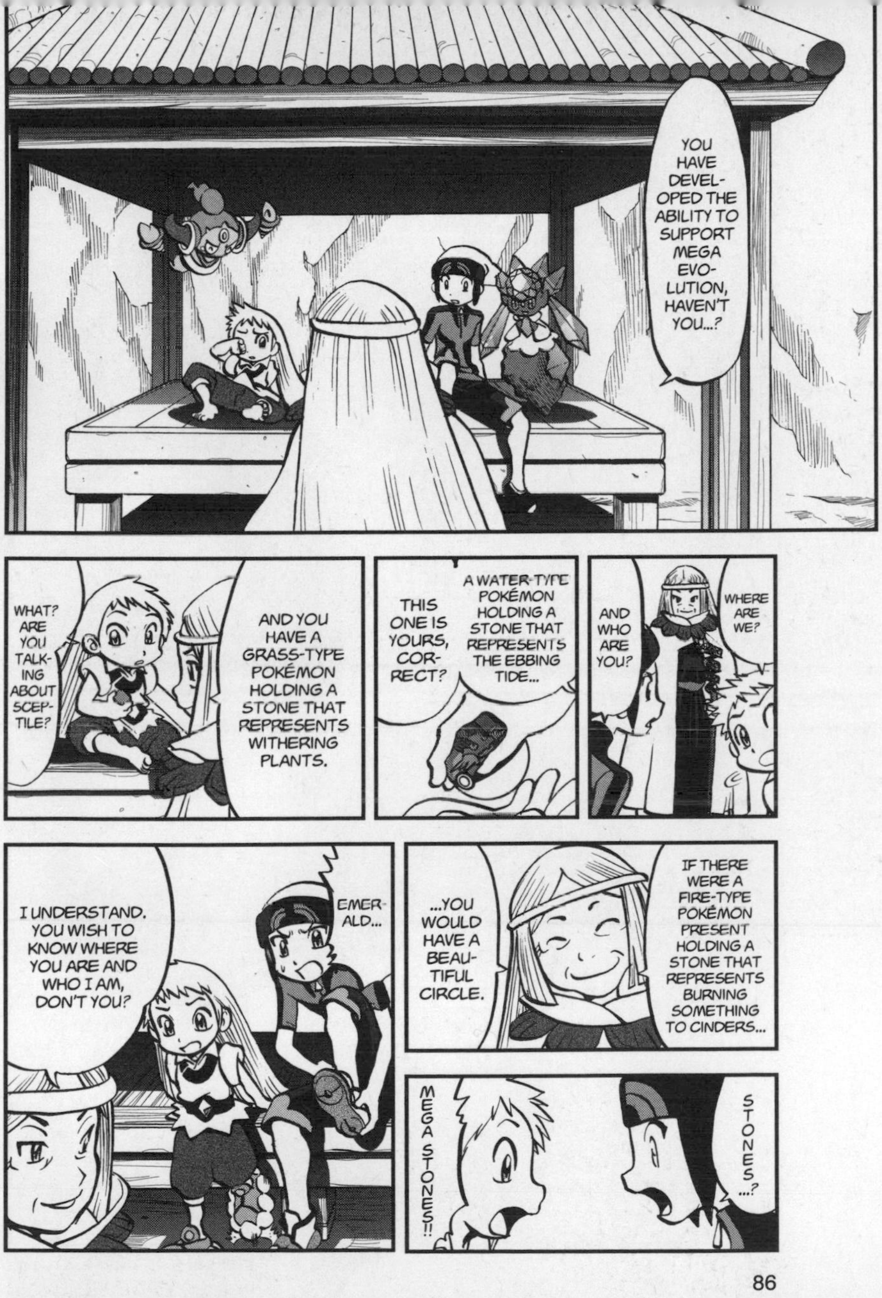
YOU HAVE DEVEL-OPED THE ABILITY TO SUPPORT MEGA EVO-LUTION, HAVEN'T YOU...?
WHERE ARE WE?
AND WHO ARE YOU?
A WATER-TYPE POKÉMON HOLDING A STONE THAT REPRESENTS THE EBBING TIDE...
THIS ONE IS YOURS, CORRECT?
AND YOU HAVE A GRASS-TYPE POKÉMON HOLDING A STONE THAT REPRESENTS WITHERING PLANTS.
WHAT? ARE YOU TALKING ABOUT SCEPTILE?
IF THERE WERE A FIRE-TYPE POKÉMON PRESENT HOLDING A STONE THAT REPRESENTS BURNING SOMETHING TO CINDERS...
...YOU WOULD HAVE A BEAUTIFUL CIRCLE.
STONES...?
MEGA STONES!!
EMERALD...
I UNDERSTAND. YOU WISH TO KNOW WHERE YOU ARE AND WHO I AM, DON'T YOU?

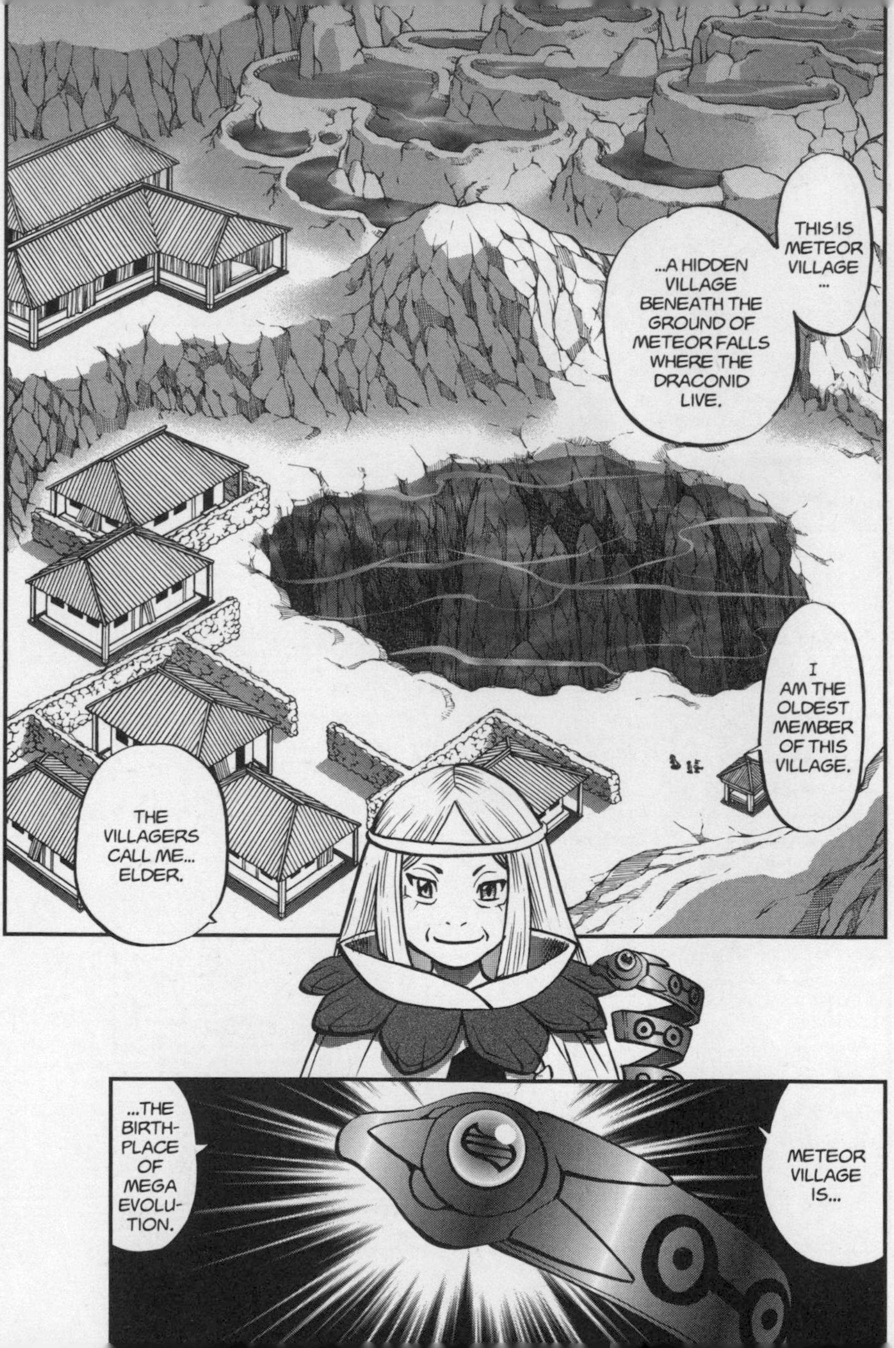
THIS IS METEOR VILLAGE...
...A HIDDEN VILLAGE BENEATH THE GROUND OF METEOR FALLS WHERE THE DRACONID LIVE.
I AM THE OLDEST MEMBER OF THIS VILLAGE.
THE VILLAGERS CALL ME... ELDER.
METEOR VILLAGE IS...
...THE BIRTH-PLACE OF MEGA EVOLU-TION.

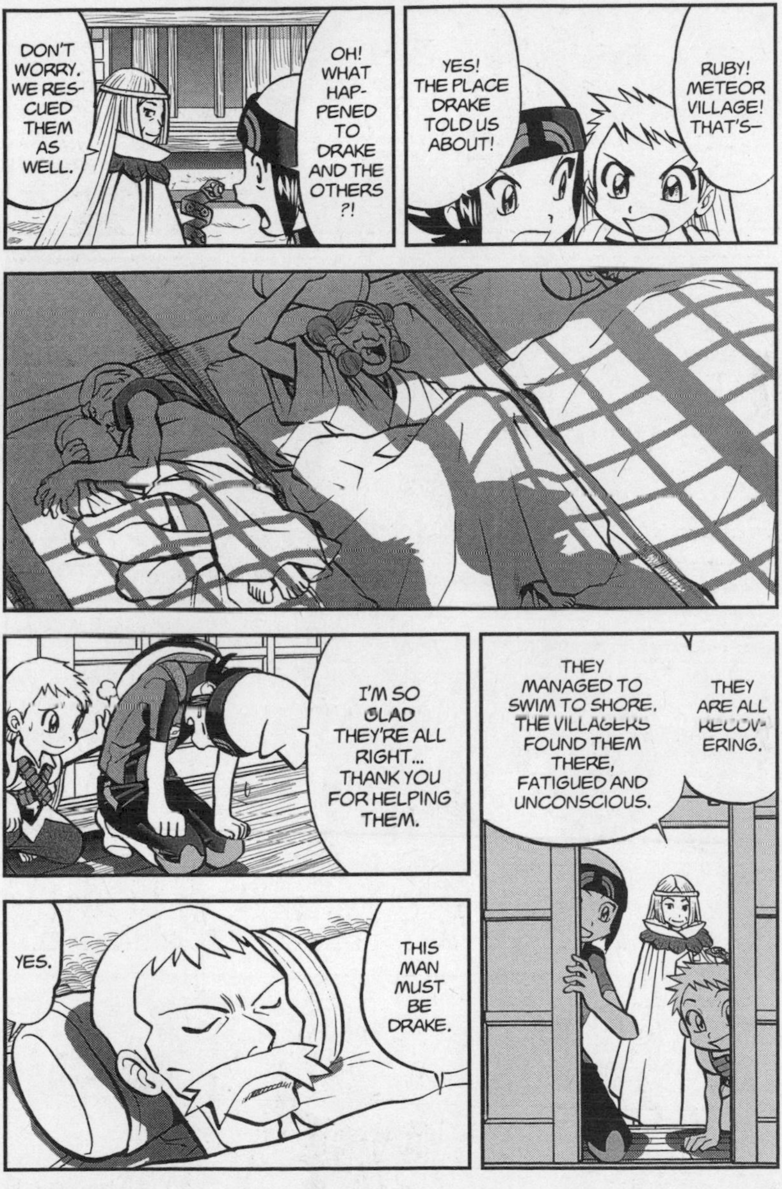
RUBY! METEOR VILLAGE! THAT'S—
YES! THE PLACE DRAKE TOLD US ABOUT!
OH! WHAT HAP-PENED TO DRAKE AND THE OTHERS?!
DON'T WORRY. WE RES-CUED THEM AS WELL.
THEY ARE ALL RECOV-ERING.
THEY MANAGED TO SWIM TO SHORE. THE VILLAGERS FOUND THEM THERE, FATIGUED AND UNCONSCIOUS.
I'M SO GLAD THEY'RE ALL RIGHT... THANK YOU FOR HELPING THEM.
THIS MAN MUST BE DRAKE.
YES.

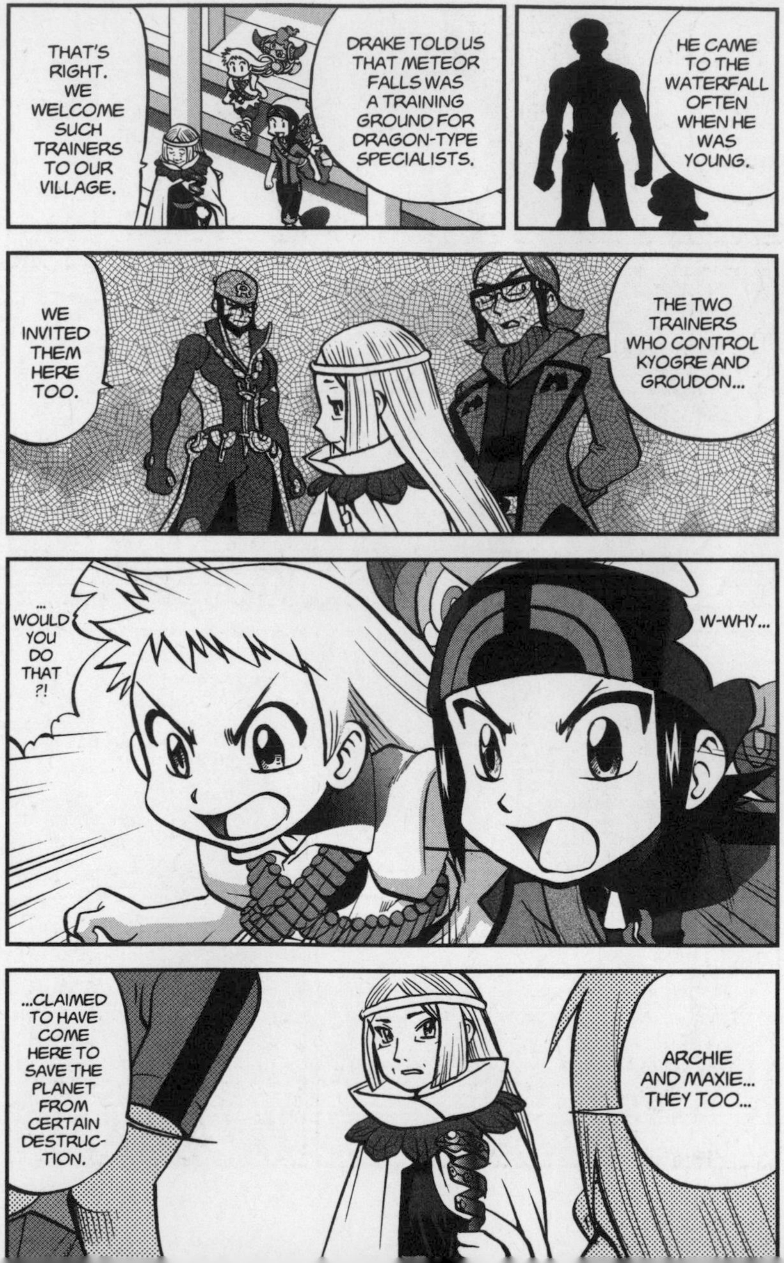
HE CAME TO THE WATERFALL OFTEN WHEN HE WAS YOUNG.
DRAKE TOLD US THAT METEOR FALLS WAS A TRAINING GROUND FOR DRAGON-TYPE SPECIALISTS.
THAT'S RIGHT. WE WELCOME SUCH TRAINERS TO OUR VILLAGE.
THE TWO TRAINERS WHO CONTROL KYOGRE AND GROUDON...
WE INVITED THEM HERE TOO.
W-WHY...
...WOULD YOU DO THAT?!
ARCHIE AND MAXIE... THEY TOO...
...CLAIMED TO HAVE COME HERE TO SAVE THE PLANET FROM CERTAIN DESTRUCTION.

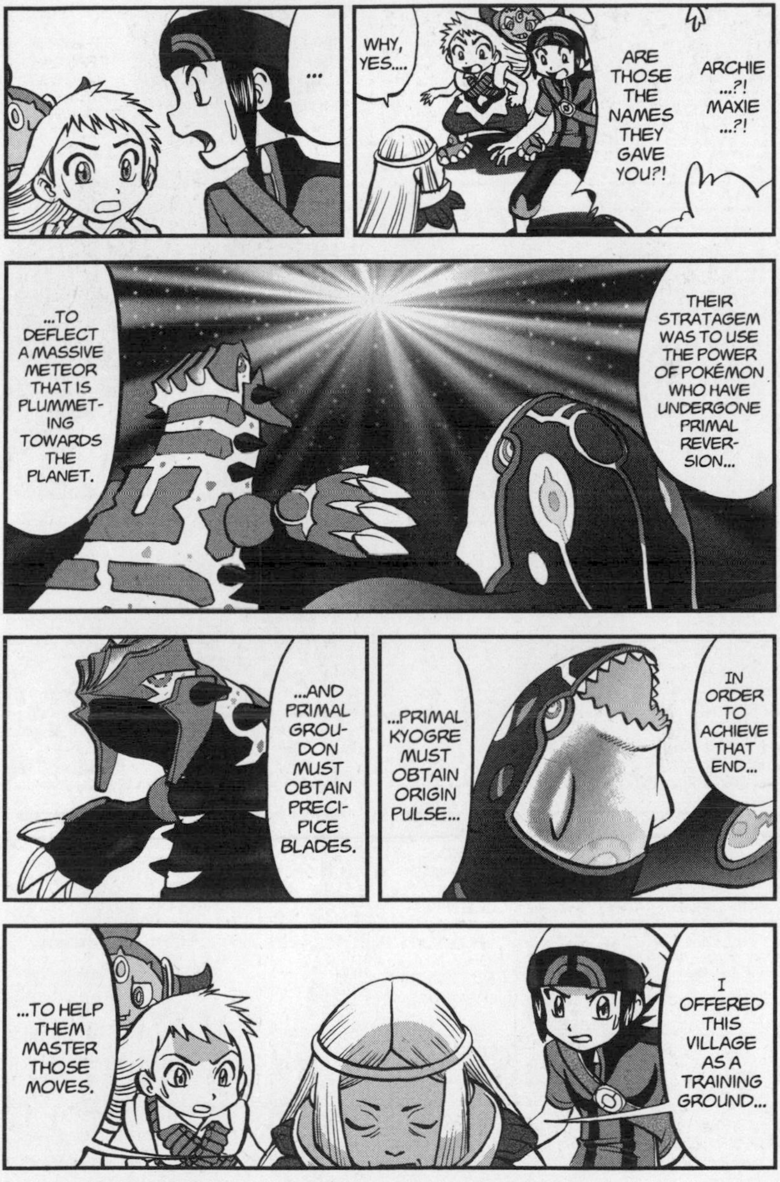
ARCHIE ...?! MAXIE ...?!
ARE THOSE THE NAMES THEY GAVE YOU?!
WHY, YES....
...
THEIR STRATAGEM WAS TO USE THE POWER OF POKÉMON WHO HAVE UNDERGONE PRIMAL REVERSION...
...TO DEFLECT A MASSIVE METEOR THAT IS PLUMMETING TOWARDS THE PLANET.
IN ORDER TO ACHIEVE THAT END...
...PRIMAL KYOGRE MUST OBTAIN ORIGIN PULSE...
...AND PRIMAL GROUDON MUST OBTAIN PRECIPICE BLADES.
I OFFERED THIS VILLAGE AS A TRAINING GROUND...
...TO HELP THEM MASTER THOSE MOVES.

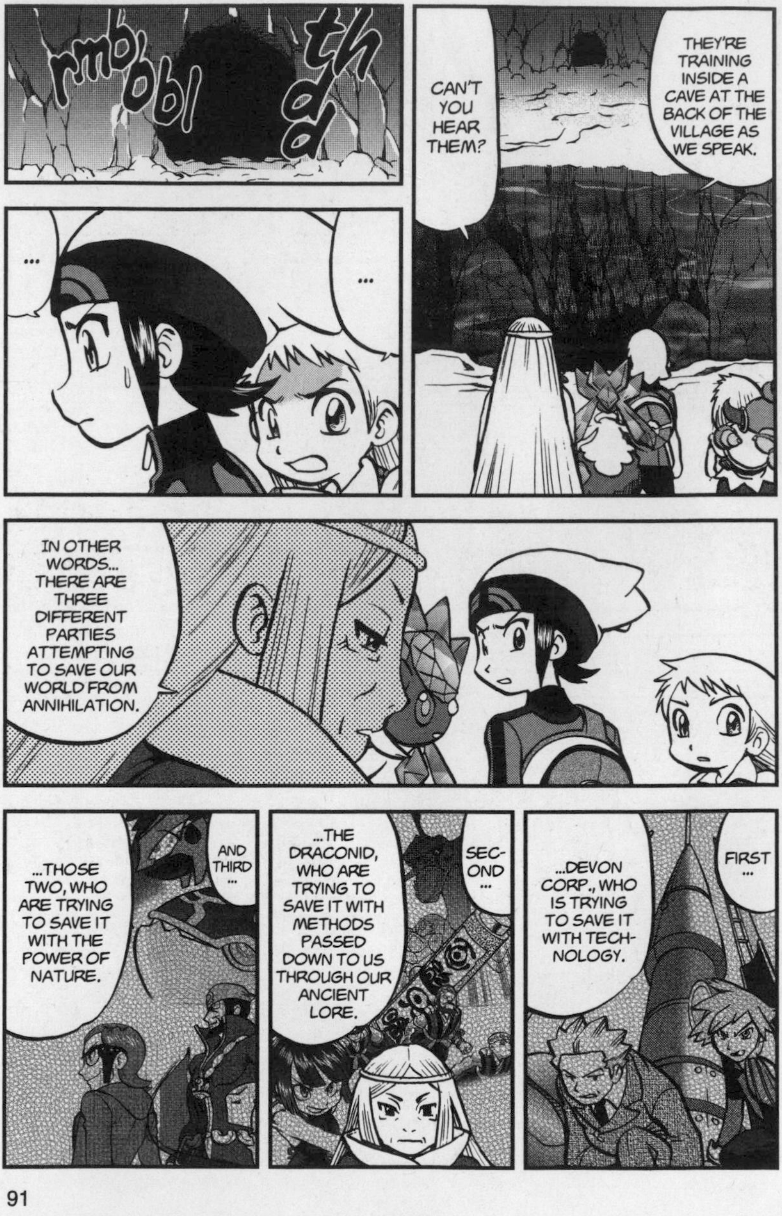
THEY'RE TRAINING INSIDE A CAVE AT THE BACK OF THE VILLAGE AS WE SPEAK.
CAN'T YOU HEAR THEM?
rmbl bl
thd
...
...
IN OTHER WORDS... THERE ARE THREE DIFFERENT PARTIES ATTEMPTING TO SAVE OUR WORLD FROM ANNIHILATION.
FIRST...
...DEVON CORP., WHO IS TRYING TO SAVE IT WITH TECH-NOLOGY.
SEC-OND...
...THE DRACONID, WHO ARE TRYING TO SAVE IT WITH METHODS PASSED DOWN TO US THROUGH OUR ANCIENT LORE.
AND THIRD...
...THOSE TWO, WHO ARE TRYING TO SAVE IT WITH THE POWER OF NATURE.

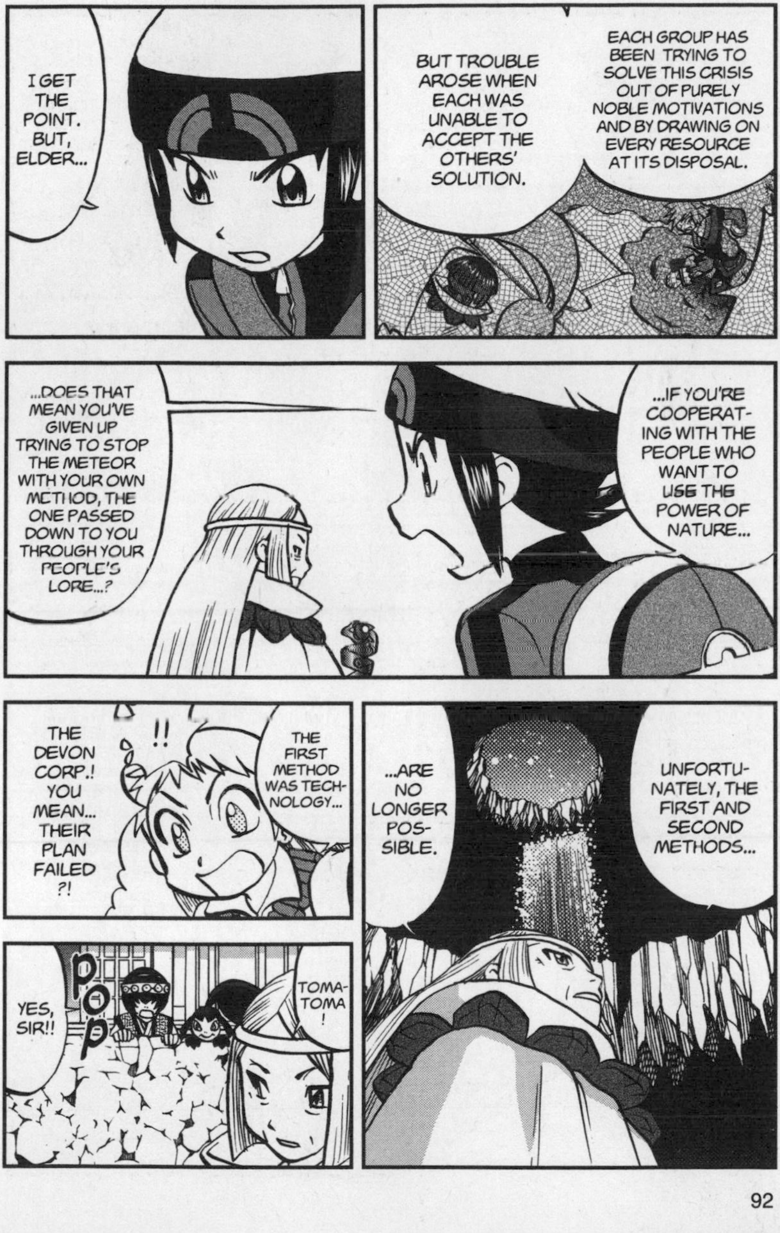
EACH GROUP HAS BEEN TRYING TO SOLVE THIS CRISIS OUT OF PURELY NOBLE MOTIVATIONS AND BY DRAWING ON EVERY RESOURCE AT ITS DISPOSAL.
BUT TROUBLE AROSE WHEN EACH WAS UNABLE TO ACCEPT THE OTHERS' SOLUTION.
I GET THE POINT. BUT, ELDER...
...IF YOU'RE COOPERATING WITH THE PEOPLE WHO WANT TO USE THE POWER OF NATURE...
...DOES THAT MEAN YOU'VE GIVEN UP TRYING TO STOP THE METEOR WITH YOUR OWN METHOD, THE ONE PASSED DOWN TO YOU THROUGH YOUR PEOPLE'S LORE...?
UNFORTUNATELY, THE FIRST AND SECOND METHODS...
...ARE NO LONGER POSSIBLE.
THE FIRST METHOD WAS TECHNOLOGY...
!!
THE DEVON CORP.! YOU MEAN... THEIR PLAN FAILED?!
TOMA-TOMA!
POP
POP
YES, SIR!!

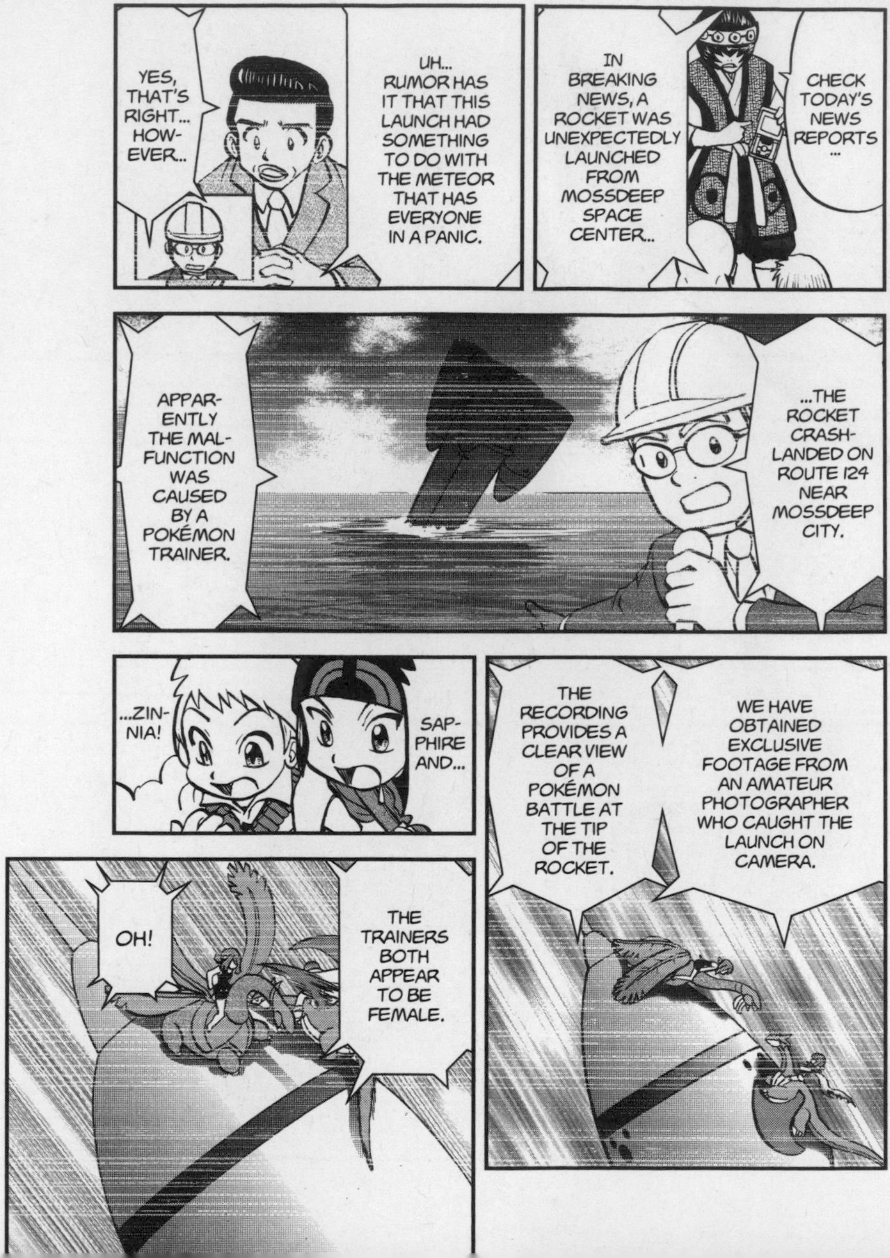
CHECK TODAY'S NEWS REPORTS...
IN BREAKING NEWS, A ROCKET WAS UNEXPECTEDLY LAUNCHED FROM MOSSDEEP SPACE CENTER...
UH... RUMOR HAS IT THAT THIS LAUNCH HAD SOMETHING TO DO WITH THE METEOR THAT HAS EVERYONE IN A PANIC.
YES, THAT'S RIGHT... HOWEVER...
...THE ROCKET CRASH-LANDED ON ROUTE 124 NEAR MOSSDEEP CITY.
APPARENTLY THE MALFUNCTION WAS CAUSED BY A POKÉMON TRAINER.
WE HAVE OBTAINED EXCLUSIVE FOOTAGE FROM AN AMATEUR PHOTOGRAPHER WHO CAUGHT THE LAUNCH ON CAMERA.
THE RECORDING PROVIDES A CLEAR VIEW OF A POKÉMON BATTLE AT THE TIP OF THE ROCKET.
SAPPHIRE AND...
...ZINNIA!
THE TRAINERS BOTH APPEAR TO BE FEMALE.
OH!

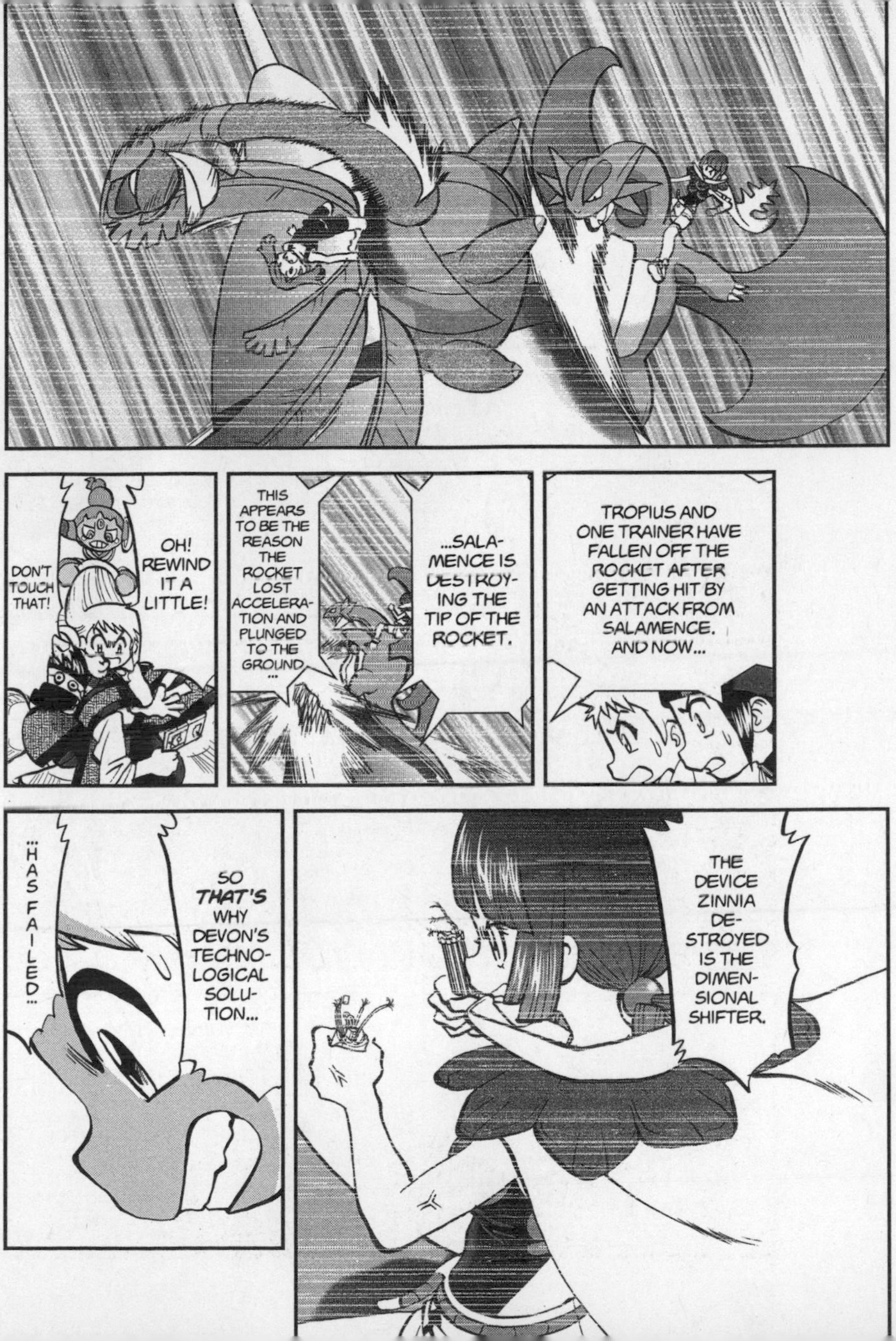
TROPIUS AND ONE TRAINER HAVE FALLEN OFF THE ROCKCT AFTER GETTING HIT BY AN ATTACK FROM SALAMENCE. AND NOW...
...SALAMENCE IS DESTROYING THE TIP OF THE ROCKET.
THIS APPEARS TO BE THE REASON THE ROCKET LOST ACCELERATION AND PLUNGED TO THE GROUND...
OH! REWIND IT A LITTLE!
DON'T TOUCH THAT!
THE DEVICE ZINNIA DESTROYED IS THE DIMENSIONAL SHIFTER.
SO *THAT'S* WHY DEVON'S TECHNOLOGICAL SOLUTION...
...HAS FAILED...

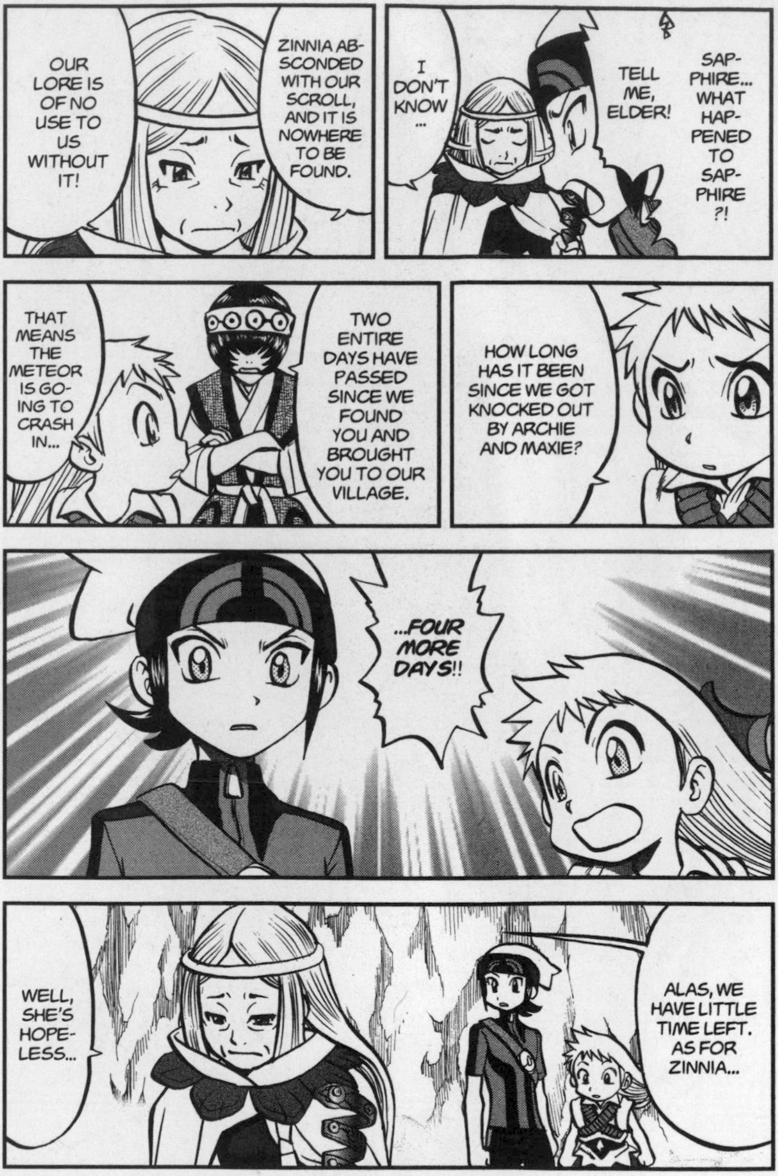
SAPPHIRE... WHAT HAPPENED TO SAPPHIRE?!
TELL ME, ELDER!
I DON'T KNOW...
ZINNIA ABSCONDED WITH OUR SCROLL, AND IT IS NOWHERE TO BE FOUND.
OUR LORE IS OF NO USE TO US WITHOUT IT!
HOW LONG HAS IT BEEN SINCE WE GOT KNOCKED OUT BY ARCHIE AND MAXIE?
TWO ENTIRE DAYS HAVE PASSED SINCE WE FOUND YOU AND BROUGHT YOU TO OUR VILLAGE.
THAT MEANS THE METEOR IS GOING TO CRASH IN...
...FOUR MORE DAYS!!
ALAS, WE HAVE LITTLE TIME LEFT. AS FOR ZINNIA...
WELL, SHE'S HOPELESS...

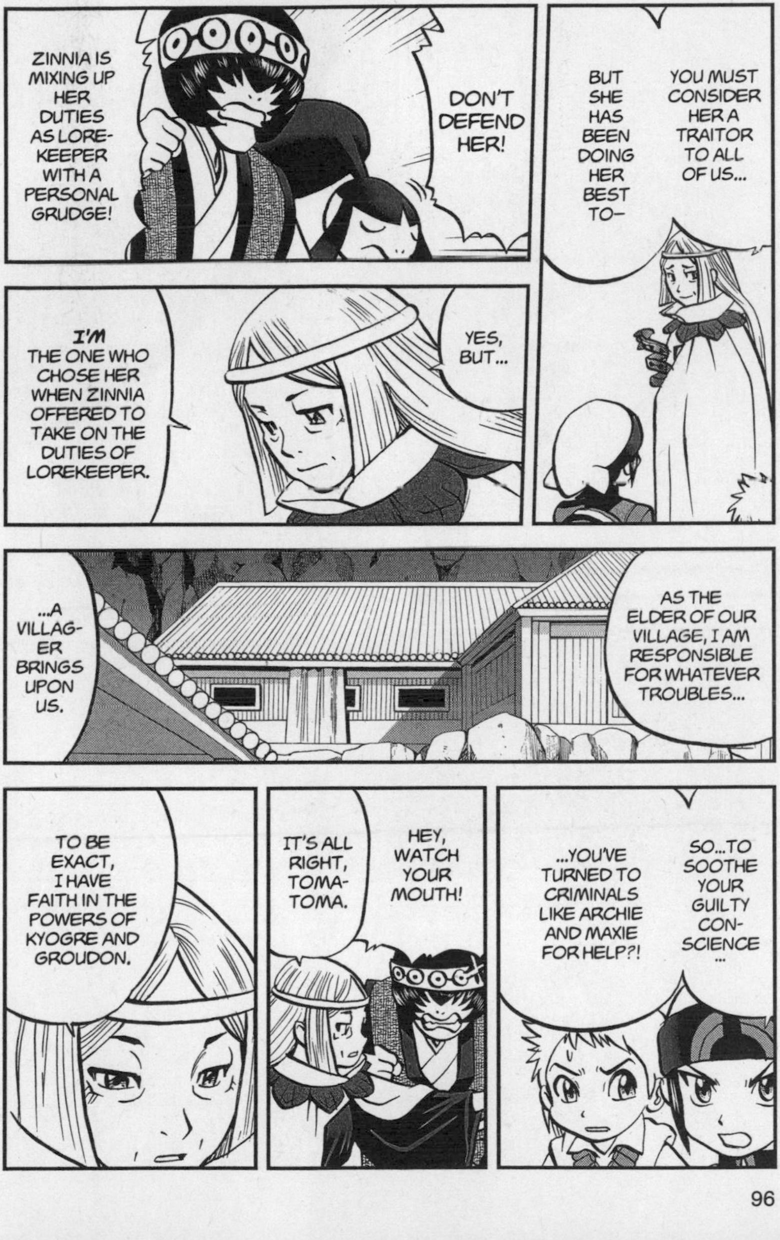
YOU MUST CONSIDER HER A TRAITOR TO ALL OF US...
BUT SHE HAS BEEN DOING HER BEST TO—
DON'T DEFEND HER!
ZINNIA IS MIXING UP HER DUTIES AS LORE-KEEPER WITH A PERSONAL GRUDGE!
YES, BUT...
I'M THE ONE WHO CHOSE HER WHEN ZINNIA OFFERED TO TAKE ON THE DUTIES OF LOREKEEPER.
AS THE ELDER OF OUR VILLAGE, I AM RESPONSIBLE FOR WHATEVER TROUBLES...
...A VILLAG-ER BRINGS UPON US.
SO...TO SOOTHE YOUR GUILTY CON-SCIENCE...
...YOU'VE TURNED TO CRIMINALS LIKE ARCHIE AND MAXIE FOR HELP?!
HEY, WATCH YOUR MOUTH!
IT'S ALL RIGHT, TOMA-TOMA.
TO BE EXACT, I HAVE FAITH IN THE POWERS OF KYOGRE AND GROUDON.

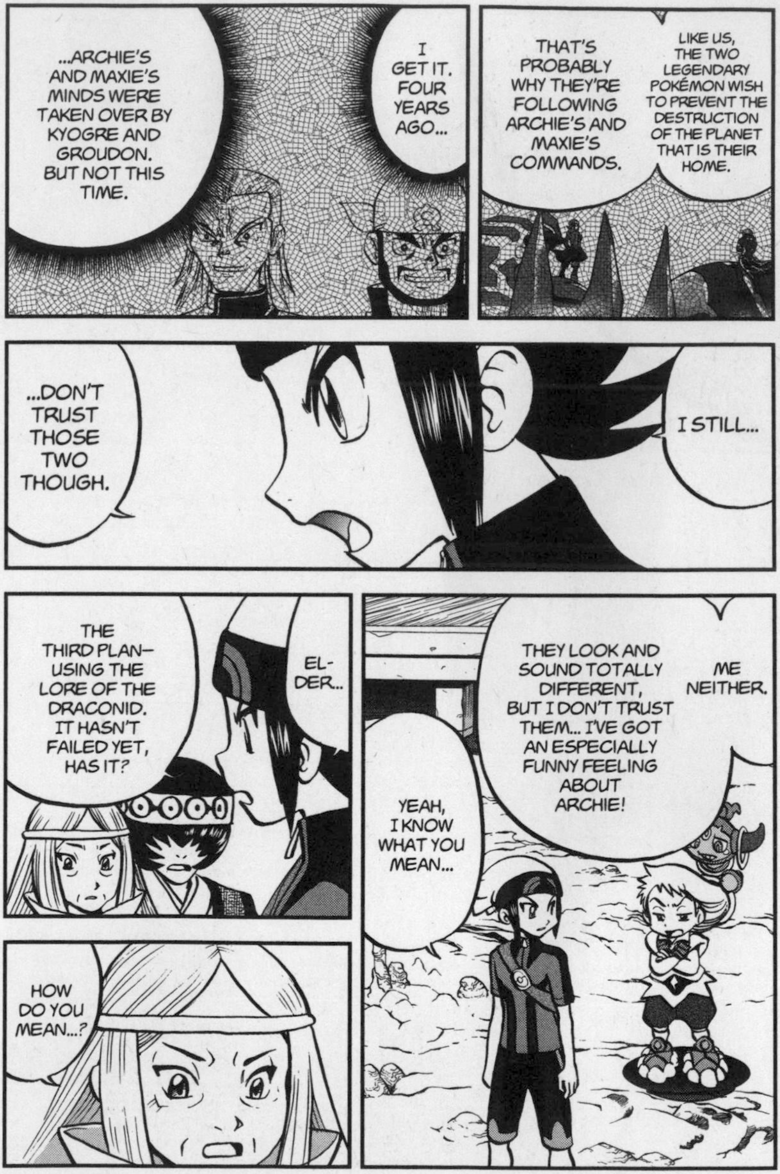
LIKE US, THE TWO LEGENDARY POKéMON WISH TO PREVENT THE DESTRUCTION OF THE PLANET THAT IS THEIR HOME.
THAT'S PROBABLY WHY THEY'RE FOLLOWING ARCHIE'S AND MAXIE'S COMMANDS.
I GET IT. FOUR YEARS AGO...
...ARCHIE'S AND MAXIE'S MINDS WERE TAKEN OVER BY KYOGRE AND GROUDON. BUT NOT THIS TIME.
I STILL...
...DON'T TRUST THOSE TWO THOUGH.
ME NEITHER.
THEY LOOK AND SOUND TOTALLY DIFFERENT, BUT I DON'T TRUST THEM... I'VE GOT AN ESPECIALLY FUNNY FEELING ABOUT ARCHIE!
YEAH, I KNOW WHAT YOU MEAN...
EL-DER...
THE THIRD PLAN— USING THE LORE OF THE DRACONID. IT HASN'T FAILED YET, HAS IT?
HOW DO YOU MEAN...?

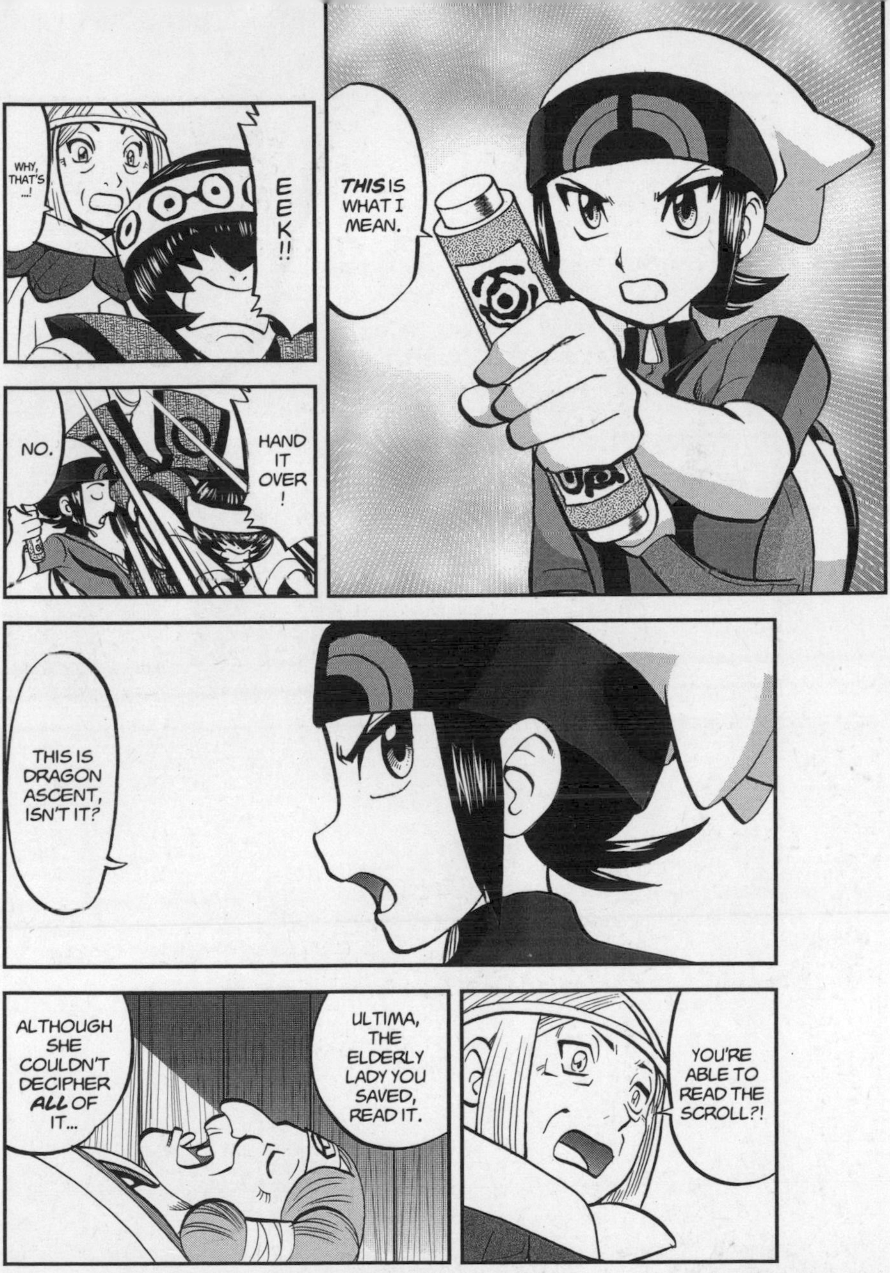
THIS IS WHAT I MEAN.
EEK!!
WHY, THAT'S ...!
HAND IT OVER!
NO.
THIS IS DRAGON ASCENT, ISN'T IT?
YOU'RE ABLE TO READ THE SCROLL?!
ULTIMA, THE ELDERLY LADY YOU SAVED, READ IT.
ALTHOUGH SHE COULDN'T DECIPHER ALL OF IT...

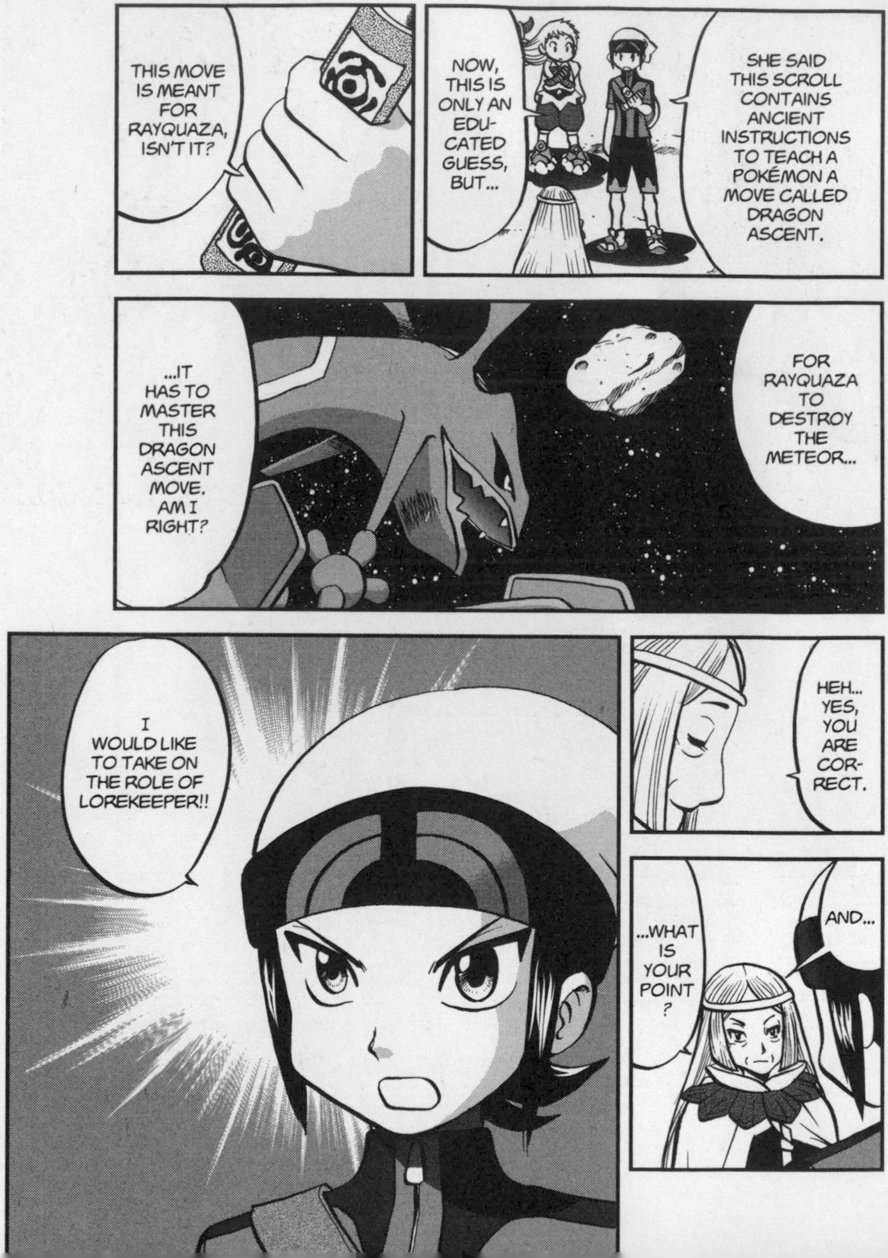
SHE SAID THIS SCROLL CONTAINS ANCIENT INSTRUCTIONS TO TEACH A POKÉMON A MOVE CALLED DRAGON ASCENT.
NOW, THIS IS ONLY AN EDU-CATED GUESS, BUT...
THIS MOVE IS MEANT FOR RAYQUAZA, ISN'T IT?
FOR RAYQUAZA TO DESTROY THE METEOR...
...IT HAS TO MASTER THIS DRAGON ASCENT MOVE. AM I RIGHT?
HEH... YES, YOU ARE COR-RECT.
AND...
...WHAT IS YOUR POINT?
I WOULD LIKE TO TAKE ON THE ROLE OF LOREKEEPER!!

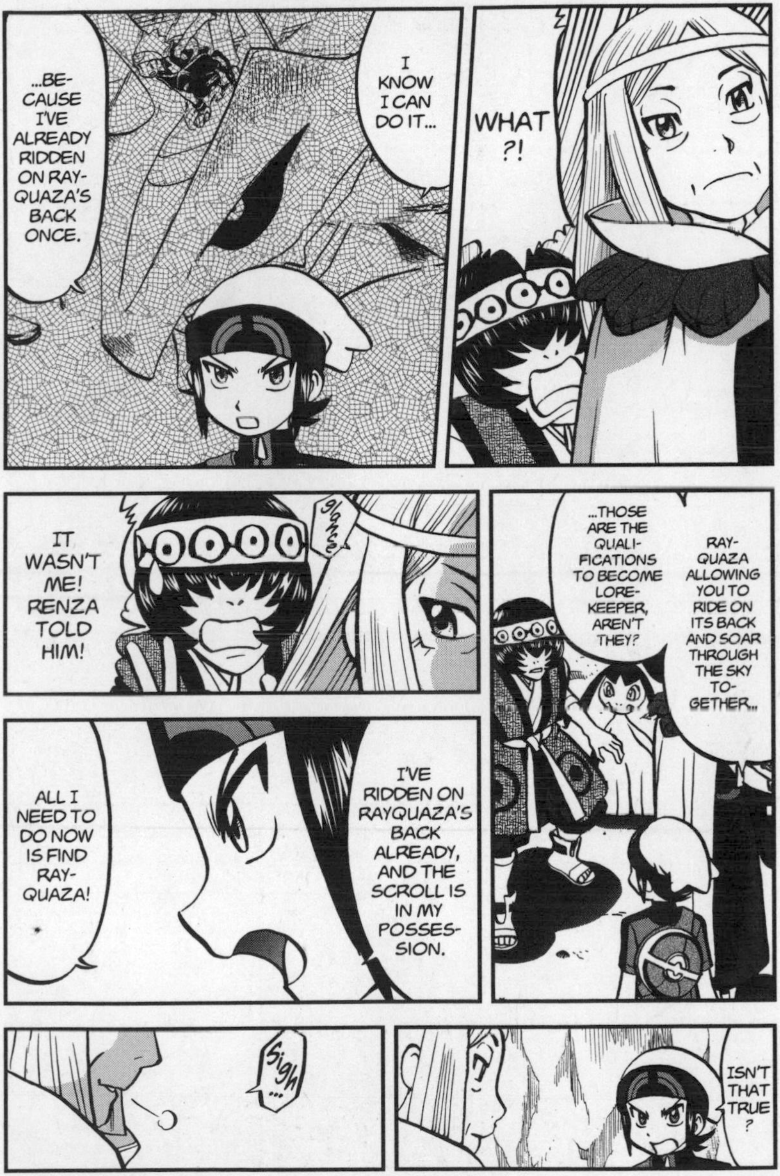
I KNOW I CAN DO IT...
...BE-CAUSE I'VE ALREADY RIDDEN ON RAY-QUAZA'S BACK ONCE.
WHAT ?!
IT WASN'T ME! RENZA TOLD HIM!
glance
RAY-QUAZA ALLOWING YOU TO RIDE ON ITS BACK AND SOAR THROUGH THE SKY TO-GETHER...
...THOSE ARE THE QUALI-FICATIONS TO BECOME LORE-KEEPER, AREN'T THEY?
I'VE RIDDEN ON RAYQUAZA'S BACK ALREADY, AND THE SCROLL IS IN MY POSSES-SION.
ALL I NEED TO DO NOW IS FIND RAY-QUAZA!
ISN'T THAT TRUE ?
Sigh...

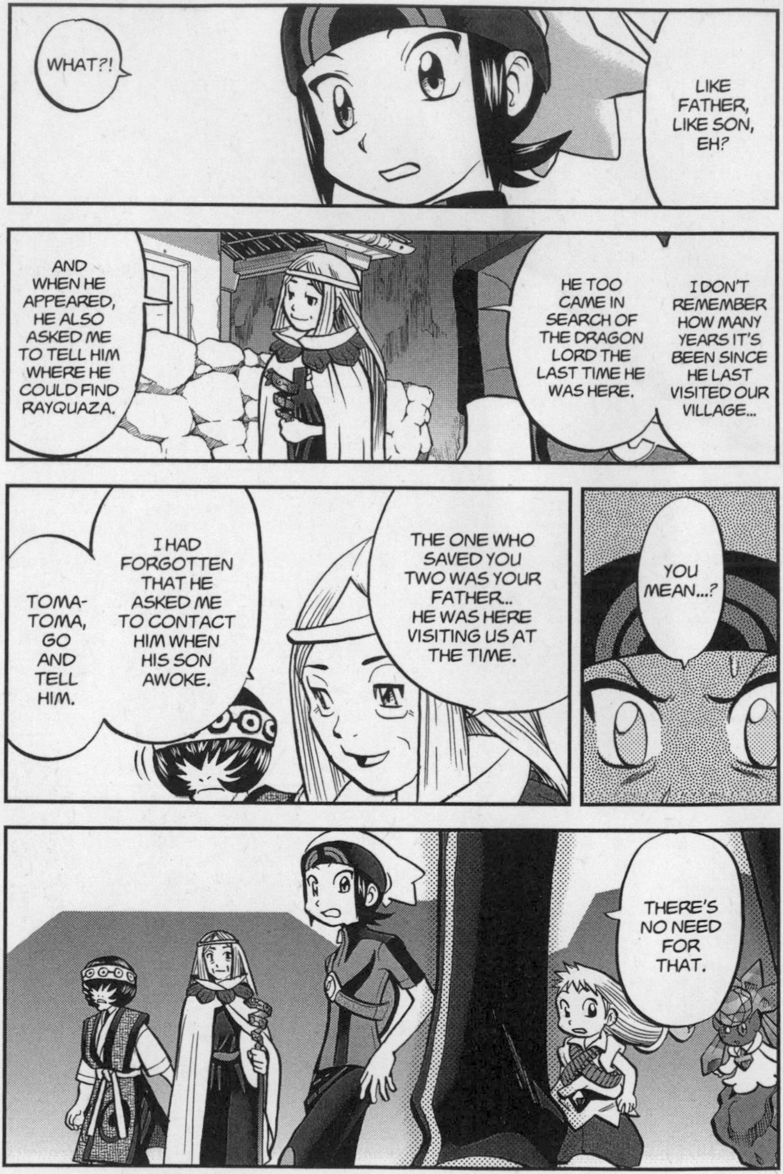
LIKE FATHER, LIKE SON, EH?
WHAT?!
I DON'T REMEMBER HOW MANY YEARS IT'S BEEN SINCE HE LAST VISITED OUR VILLAGE...
HE TOO CAME IN SEARCH OF THE DRAGON LORD THE LAST TIME HE WAS HERE.
AND WHEN HE APPEARED, HE ALSO ASKED ME TO TELL HIM WHERE HE COULD FIND RAYQUAZA.
YOU MEAN...?
THE ONE WHO SAVED YOU TWO WAS YOUR FATHER... HE WAS HERE VISITING US AT THE TIME.
I HAD FORGOTTEN THAT HE ASKED ME TO CONTACT HIM WHEN HIS SON AWOKE.
TOMA-TOMA, GO AND TELL HIM.
THERE'S NO NEED FOR THAT.

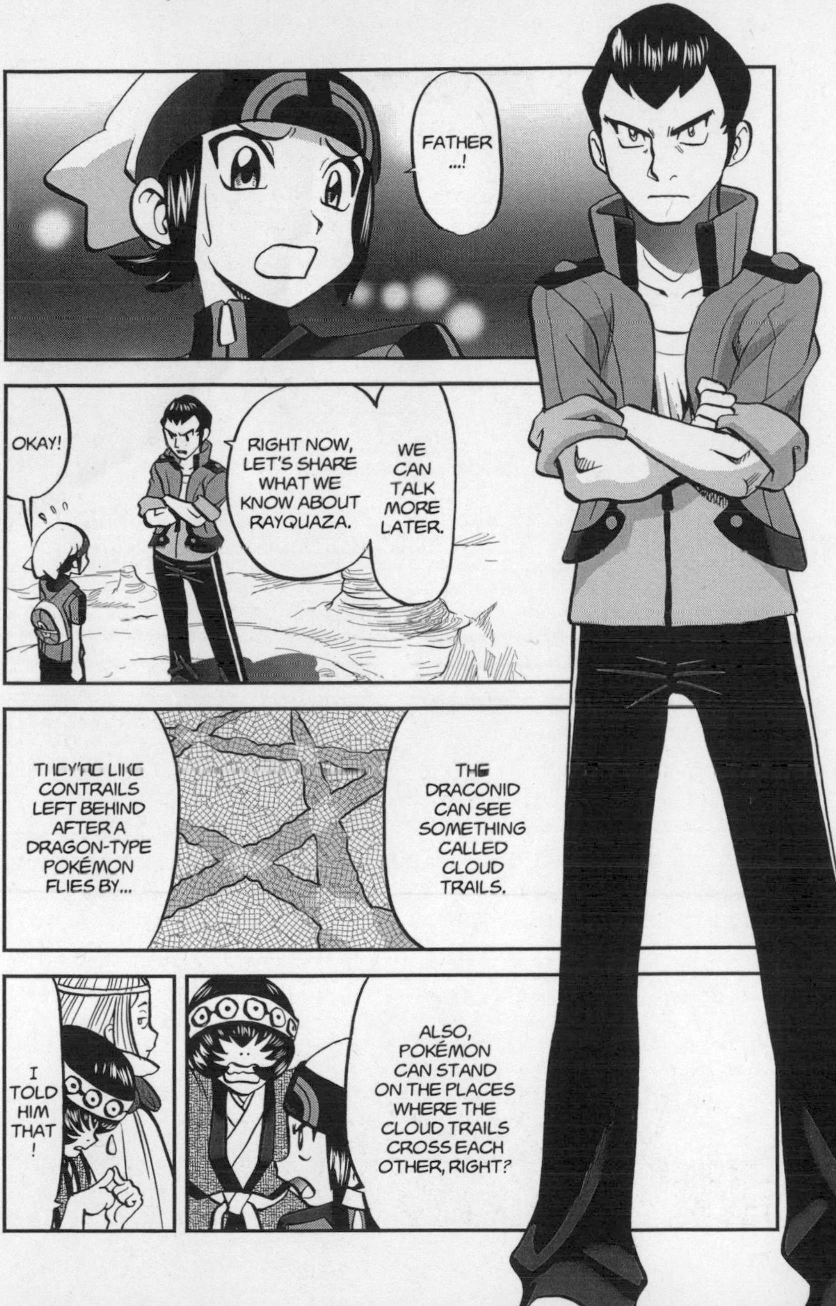
FATHER ...!
WE CAN TALK MORE LATER.
RIGHT NOW, LET'S SHARE WHAT WE KNOW ABOUT RAYQUAZA.
OKAY!
THE DRACONID CAN SEE SOMETHING CALLED CLOUD TRAILS.
THEY'RE LIKE CONTRAILS LEFT BEHIND AFTER A DRAGON-TYPE POKÉMON FLIES BY...
ALSO, POKÉMON CAN STAND ON THE PLACES WHERE THE CLOUD TRAILS CROSS EACH OTHER, RIGHT?
I TOLD HIM THAT!

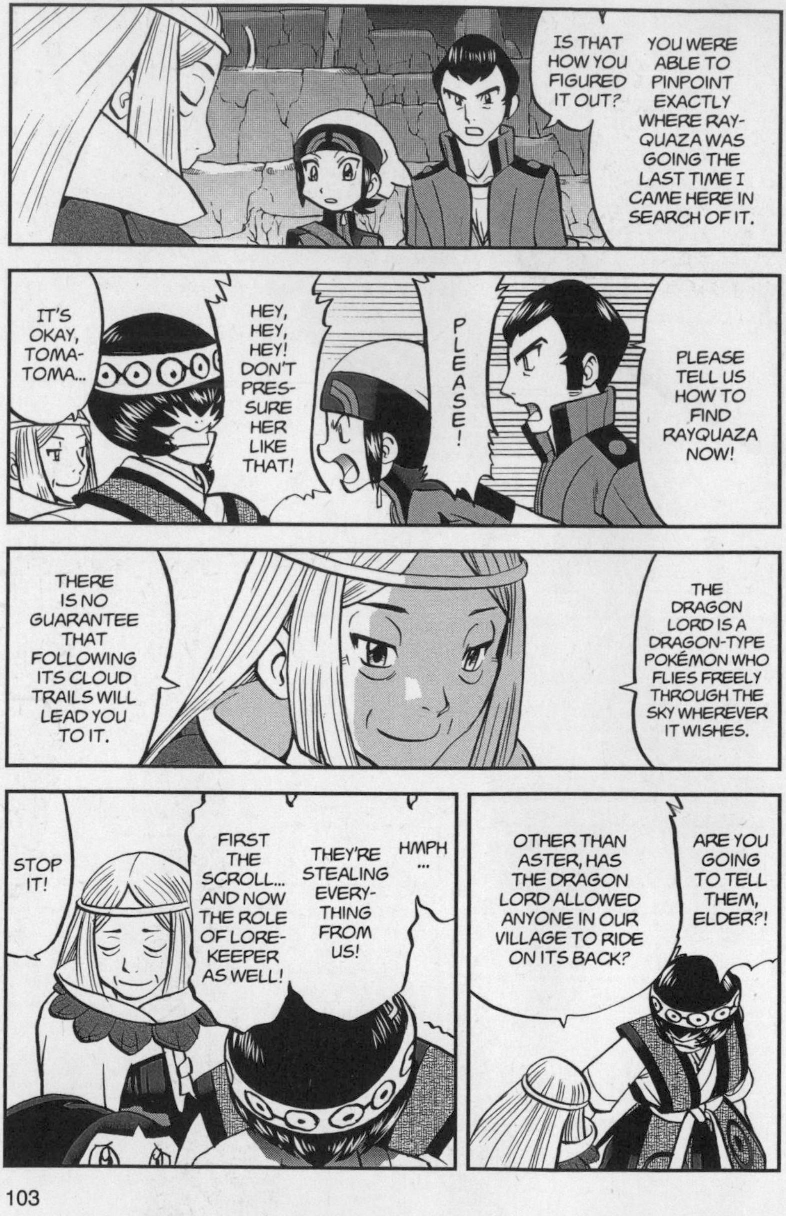
YOU WERE ABLE TO PINPOINT EXACTLY WHERE RAYQUAZA WAS GOING THE LAST TIME I CAME HERE IN SEARCH OF IT.
IS THAT HOW YOU FIGURED IT OUT?
PLEASE TELL US HOW TO FIND RAYQUAZA NOW!
PLEASE!
HEY, HEY, HEY! DON'T PRESSURE HER LIKE THAT!
IT'S OKAY, TOMA-TOMA...
THE DRAGON LORD IS A DRAGON-TYPE POKÉMON WHO FLIES FREELY THROUGH THE SKY WHEREVER IT WISHES.
THERE IS NO GUARANTEE THAT FOLLOWING ITS CLOUD TRAILS WILL LEAD YOU TO IT.
ARE YOU GOING TO TELL THEM, ELDER?!
OTHER THAN ASTER, HAS THE DRAGON LORD ALLOWED ANYONE IN OUR VILLAGE TO RIDE ON ITS BACK?
HMPH ...
THEY'RE STEALING EVERYTHING FROM US!
FIRST THE SCROLL... AND NOW THE ROLE OF LOREKEEPER AS WELL!
STOP IT!

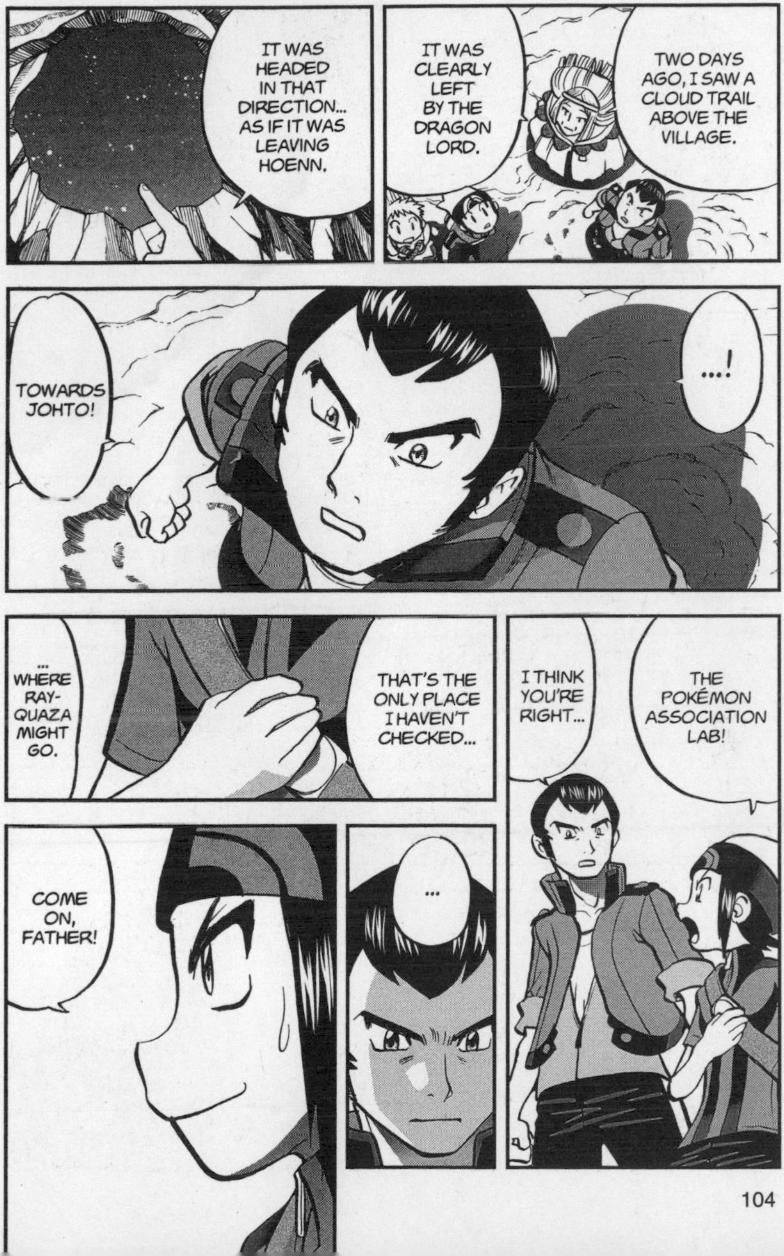

TWO DAYS AGO, I SAW A CLOUD TRAIL ABOVE THE VILLAGE.
IT WAS CLEARLY LEFT BY THE DRAGON LORD.
IT WAS HEADED IN THAT DIRECTION... AS IF IT WAS LEAVING HOENN.
...!
TOWARDS JOHTO!
THE POKÉMON ASSOCIATION LAB!
I THINK YOU'RE RIGHT...
THAT'S THE ONLY PLACE I HAVEN'T CHECKED...
... WHERE RAY-QUAZA MIGHT GO.
...
COME ON, FATHER!

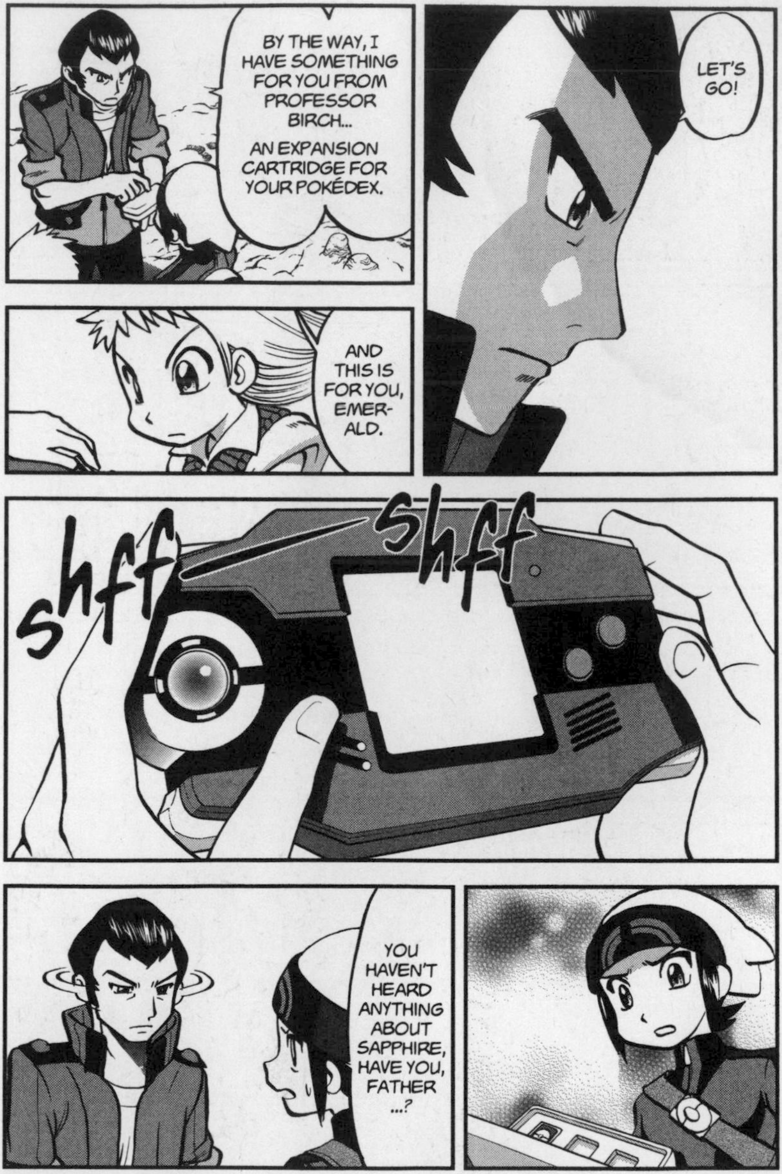
LET'S GO!
BY THE WAY, I HAVE SOMETHING FOR YOU FROM PROFESSOR BIRCH...
AN EXPANSION CARTRIDGE FOR YOUR POKÉDEX.
AND THIS IS FOR YOU, EMER-ALD.
shff
shff
YOU HAVEN'T HEARD ANYTHING ABOUT SAPPHIRE, HAVE YOU, FATHER ...?

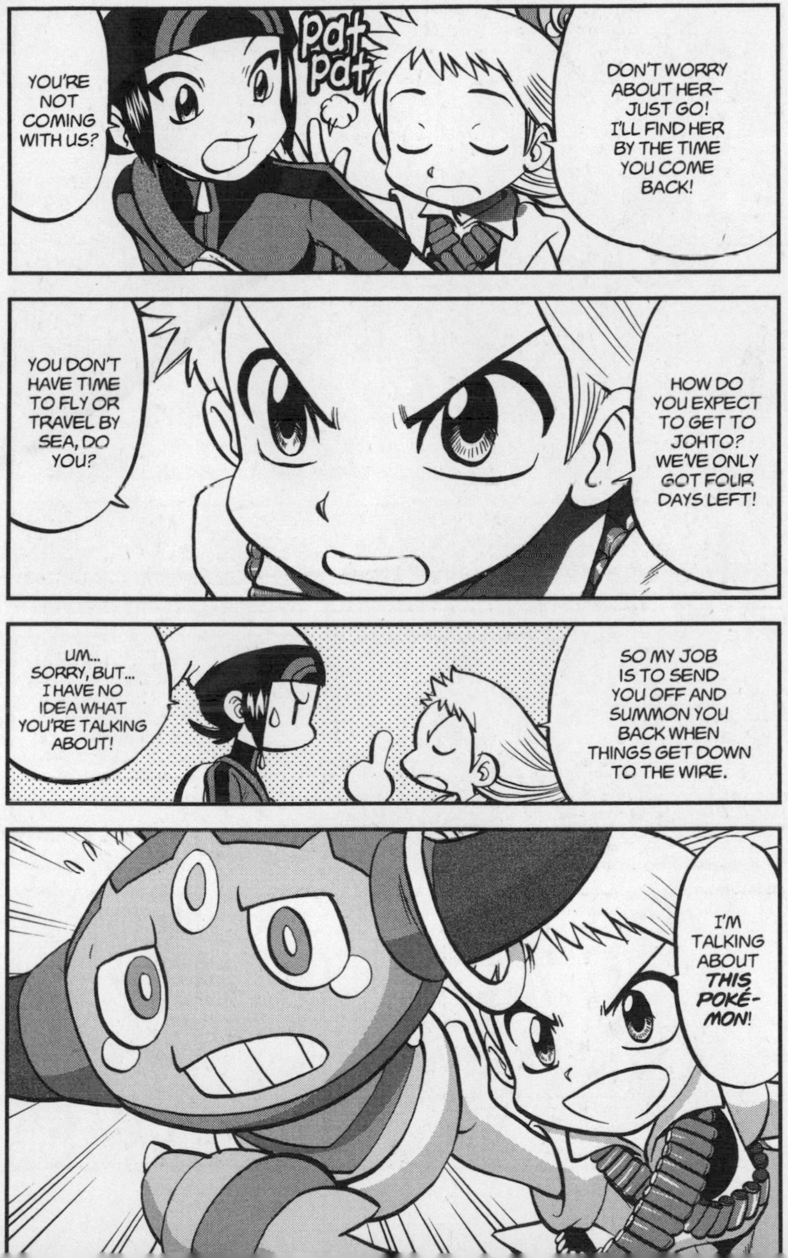
DON'T WORRY ABOUT HER— JUST GO! I'LL FIND HER BY THE TIME YOU COME BACK!
pat pat
YOU'RE NOT COMING WITH US?
HOW DO YOU EXPECT TO GET TO JOHTO? WE'VE ONLY GOT FOUR DAYS LEFT!
YOU DON'T HAVE TIME TO FLY OR TRAVEL BY SEA, DO YOU?
SO MY JOB IS TO SEND YOU OFF AND SUMMON YOU BACK WHEN THINGS GET DOWN TO THE WIRE.
UM... SORRY, BUT... I HAVE NO IDEA WHAT YOU'RE TALKING ABOUT!
I'M TALKING ABOUT *THIS POKÉMON*!

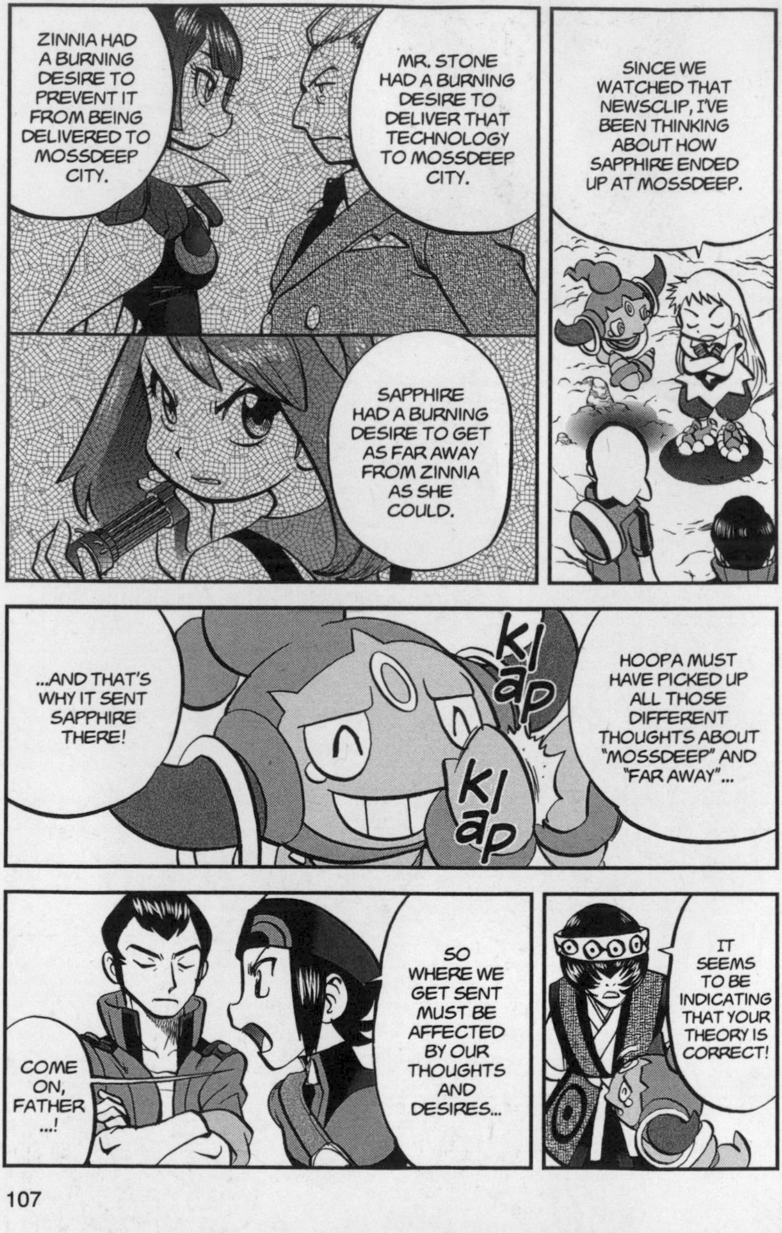
SINCE WE WATCHED THAT NEWSCLIP, I'VE BEEN THINKING ABOUT HOW SAPPHIRE ENDED UP AT MOSSDEEP.
MR. STONE HAD A BURNING DESIRE TO DELIVER THAT TECHNOLOGY TO MOSSDEEP CITY.
ZINNIA HAD A BURNING DESIRE TO PREVENT IT FROM BEING DELIVERED TO MOSSDEEP CITY.
SAPPHIRE HAD A BURNING DESIRE TO GET AS FAR AWAY FROM ZINNIA AS SHE COULD.
HOOPA MUST HAVE PICKED UP ALL THOSE DIFFERENT THOUGHTS ABOUT "MOSSDEEP" AND "FAR AWAY"...
klap
klap
...AND THAT'S WHY IT SENT SAPPHIRE THERE!
IT SEEMS TO BE INDICATING THAT YOUR THEORY IS CORRECT!
SO WHERE WE GET SENT MUST BE AFFECTED BY OUR THOUGHTS AND DESIRES...
COME ON, FATHER ...!

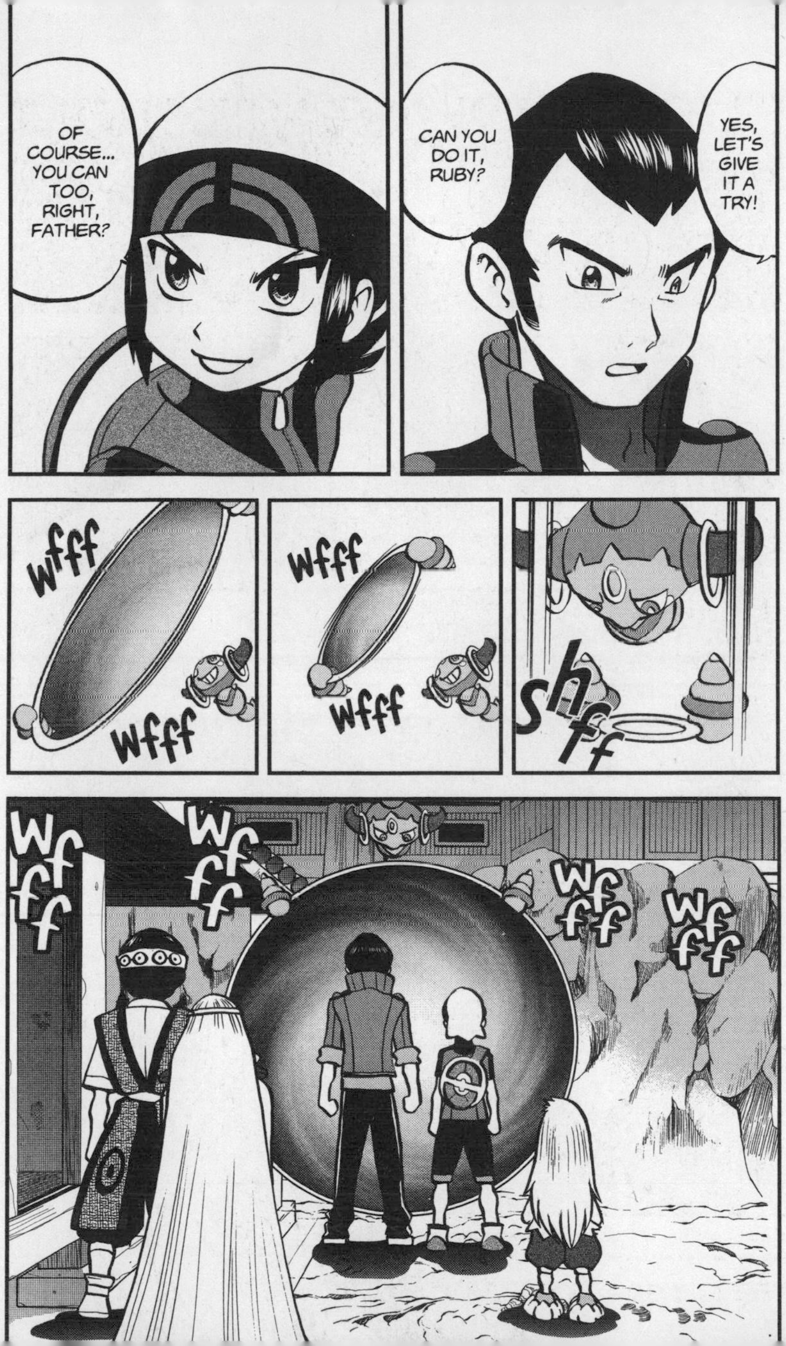

YES, LET'S GIVE IT A TRY!
CAN YOU DO IT, RUBY?
OF COURSE... YOU CAN TOO, RIGHT, FATHER?
shff
wfff
wfff
wfff
wfff
Wfff
Wfff
Wfff
Wfff

Ruby and his absentee father search for Rayquaza in hopes of teaching the Legendary Pokémon the move Dragon Ascent and saving the world. Emerald passes through Legendary Pokémon Hoopa's ring to join Sapphire but accidentally brings along three squabbling Pokémon—and a whole lot of trouble!

Will Sapphire ever forgive Ruby for withholding the truth about the meteor?

VOLUME 5 AVAILABLE NOVEMBER 2017!

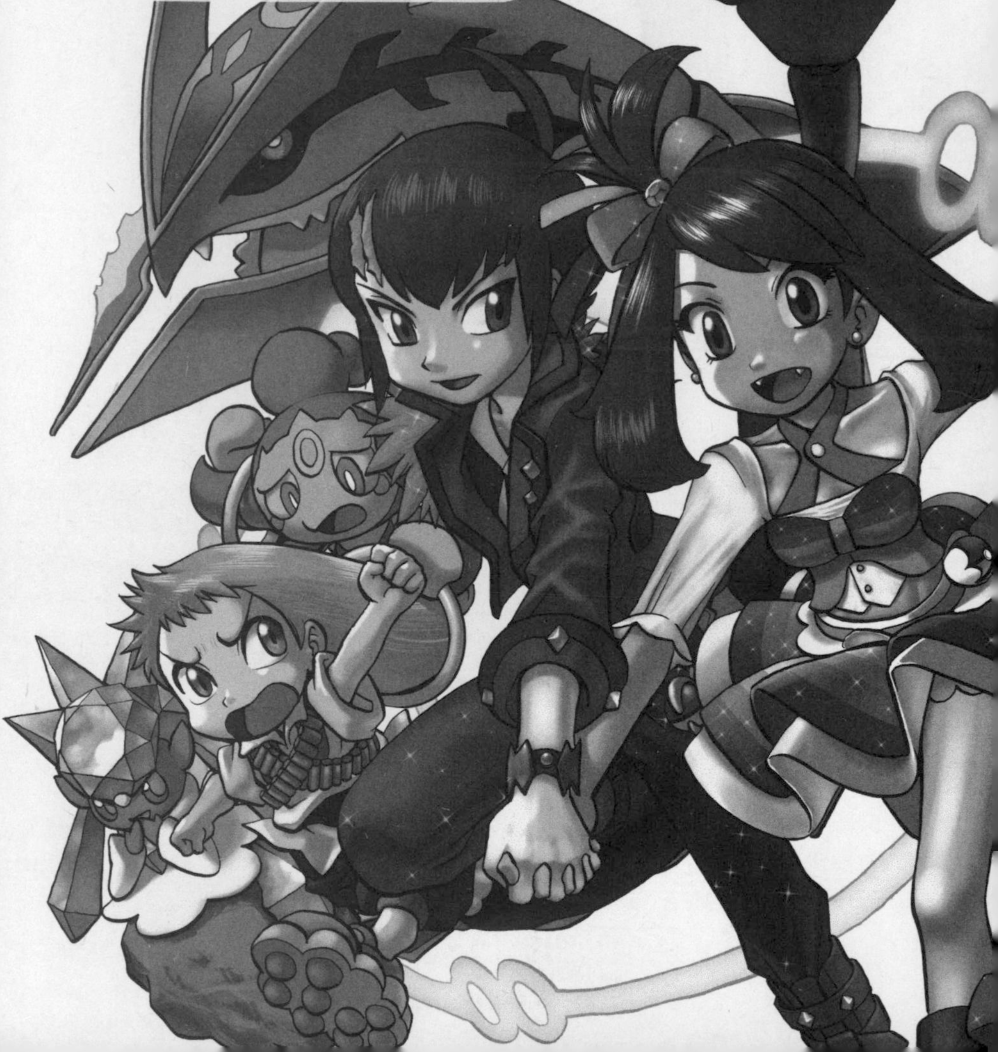

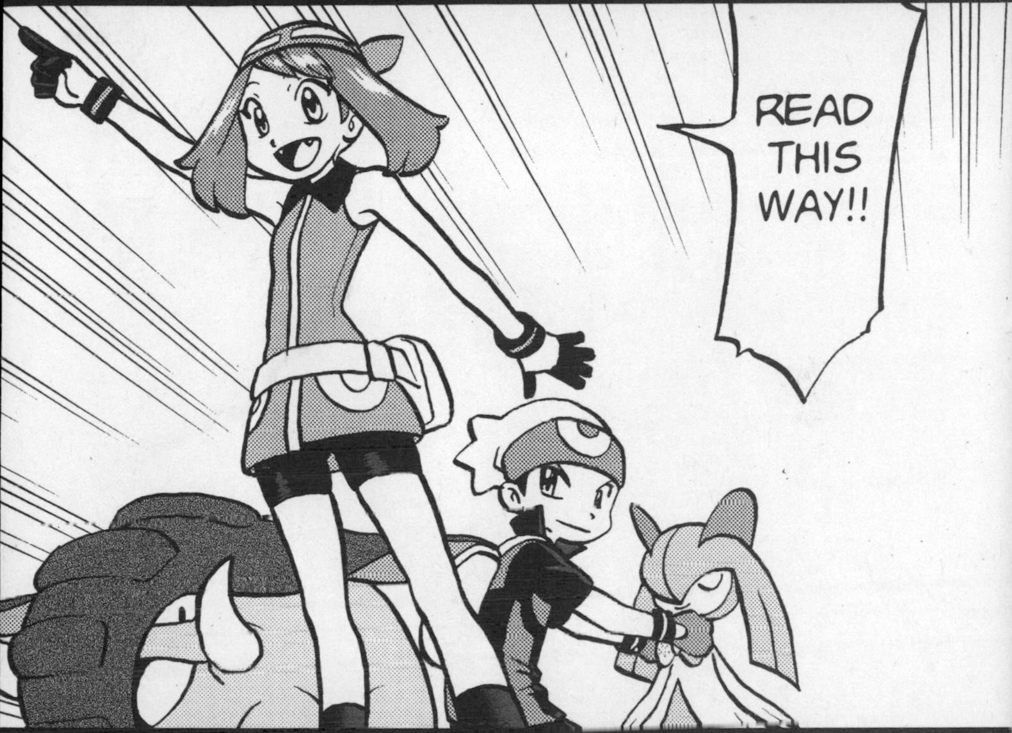
READ THIS WAY!!

THIS IS THE END OF THIS GRAPHIC NOVEL!

To properly enjoy this VIZ Media graphic novel, please turn it around and begin reading from right to left.

This book has been printed in the original Japanese format in order to preserve the orientation of the original artwork. Have fun with it!

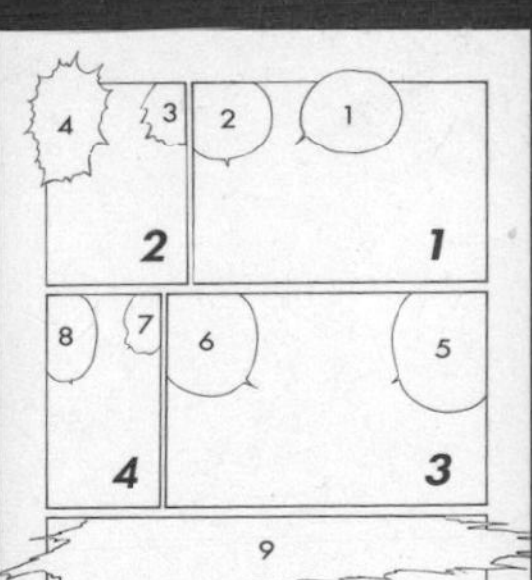
1
2
3
4
5
6
7
8
9

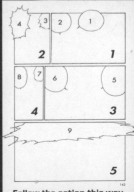

Follow the action this way.

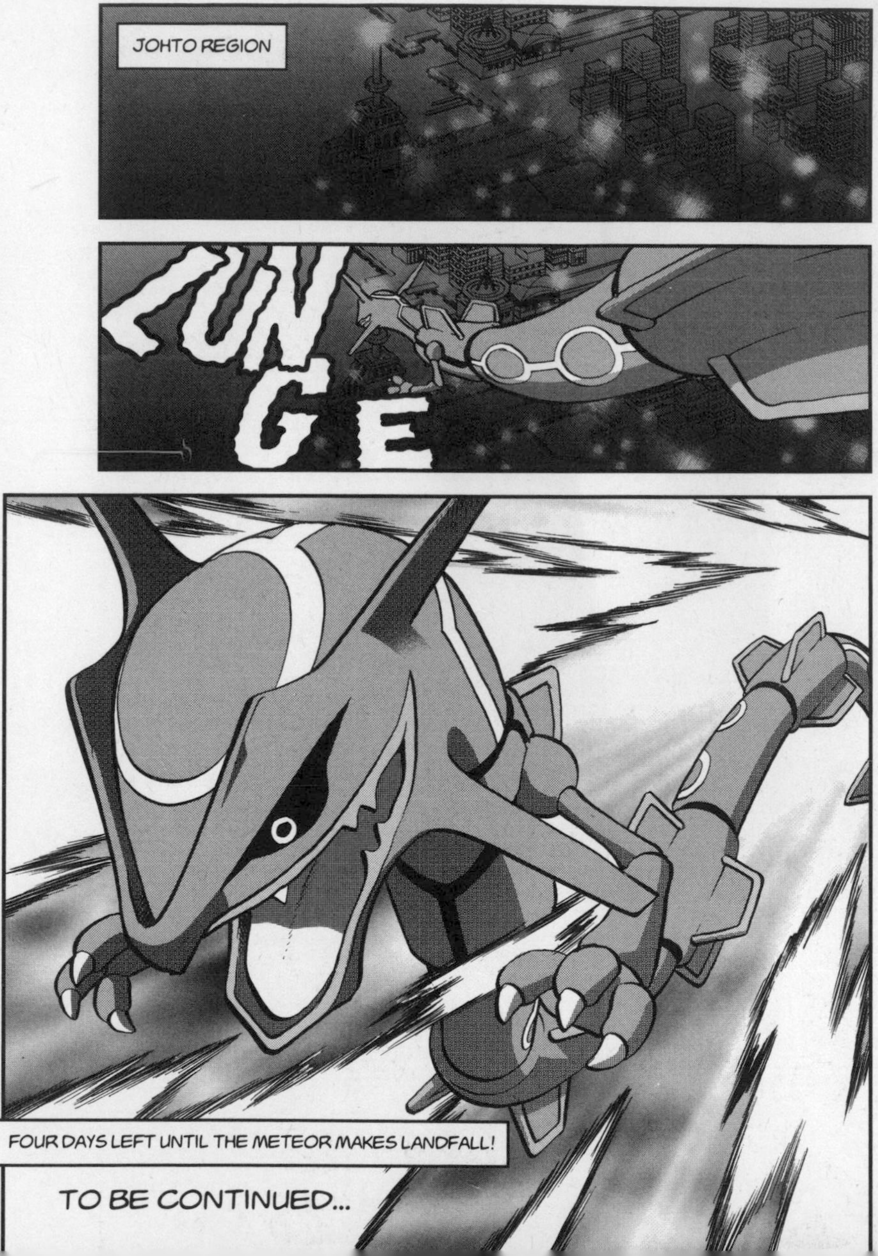
JOHTO REGION
ZUNGE
FOUR DAYS LEFT UNTIL THE METEOR MAKES LANDFALL!
TO BE CONTINUED...

P9-DOB-725

Pokémon ΩRuby • αSapphire
Volume 4
VIZ Media Edition

Story by HIDENORI KUSAKA
Art by SATOSHI YAMAMOTO

Translation—Tetsuichiro Miyaki
English Adaptation—Bryant Turnage
Touch-Up & Lettering—Susan Daigle-Leach
Design—Shawn Carrico
Editor—Annette Roman

Printed in the U.S.A.

Published by
VIZ Media, LLC
P.O. Box 77010
San Francisco, CA 94107

10 9 8 7 6 5 4 3 2 1
First printing, July 2017

www.viz.com

RATED A FOR ALL AGES

PARENTAL ADVISORY
POKÉMON ADVENTURES
is rated A and is suitable
for readers of all ages.
ratings.viz.com

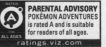